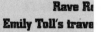

### FALL INTO DEATH

"Toll's writing is enjoyable and the characters believable. Reading this book is like taking a personal tour of the fall foliage in New England. It is entertaining, interesting and full of little tidbits about famous authors. Highly recommended."
—*I Love a Mystery*

"Traveling with Lynne and company should satisfy any armchair traveler with a taste for suspense along with their fall color."
—*Mysterious Galaxy*

"This is a book you need to read with a notepad nearby. Not to keep notes about the characters, plot, etc. You will want to go to many of the places made very appealing, and try some of the food described. Read this book with an overnight bag packed and ready to go."
—*Deadly Pleasures*

### MURDER PANS OUT

"A truly delightful cozy with a great deal of Gold Rush lore thrown in."
—*I Love a Mystery*

"Toll is a marvelous writer, with a feel for language, a wry sense of humor, a sensitivity to human emotions, a no-nonsense narrative style and the ability to pack several mysteries into the narrow confines of one novel. *Murder Pans Out* is a thoroughly enjoyable work, with an implicit moral included: Don't mess with a bunch of women school teachers."
—*New Mystery Lovers Magazine*

"Each of the characters is entirely three-dimensional and will remind you of someone you know. Even the bad guy has a fascinating and multi-faceted personality. The mystery is well done, and the pace never flags."
—*The Romance Reader's Connection*

*continued . . .*

## MURDER WILL TRAVEL

"A clever, charming novel that readers will relish on many levels. Its wine country setting is both exciting and fun while its complex plot will satisfy the most discriminating mystery buff. An admirable and delightful addition to the mystery world."　　—Earlene Fowler, author of *Broken Dishes*

"A splendid new series brimming with excitement and atmosphere. Rich and full-bodied . . . an exciting and thoroughly original mystery."
　　　　　—Tamar Myers, author of *Thou Shalt Not Grill*

"Flawless. The plotting is tight and realistic; it's a pleasure to read a mystery that doesn't require a conscious suspension of disbelief. . . . Toll perfectly captures the Sonoma Valley—its scenery, its history, its atmosphere. All of Toll's characters are fully rendered, which is a particularly notable accomplishment in a novel with a cast of about twenty . . . An auspicious award-worthy kick-off for a new series."
　　　　　　　　　　　　　　—BookBrowser.com

"Delightful . . . *Murder Will Travel* is a classic who-done-it and Lynne is a character I'm looking forward to meeting again. Toll's story is rich in plot, character development and history and I'd recommend this to all who love classic mysteries."　　　　　　　　　—*I Love A Mystery*

"Wine fans take note—I recommend having a glass of your favorite wine at hand while reading *Murder Will Travel,* with its many evocations of the Sonoma Wine Country and its vineyards and their products. *Murder Will Travel* introduces amateur sleuth Lynne Montgomery: tour guide, widowed mother, and a well-rounded, mature woman I very much enjoyed spending time with."
　　　　　　　　　　　　　　—*Mysterious Galaxy*

# KEYS TO
## *Death*

*Emily Toll*

BERKLEY PRIME CRIME, NEW YORK

**THE BERKLEY PUBLISHING GROUP**
**Published by the Penguin Group**
**Penguin Group (USA) Inc.**
**375 Hudson Street, New York, New York 10014, USA**
Penguin Group (Canada), 10 Alcorn Avenue, Toronto, Ontario, M4V 3B2, Canada
(a division of Pearson Penguin Canada Inc.)
Penguin Books Ltd, 80 Strand, London WC2R 0RL, England
Penguin Group Ireland, 25 St. Stephen's Green, Dublin 2, Ireland
(a division of Penguin Books Ltd.)
Penguin Group (Australia), 250 Camberwell Road, Camberwell, Victoria 3124,
Australia (a division of Pearson Australia Group Pty. Ltd.)
Penguin Books India Pvt. Ltd., 11 Community Centre, Panchsheel Park, New Delhi—
110 017, India
Penguin Group (NZ), Cnr. Airborne and Rosedale Roads, Albany, Auckland 1310, New Zealand (a
division of Pearson New Zealand Ltd.)
Penguin Books (South Africa) (Pty.) Ltd., 24 Sturdee Avenue, Rosebank, Johannesburg 2196, South
Africa

Penguin Books Ltd, Registered Offices: 80 Strand, London WC2R 0RL, England

KEYS TO DEATH

A Berkley Prime Crime Book / published by arrangement with the author

PRINTING HISTORY
Berkley Prime Crime mass-market edition / May 2005

Copyright © 2005 Taffy Cannon.
Cover design by George Long.
Cover art by Dave Schweitzer.

ISBN: 0-425-20294-1

Berkley Prime Crime Books are published by The Berkley Publishing Group,
a division of Penguin Group (USA) Inc.,
375 Hudson Street, New York, New York 10014.
The name BERKLEY PRIME CRIME and the BERKLEY PRIME CRIME design
are trademarks belonging to Penguin Group (USA) Inc.

PRINTED IN THE UNITED STATES OF AMERICA

10  9  8  7  6  5  4  3  2  1

*For Carol Tico*

*Chapter 1*

**THE** alligator lying on the boat ramp wasn't sunning itself.

It wasn't an alligator, either.

❧

**LYNNE** Montgomery closed her eyes for a moment, hoping that when she looked again it would be gone, an apparition caused by too much wine the night before in an unfamiliar tropical environment.

When she opened her eyes again, however, it was still there, and it was still not an alligator. Funny how quickly your perceptions can change. Until yesterday in the Everglades, Lynne had never seen an alligator outside a zoo. Now she was wishing that one lay sprawled in all its ungainly reptilian splendor at her feet, because the alternative was even less desirable.

She moved warily toward the ramp. Here on the shore of Little Sister Key, Florida Bay spread out before her, its crystalline blue waters stretching placidly toward the southernmost Florida mainland and the Everglades. Sea birds swooped gracefully above, riding invisible air currents. The morning glowed warm and balmy, a perfect tropical December day.

Except, of course, for the alligator. The alligator that wasn't.

As Lynne reached the edge of the boat ramp, she could no longer deny what was lying there, half in and half out of the water. Despite her wishful thinking, Lynne had known at first glance that she wasn't looking at any crocodilian. This was a female homo sapien lying here, face down on the concrete, the bay waters lapping at her legs.

She moved forward cautiously. One motionless arm was stretched toward her. She thought she recognized the woman but deliberately avoided looking at her face as she gingerly wrapped her fingers around the cold wrist, searching for a pulse.

No pulse.

No warmth in the body, either. The slim, tanned wrist wore a small gold watch rimmed with diamonds, but the chilly hand attached to that wrist was stiff and unyielding. The fingernails were freshly manicured and polished in a cheery tangerine, with no signs of the damage that a struggle might have caused.

Indeed, up close, Lynne could see no signs of violence of any sort. No obvious blood or rips or holes in the fabric of the loose, flowing, dark green dress twisted and tangled around the woman's ankles. Flimsy dark green sandals remained on her feet, exposing tangerine-painted toenails.

Lynne had postponed confirming her snap identification as long as she could. Now she steeled herself to back off and look at the entire picture, not merely its components. She took a deep breath and moved away.

There was no question, no doubt.

This was Peggy's friend who had stopped by last night while they were having drinks and hors d'oeuvres.

Lynn struggled now to remember the woman's name. Sandy? Debbie? It was one of those old-style cheerleader names like Barbie and Susie, names that nobody under forty had anymore.

Darcy. That was it. Darcy. Who had dropped off the schedule for a holiday tennis tournament, a tournament Darcy would not play in.

Welcome to the Keys.

# Chapter 2

**THE** *Previous Morning*

As the red Mustang convertible headed up out of the Everglades, Jenna Montgomery caught herself checking her watch and issued a mental reprimand.

This was a vacation.

She didn't need to worry about the time or the day or where she was headed or how she was going to pay for it. Everything was taken care of, courtesy of her mother, the Booked for Travel agency, and Peggy Parker, her mother's old PTA buddy from Floritas, California. Jenna's role was simple enough: work on her tan, do a little diving, eat large quantities of crab meat, drink some beer, work on the tan a bit more.

And keep her mother company, of course, but that was no chore. Lynne Montgomery was a paragon among mothers—at least among the mothers of Jenna's twenty-something friends. She wasn't the kind of mom who made unreasonable demands, asked pointed questions about marriage and grandchildren, reminded her daughter of past failings and present uncertainties and future . . . well, that was actually a big part of the problem. Jenna couldn't even supply a noun to go along with the adjective "future."

The fact of the matter was that Jenna's future was problematic at best. She'd been drifting along for a few years now, sharing a Santa Monica apartment with a couple of girlfriends, working at an independent bookstore in West L.A., wondering occasionally what she might want to do with her life. Realizing, deep down, that this *was* what she was doing with her life, and that she had a degree with honors in English literature from UCLA, and probably ought to be doing something a bit more focused. And now Booker T, the wonderful indy bookstore that had allowed her to avoid confronting her future, was going out of business. Closing its doors for good at the end of January, its financial hemorrhage so intense that Jenna's boss had seemed relieved not to have to pay her for the two weeks she'd be gone.

"Just one more stop," her mother said now, as they approached the Royal Palm Visitor's Center, near the Everglades National Park exit.

"Whatever." Jenna knew that it would be useless to complain. Her mother was on autopilot here, too thorough and compulsive a traveler not to stop automatically and scope out any place with a trail, a gift store, or a nature exhibit.

While this was the second complete day of their Florida trip, Jenna had found most of what had occurred since leaving Southern California disjointed and disorienting. They'd flown into Miami the night before last on a flight delayed so long that economy passengers were actually offered a free drink when the plane finally got off the ground.

The flight itself had a decidedly Caribbean flavor, with announcements in both English and Spanish and a general lack of concern about time, though passengers connecting to Rio de Janiero and Sao Paulo were assured that they would make their connections. The view coming into Miami was a breathtaking swath of lights glittering through air newly cleared by rain. A few residual low clouds floated below the plane, occasionally obscuring the vista of skyscrapers, including one lit in wavy contours of periwinkle blue.

The reality, alas, had been considerably less enticing: a tired terminal with stained carpets and half the stalls in the ladies room bearing paper towels hung over closed doors announcing they were out of order—a perfect segue into their airport-adjacent motel, a place so seedy that the parking lot required a full-time attendant who was probably armed with an Uzi. The motel was just a stone's throw away from the Pink Pussycat, featuring nude dancers, its roof decorated with huge plastic palm trees of varying sizes in orange, red, and green.

In the morning, her mother had insisted on detouring through Miami Beach, and Jenna had been surprised and delighted by South Beach, where they stopped for breakfast. The Art Deco architecture was spiffed up and fresh, the buildings small and precious, all painted in tropical colors reminiscent of fruits: lemon, peach, salmon, and mango. Plus aqua. Lots of aqua. It was, she'd realized with a start, the same color scheme as the Mad Hatter's Teacups in Disneyland.

As they wound their way out of Miami, billboards everywhere proclaimed WE BUY UGLY HOUSES, a commodity that appeared to be in limitless supply. The contrast was stunning as they escaped into the Everglades, going from

Florida's most highly developed space to its least developed in the span of a few hours. They picked up a selection of unfamiliar tropical fruits at a whimsical stand called Robert Is Here, then they meandered along the winding two-lane park road at a pace that delivered them to their lodgings at Flamingo just in time for a spectacular sunset.

Now, on their way out of the park, Jenna resisted the impulse to slather on one last coat of Everglades Everyday insect repellent. Mosquitoes were rarely a problem in Southern California, which was essentially, under its veneer of expansive irrigated lawns, a desert.

South Florida, on the other hand, was essentially a swamp. The dockside shop at Flamingo had offered half a dozen varieties of bug dope, and Jenna had coated herself repeatedly. The shop also sold some remarkably constructed clothing designed to protect wearers against skeeters, and she had been tempted to buy a mosquito netting hat to protect the tender flesh of her face. She had no trouble, however, passing up the T-shirt bearing a hideous, gargantuan mosquito asking, GOT BLOOD?

No need for special clothing, it turned out. Gator repellant would have been more useful. From the fifteen-foot crocodile lolling about at the Flamingo dock to the dozens of alligators and crocs they passed on the Backwater Cruise down ramrod straight channels into the wild, there'd been no shortage of creepy reptiles. "Can't remember when I've seen so many," the taciturn boat captain told them.

And then there were still more as they walked along raised wooden pathways winding into the swamp.

"You know, Mom," Jenna said, "I think it's time to get

out of the Everglades. I can actually tell the difference between an alligator and a crocodile."

"Well, I don't think there *are* any crocodiles this far from the sea," her mother responded. "They're salt water creatures, remember, or at least brackish, mixed with fresh water. And alligators are fresh water. This far away from the ocean, all of the ones you see here are bound to be alligators."

"That's not the point," Jenna told her, astonished to be arguing such an esoteric reptilian issue. She waved at the alligator lying at water's edge some thirty feet away. The guide this morning had explained that on cool days the creatures would lie out to obtain a "solar gain," a term Jenna instantly recognized as synonymous with sunbathing. "Wide snout, no snaggleteeth. That's definitely a gator."

"Ready for the Keys, then?"

"Absolutely. How long is it going to take to get there?"

Her mother shrugged. "A few hours? I can't really tell. But there's only one road, and I say it's time to get on it."

❧

**MOVING** south along the road that would become the Overseas Highway as soon as they left the Florida mainland, Lynne sneaked a look at Jenna. Her daughter had her seat back at a forty-five-degree angle and was lying with her eyes closed, efficiently catching rays while they hurtled through mangrove swamps.

Jenna was a beautiful girl, pure California with her blond hair, blue eyes, and long, eternally tanned legs.

Lynne had grown accustomed to having heads turn when the two of them walked together, a phenomenon that did not occur when Lynne walked alone, except occasionally on early morning strolls along the Floritas seawall, when men of a certain age were exercising. Indeed, Lynne had come to relish the attention, felt a rush of maternal, almost primeval pride in her role in the creation of this splendid young woman.

Looking at her now, Lynne could see Monty's profile superimposed on Jenna—the same slant of forehead, slightly tilted nose, slightly more determined jaw. She felt a momentary twinge of pain and grief, the sensation of helpless loss that still overcame her unexpectedly, years after Monty's sudden death.

The experts claimed that time would dull the sense of overwhelming despair that came with unanticipated widowhood. Lynne could grudgingly concede that she had reached some accommodation to the irretrievable loss she had experienced that January morning when Monty carried his surfboard out of the ocean onto the Pacific shore, then suffered the massive heart attack that left him dead before he ever hit the sand. He had still been in his wetsuit when she reached the hospital, forced her way into the emergency room cubicle where he lay lifeless, took his hand into her own, and collapsed sobbing on his forever-still chest, clad in cold black neoprene.

She shook herself from the memories, came back to Highway 1. They had the road pretty much to themselves on this straight shot from Florida City to the Upper Keys. Lynne had never been there as an adult and had only a vague sense of what to expect. But she smiled as she saw the sign for Surprise Lake, named by the laborers hacking their way through mangrove jungle to make way for Henry Flagler's outrageous Overseas Railway. The lake had been named for the most fundamental of reasons: nobody knew it was there until they came upon it in the steamy heat of South Florida expansionism.

The area was proving to be a world of surprises, a mishmash of cultural and economic themes, many of them flatout loony. Lynne had somehow expected South Florida to be like Southern California—both noted repositories for sun-loving nutcases—but there was an edge of wild abandon in Florida that felt totally unfamiliar.

Florida, it seemed, was the endgame for the American Dream.

✿

**JENNA** awoke surrounded by gas stations and fast food restaurants and shops that offered SEASHELLS! BAIT! SANDALS! BIKINIS! They were crawling down a busy highway, the sun bright overhead.

"Where are we?" she asked, shaking her head to dismiss the cobwebs that always muddled her when she fell asleep midday. Some folks could nap easily, but upon waking Jenna always found herself disoriented rather than refreshed. In this case, she had every reason to feel disoriented. She was somewhere in South Florida, in a red convertible with the top down, fleeing swamps full of alligators and mosquitoes.

"Key Largo," Lynne answered. "Welcome to the Keys. We've officially arrived."

Jenna swiveled her head, still groggy. "Pennecamp Park?" The John Pennecamp Coral Reef State Park was reputed to have extraordinary diving, and it was, ultimately, the prospect of the diving that had tipped the scales toward coming along on this trip, though Jenna knew she hadn't exactly been a hard sell.

"Behind us, mostly." Lynne waved her left hand toward

the south. "It looks like there are about four hundred dive shops around here. I'd just as soon not stop right now, though. We can come back in a day or so, or you can swing back through without me. Peggy says there's some incredible diving closer to Little Sister Key, so you may be content with that."

"You can tell me how to find this again?" Jenna asked.

Lynne laughed. "Honey, there's only one road, and we're on it. You can keep track of where we are by the Mile Marker signs. They start at zero in Key West and end in Miami with one twenty-six. We're right around one hundred now. Little Sister Key, where we're going to be staying, is Mile Marker Twenty-Six."

Jenna attempted to absorb and file this information. She had done so little planning for this trip that she had barely managed to collect her swimsuits and sunscreen. "Key Largo. Is that where they shot the Bogart movie?"

"Nope. That was classic Hollywood, shot almost entirely in California, your basic 1940s sound stage special. They actually didn't even call this place Key Largo until after the movie came out. It had some other name before that—Rock Harbor, I think. I believe, however, that somewhere along here is the original boat they used to shoot *The African Queen*. For those who need a Bogart fix regardless of the movie."

"I can pass," Jenna said, pulling her seat to a more upright position and looking around. This was all considerably more crowded than she had anticipated. And not very charming, either. There were too many beat-up old buildings, paint-peeling motor courts, funky little shops selling souvenirs that were probably made in China. A jarring nod to the holiday season was evident in occasional blow-up

Santas and snowmen, outside shops frantically competing for the tourist dollar.

A roadside sign from the American Red Cross warned: 169 DAYS UNTIL HURRICANE SEASON. A jackass in a red car as bright as their own hurtled down the center divide of the highway and passed them, disappearing ahead, then making a satisfying reappearance: stopped on the right shoulder in front of a Monroe County Sheriff's car with its lights flashing.

And then something almost magical happened.

As they moved farther down into the Keys, everything seemed to slowly change. The commercial elements receded, the natural ones coming to the forefront. They passed through areas of low vegetation that suddenly broke into expanses of clear blue water.

The world flattened out. There was water everywhere, the road skimming along on the merest suggestions of islands. They stopped for lunch at a roadside diner with passable conch chowder—pretty much indistinguishable from clam chowder, which Jenna didn't care for either—and an incredible view of mangrove hammocks and rippling waters, seabirds suddenly lunging into the waters to catch fish.

After lunch, the road seemed to simply disappear. The bridges grew longer and longer, stretching ahead toward only the promise of more land.

"This is amazing," Jenna said. "It's like there's more bridge here than land."

"That's because in the middle keys there just about *is* more bridge than land. We'll be coming up to the Seven Mile Bridge soon. Which is just exactly what it sounds like."

Jenna looked around. "This is all nice and everything, but *why?*"

Her mother laughed. "Because Henry Flagler was a very determined man. He pretty much invented modern Florida, which I'm not sure is something to be proud of. But never mind that. Flagler came here at the end of the nineteenth century when it was mostly uninhabitable and certainly uninhabited by Anglo-Americans. He'd made buckets of money as John D. Rockefeller's partner, and he started putting it into the construction of hotels on the eastern Florida coast, working his way down from St. Augustine and building railroads to link them up to what was then considered civilization, up north."

"I still don't see what that has to do with putting up seven-mile-long bridges that don't really go anywhere."

"Well, that's the thing, Jenna. Henry Flagler didn't think that it was going nowhere. He had a plan to develop Key West as a major shipping port because it had an excellent harbor and was close to Havana and the Panama Canal. Miami didn't have a deep-water harbor at the time. So Flagler built this as an Overseas Railway with the idea that he could ship stuff down to Key West and then send it off into the world. The railroad ran for a couple of decades, then it got wiped out in a hurricane in 1935, along with hundreds of men who were working on a road to go alongside it.

"And that was that, the end of the railroad. This was during the Depression, and the railroad had been too expensive to build in the first place. So they slapped a highway on top of what remained of the railway. Most of the bridges had survived, actually, which was pretty impressive engineering."

They were coming onto the Seven Mile Bridge now, and

Jenna looked around in amazement. "This is kind of scary, you know?"

Her mother looked over. "Scary how, Jen?"

"Scary like there's nothing in sight but water."

"Well, there's also the old bridge." Lynne pointed off to the right, where another roadway ran parallel to the bridge they were traveling on. A dozen snowy egrets flew past, graceful as ballerinas. "I believe they blew up part of it to make the movie *True Lies*, back before Arnold Schwarzenegger went into politics."

There was, indeed, a section of the bridge missing. But beyond that, there was nothing to be seen in any direction. They were probably halfway across the bridge before Jenna realized she was clenching her hands so tightly that her nails were leaving white marks across her palm. In a pattern not unlike the Keys.

❧

**LYNNE** hadn't expected to find the Keys familiar, exactly, even though she knew she'd been there as a child and had photographic evidence of the visit. She had some very specific memories, too, from the period when her Navy pilot daddy had been stationed at Key West. She had pieced together the dates from her memories of having just started first grade.

Her thrice-widowed mother Priscilla was no help at all reconstructing the Key West recollections. Priscilla had moved so many times before and after Key West that she swore entire decades were a blur. Given her mother's predilection for embroidered historical memories, it probably didn't matter much that Priscilla was vague about Key West. If she'd claimed to remember it in detail, Lynne knew, those details were likely to be hopelessly out of line with whatever the reality might have been.

Now she could feel herself relaxing, her heartbeat slowing, her breathing becoming more languid. The Keys actually *felt* different. The very essence of the journey metamorphosed as they passed across this string of islands, stitched together by the bridges built for that cockamamie railway.

The air seemed softer here, the light more tempered, the waters impossibly blue. And everything was wide and flat—really flat, elevation above sea level being measured in inches for the most part—and the water itself remarkably shallow. "If you were ten feet tall," the Everglades guide had said, "you could walk to Key West." No mountains here, no sudden offshore drop-offs, no pounding surf, not even much resembling waves in the pale turquoise waters. It was a world apart from Southern California, alike only in that both featured a junction between water and land.

Magnificent cloud formations floated above azure waters, tiny uninhabited islands speckled the horizon, large confident birds swooped and dove into the sea, emerging triumphant with fish flapping in their beaks. The landscape was at once foreign and familiar, and Lynne was glad she had come.

"I think we'll be getting there pretty soon," Lynne told Jenna now. They had just crossed onto Big Pine Key, where signs everywhere warned to watch out for Key Deer, indigenous creatures that had flirted with extinction but were apparently now on the road to species recovery. They were tiny by normal deer standards and extremely cute, both factors that had endangered them over time, along with a tendency to get too chummy with tourists and lose their fear of man. "Little Sister Key is just a couple more islands over, past Rampart Key."

It seemed like only a few more minutes before Jenna exclaimed, "Hey!" She pointed at a sign for Dos Hermanas Resort, off to the right. "Ask me, 'Are we there yet?'"

Lynne smiled. *Are we there yet?* had been a family joke, Monty's inevitable plaint when they were headed anywhere, even to visit his parents or siblings, all of whom lived in San Diego county, a stone's throw from Floritas. He'd lacked Lynne's spirit of travel, had wholeheartedly believed that their corner of Southern California was already the finest place on earth.

Which might just have been true, but until she'd seen lots more of the globe, Lynne wasn't willing to concede that point.

*Chapter 3*

THE main office of Dos Hermanas Resort was nestled in a stand of palm trees on the left-hand side of the road, facing southeast. A sign promised VACANCY, but Lynne knew they were expecting to fill up by the week before Christmas and stay full for months to follow. When the north wind doth blow, folks from Maine to Minnesota looked south, and those who looked as far south as they could go without benefit of passport often headed for the Keys.

Lynne smiled at the five-foot-tall manatee mailbox holder that stood out front. It was a particularly idealized and pristine representation of a species that Lynne had seen alive only in damaged form, recuperating in various aquaria, flesh stitched with scars from encounters with man and man's boats. The manatee was neither particularly bright nor attractive, but nonetheless beloved among Floridian environmentalists, a kind of stand-in, she suspected, for their love-hate relationship with tourists.

She parked by the office door, then walked inside with

Jenna, feeling almost giddy with anticipation. Peggy Parker was a real friend, the kind of person you could pick up with instantly after a separation of years, as if you'd been together just a day or two ago. It had been close to twenty years since the Parkers had left Floritas, one of many stops on Rick Parker's rise up various corporate ladders. Peggy and Lynne spoke on the phone occasionally, emailed each other news and photos of grandchildren.

A young man stood behind the front desk of the small office, but before Lynne could speak, the door opened behind him and Peggy hurried out, beaming. "You're here!" She came around the counter and offered a warm hug. "How great to see you!"

"And look at you!" Lynne returned the hug with enthusiasm. She hadn't seen Peggy in person for many years, but she would have recognized her face anywhere. What she hadn't expected, hadn't even considered, was that her friend would have white hair. Not gray, not silver, but a bright incandescent white. It made her look . . . well, not older, exactly, though this woman was clearly of middle age and then some. It made her look stately, mature. And, in conjunction with a light tan, a bit foxy.

"And this is Jenny! Or Jenna, your mom says you're called now. My heavens, girl, you're even prettier than your pictures." Peggy hugged Jenna, then turned to face them both. "Let me show you your rooms, and then we can reminisce. I've got you in Hyacinth, my top-of-the-line cottage. It isn't rented until just before Christmas."

She led them across quiet, spacious grounds, shaded by palm trees and unfamiliar shrubs with vivid tropical flowers. A young couple lounged in one of the hot tubs and waved at Peggy as they passed. Another couple was swinging gently in a multicolored Yucatan string hammock strung between two tall palms.

The grounds were a knockout, but what made them so special was the setting. Florida Bay spread out before them in warm inviting shades of aquamarine, as graceful birds swooped and soared above the water, riding the thermals, sometimes abruptly diving headfirst into the bay and emerging with a silver fish flopping in a built-for-action beak. Peggy led them past cages camouflaged into the shrubbery and filled with parrots and other tropical birds. As they passed, a couple of old-style wolf whistles came from one of the cages.

Lynne laughed as she looked back at the cages. "I can't take Jenna anywhere without exciting the natives."

"Mom!"

"They whistle at just about anybody," Peggy said. "It's actually good for business, I think." She stopped at a cottage fronting on the bay and waved hellos to a couple of old boys in ball caps bringing a boat full of fishing tackle into the Dos Hermanas harbor. No other boats were currently tied up at the three docks.

"Catch anything special?" Peggy called to the fishermen.

One of them grunted as he cut the motor and tied up to the dock. His companion grinned in the sudden silence. "Everything I catch is special, Peggy. I caught Madeline and my luck's held ever since."

Peggy chuckled as she turned back to Lynne and Jenna. "They come for a month to fish, have for years. Their wives come for the first two weeks, then take off on a trip of their own. They just left for Charleston, and they'll all meet up for Christmas again, back in Ohio."

She climbed two steps to a screened porch and unlocked

the door. Inside were two bedrooms, a kitchenette, and a modest living room. "We'll have dinner tonight at our place if that's all right."

"Absolutely!" Lynne told her.

"Good, then. It'll be fun. Rick's going to barbecue. He's become quite the chef—turned into one of those guys who suddenly discover cooking and think it's always fun. For his birthday, I got him one of those massive stainless steel grills. You know, the ones that look like a car on a high-speed train. Only one small glitch for tonight. Our sister-in-law Gloria's here, I'm afraid. Rick's brother's wife. She'll be at dinner, too."

"Did you mention her before?" Lynne asked, quite certain that Peggy had not.

Peggy shook her head. "I guess I was hoping she'd evaporate, or go back to Connecticut or something. But no such luck. She's here for the winter, it seems, and there's not a damn thing I can do about it."

She looked around, as if checking for eavesdroppers. "Gloria is, well, a little difficult. No, I take that back. She's a *lot* difficult. She acts like she's really slumming to be here, instead of Palm Beach, which she seems to believe is her birthright. But there's this little problem about her husband being in jail for eighteen months for insider trading, and some kind of whopping fine that's left her destitute. Her version of destitute, anyway. She's a royal pain in the butt, actually, but Rick feels an obligation to have her here, his brother's wife and all."

Lynne laughed. "You make her sound so appealing."

Peggy showed them around the cottage, then stepped over to the living room window and pointed. "Our house is over there, Bougainvillea, with a big stand of guess-what coming up by the patio. You probably don't remember, but our place in Floritas had bougainvillea spilling over the backyard fence, blooming year round. The buildings here are almost all named for flowers, which is part of why I liked Dos Hermanas from the beginning when we started looking for a place to buy. Gloria's on the point there, upstairs in Jasmine, with an incredible view. I could get a lot of money for that unit, but hey, I've learned to pick my battles. So why don't you freshen up, or nap or whatever, then come over around five. We can watch the sun set and get drunk and talk about the olden days."

❧

**RICK** was fifty pounds heavier than he'd been in Floritas, but he still had a full head of sandy hair and a salesman's easy good nature. He offered a bear hug to Lynne when she and Jenna arrived at Bougainvillea at five.

"You look great, Lynne! And Jenna, you're all grown up." Keeping his left arm around Lynne, he extended a hand to Jenna, who looked startled at first, then pleased as she shook hands with him. He led them out to the patio, cut off from the rest of the Dos Hermanas property by three colors of bougainvillea—amber, purple, and deep red—all grown together in an impenetrable, spiky tangle. On the other side of the patio an enormous banyan tree had put down huge aerial roots.

"We're cut off from the rest of the resort back here," he explained. "It's one thing to run a resort, and something else altogether to live there as well. That's something I never really thought about before. We like being able to lock the door and come out here where there's no hint of anybody else in the world."

It was, Lynne agreed, a spectacular view. An expanse of rich blue waters swept past, heading for the horizon. A few miles out, heavy vegetation on another island hid whatever development might be there, giving an utterly unspoiled vista. And a vista where the sun was beginning to set, some random clouds making interesting obstacles for the disappearing rays.

"Nice sunset," Lynne said. "You order that special for us?" She took a sip of wine as she watched Jenna take a swig of beer. Jenna had asked for St. Pauli Girl, which surprised Lynne a little. She'd expected Jenna to ask for a margarita. This patio and this view had certainly wiped out any doubt in Lynne's mind that they had safely arrived in Margaritaville.

"Back here," Rick told them, pulling aside a croton bush's red and gold foliage, just in front of the banyan, "is where we're going to expand the family room." Piles of cinder blocks and some lumber under weatherproof canvas tarps sat expectantly, and he'd cleared away most of the shrubbery.

"Just like every place we ever lived," Peggy said. "One project after another. Basements to finish out, yards to fence, closets to build. Half the time we didn't even get these things done before we were moving again. We'd just do some kind of slapdash quick fix and call Mayflower."

"I can't help myself," Rick admitted cheerfully. "The only reason I didn't do more of this before was that I was working and on the road too much. Now that obstacle has been *ree*-moved." He rubbed his hands together with a villainous grin.

"Yoo hoo!" The gate in the bougainvillea wall opened and a statuesque woman strode in, wafting a cloud of expensive-smelling perfume. She was hopelessly overdressed for a casual family dinner in a three-piece celery-colored linen pants outfit, with matching strappy sandals.

Her hair was coiffed, not combed, and her makeup looked like it had taken the better part of an hour.

As Peggy introduced Gloria Parker, the woman extended an imperial hand at an angle that suggested that perhaps Lynne was supposed to kiss it, or at the very least admire an emerald the size of a laptop key. When Lynne shook that hand, it dissolved into a delicate mini-shake, the kind that women no longer used unless troubled by arthritis. That didn't seem to be the case here. Gloria Parker was troubled only by her own presumed superiority.

"So nice to meet you," Lynne told Gloria.

"Charmed, I'm sure," Gloria responded, and Lynne heard Jenna begin a little coughing fit behind her.

"Peggy says you're here for the winter," Lynne told her.

"It gets so dreary up in Greenwich," Gloria said.

Oh yeah.

Before Gloria could share much of her tale of travail, the gate in the bougainvillea opened again to admit a bright, lively woman with silver-blond hair and skin tanned a warm gold. She wore a floral shorts outfit and turned immediately to Lynne.

"You have to be Lynne Montgomery," she said with a sunny smile, "and Jenna. I've been hearing about you for weeks. I'm Darcy. I live over in the mobile home park next door."

"Pleased to meet you," Lynne said, which, after the glacial superiority of Gloria, was certainly true. Jenna also offered a smile and an acknowledgement.

"I won't keep you," Darcy said, handing Peggy a manila envelope. "I think I've worked out the schedule for the tennis tournament, Peggy. When you get a chance to look at it, let me know if everything's okay and I'll post it here and at the Court. Will you want inserts for the guest portfolios?"

Peggy considered for a moment, then shook her head. "I think if it's posted that ought to be enough notice." She turned to Lynne. "Darcy's responsible for the folder you may have noticed in your cottage, the one with info on resort activities and Keys restaurants and stuff."

Lynne nodded. As a matter of reflexive professional curiosity, she had already examined the information in the vinyl notebook with the gaudy parrot gracing its cover. "It looked great to me. You must have put a lot of time and effort into it, Darcy."

"Not really," Darcy answered, "but thanks." Her smile was warm and genuine.

"Would you like a drink?" Rick asked, making a move toward the bar.

Darcy shook her head. "Thanks, but I've got to run. See you all tomorrow!" And she was gone as quickly as she had arrived.

❧

**THEY** watched the sunset from the patio, drinking wine and eating veggies and a hot crab dip served with thin slices of crusty French bread. The patio was comfortably private and heavily vegetated, filled with ferns and palms and colorful croton bushes. A huge staghorn fern hung on the wall, larger than what you'd encounter in most urban conservatories.

"Who'da thunk we'd end up here?" Rick said, making some kind of minute adjustment to the fresh snapper he was cooking, then closing the lid of the gargantuan gas grill.

"For a while there, I had trouble keeping track of your address from one Christmas to the next," Lynne said. Rick Parker had been in biotech sales, uprooting his family at regular intervals to facilitate his promotions. "You moved more often than a lot of military families, and I've got to say that when I was growing up, there were times when the Navy transferred my dad so often that I'd hardly get my clothes hung in the closet before it was time to move again."

"It was fun, for the most part," Peggy said. "I got to keep fixing up new houses and learn about gardening in different parts of the country."

"The family gypsies," Gloria said, in a tone that carried no affection. She was drinking Singapore Slings and had already put away quite a lot of them.

"I don't even remember where all you went," Lynne said, ignoring Gloria. "Atlanta and Milwaukee, and . . . I don't know."

Peggy ticked them off on her fingers. "From Floritas we went to Milwaukee. From Milwaukee to Dallas and then to Richmond and from there to Atlanta. The last big move was Atlanta to Miami."

"Where we cashed in all the stock options I'd been collecting with my last company, the biotech people who hit the jackpot," Rick concluded. "At which point I took early retirement, riding the old golden parachute."

"I was hoping you'd come back to Southern California," Lynne told them.

"Me, too," Peggy admitted. "Of all the places we lived, I think I liked Floritas the best. But by the time we retired, our kids and grandkids were in the Southeast. Besides, we cashed out of California real estate too long ago to ever be able to get back in at a reasonable level. At least not without tying up most of the money we got from the stock."

"The California shell game," Rick said. "You have to have done pretty well with it, Lynne, even without moving."

"That we did. Monty never wanted to leave Floritas, and we got into our place at such a steal that it never made sense to move. We just added on and remodeled a bit." The house that Lynne and Monty had bought for $41,000 was fully paid for and now worth over three-quarters of a million. It was ridiculous, but comforting.

The sunset continued in earnest, a dazzling display of purple and mauve, shot through with sprays of gold and apricot, receding behind the jagged treetops on the next key over.

"We never had sunsets anywhere that compared to the ones in Floritas, watching the sun melt into the Pacific," Peggy said. "But this is every bit as good, I think. Better, actually, since we don't have to even leave the premises to enjoy it. And not nearly as crowded. A lot of times, it seems like we're the only ones the sun's performing for. Like some kind of incredible personal presentation."

Rick nodded in agreement then hoisted his frosty beer bottle. "To sunset in paradise."

Lynne lifted her own wine glass. "To visiting old friends in paradise."

"To paradise, period," Peggy said firmly. "I think we've all learned that paradise is where you find it."

Gloria, sipping her fourth or fifth Singapore Sling, ignored the toast altogether.

❧

**LYNNE** stayed to help clean up over Peggy's protests. Jenna, who had switched to margaritas after all, claimed sudden exhaustion, but offered to assist. Lynne had raised her well. Peggy shooed her off, and Jenna put up only token resistance. Gloria had vanished at the moment there appeared to be chores, and Rick was silently slumbering in a lounge on the patio. He'd always been one to doze off if parties went on late.

"You told me on the phone you'd been having some problems around here," Lynne said as she loaded the dishwasher. Peggy had alluded in a recent email to a succession of annoyances. "A power failure or something? Vandalism?"

Peggy nodded. "Both. Vulgarities spray painted on the side of the building a couple of times. Not very inventive, actually. 'Blow me.' 'Suck this,' with a very crude illustration. And just as soon as we'd gotten that cleaned off, somebody dropped a bucketful of chum in the swimming pool and we had to empty and refill the whole thing."

"Chum?"

"Fish bait. For large fish. Big bloody chunks of organic matter. Thoroughly disgusting. Also there was the time the power went out in the middle of the night."

"Late enough that you were asleep?"

"My bedside clock stopped at three fifteen. We didn't realize it had happened until the next morning. It didn't really matter much, since everybody here is on vacation, living on island time. Some folks missed a fishing charter and my sister-in-law, missed a hair appointment in Key West. And we paid for some food that spoiled in a couple of refrigerators in the units. But at least there's nobody here on an iron lung or something."

Lynne nodded, opening a cupboard door to find where to put away the rinsed and dried wine glasses. Peggy pointed to a cabinet in the corner.

"So what did the problem turn out to be?"

"Something related to the main breaker. If that's even the right term. If you had this problem in a house, it would either be the main line into your house or some kind of outage through the whole neighborhood. The fish was the worst though. Not the chum in the pool, the ones in the saltwater tank in the breakfast room."

"What happened?"

Peggy offered a growl. "In the breakfast room over at the Orchid Lodge there's a huge fish tank, a hundred gallons, and it used to be filled with all kinds of beautiful saltwater fish. Saltwater tanks are notoriously fussy, and if you don't keep the chemical levels just right, it can be sayonara in a hurry. It was Rick's birthday present from me. I ordered the tank and we went together to Miami and bought the fish, which cost a fortune. They were beautiful, Lynne. Colors that didn't even seem real. And we had some gorgeous anemones, too, really big ones, the kind you only see if you're snorkeling or visiting a major aquarium. I told Rick he should have one of the staff take charge of it, but he insisted on doing everything himself. He was very serious about it, maintaining the chemical levels, feeding the fish, all that kind of stuff."

"Good for him!" Lynne said. You couldn't always count on the person who started a major project to handle upkeep on the project, particularly if that person happened to be in the husband category.

"It was really nice. Until one morning I walked into the breakfast room and all those beautiful fish were floating belly up on top of the water."

"What happened? Something about the chemicals?"

Peggy closed her eyes. "You could say that. Somebody poured a gallon bottle of bleach into the water. And left the empty bottle floating on top with all the dead fish."

"How awful! When did this happen?"

"About a week ago."

Just then the lights went out.

## Chapter 4

**LYNNE** woke early the next morning, feeling comfortable and restored. Outside her open window she could hear bird cries—mostly wild, interspersed with some wolf whistles and an insistent "rise and shine" repeated at regular intervals.

She was surprised to find herself up at this early hour, actually. Her internal clock was normally set to Pacific time and Southern California, but sometime in the last sixty-odd hours, she had moved into vacation time, which always seemed to find its own rhythms. This was probably just as well. She checked her watch against the clock on the stove and learned that last night's power failure had lasted close to three hours.

Still, it was nice to be on a pure vacation, to not be responsible for fixing anything. This was the first true pleasure trip she'd taken in a long time: no tours to plan or conduct, no options to offer, no activities beyond what she decided to do for her own personal enjoyment. True, she'd been invited with an eye toward referring clients here, but there was no quid pro quo, and her only obligation was to have a good time. With Jenna along, she felt she'd stacked the odds in favor of enjoyment, and as she stretched in the unfamiliar bed, she now felt tremendous contentment.

Since breakfast wasn't served until seven, she decided to take a stroll around the key, at least the parts of it accessible by foot. Whenever possible, Lynne liked to start her day with a brisk walk of a couple miles. She had meant to explore Little Sister Key more last night, but somewhere between the crab dip and her third glass of wine she'd decided it could wait until morning. Now she slipped into shorts and a ribbed sleeveless top, adding a loose, long-sleeved shirt over it in case the weather was chillier than she expected. So far the Florida December weather was deliciously warm, with none of the nighttime chill associated with Southern California's desert winter.

As she stepped out onto the grounds of Dos Hermanas, she saw nobody else. This was just the way she liked to explore a place—on her own, with no interruptions for socializing. She decided to go along the resort's shoreline, then meander through the aviary on her way out to the road. The spur on which Dos Hermanas sat came to a dead end about a quarter mile farther north, Peggy had told her.

She was wandering along the Dos Hermanas shoreline when she saw the dark green object on the boat ramp. The ramp was at the far end of the property, and she hadn't been by here at all yesterday.

For a fleeting moment she thought of the fifteen-foot-long crocodile lounging on the ramp at Flamingo before their back-country cruise yesterday morning. Crocs and alligators liked boat ramps, the guide had told them, because they resemble the "slides" they fashion for themselves

along the banks of waterways, angled to move their ungainly bulk to and from the water more smoothly.

But this wasn't an alligator. It was a woman, a woman
she was pretty sure she recognized. Lynne moved toward
her hesitantly, averting her eyes at first until she'd felt the
cold stiff wrist, ascertained that the woman was dead, and
identified her as Peggy's friend Darcy.

Now what?

Call for help, of course. Somebody was bound to be up
in the office, over in the Orchid Lodge where Peggy had
showed her the breakfast room yesterday. The breakfast
room where the saltwater fish had died.

As she turned toward the office, a strident female voice
stopped her in her tracks.

"What in the name of heaven is *that?*"

No mistaking that petulant tone of entitlement. Lynne
turned and offered a nod to Gloria Parker. Under the circumstances, a smile seemed to be in poor taste. Gloria was
wearing a lavender velour warm-up suit, its jacket zipped.
Her hair, apparently cemented in position, looked exactly
as it had the night before, though her makeup was more
abbreviated. In the morning light, some odd facial lumps
that Lynne had wondered about last night seemed more
pronounced.

"It's Peggy's friend Darcy," Lynne answered, careful to
avoid looking again at the poor woman lying splayed on
the concrete, "and I believe she's dead."

Gloria gasped and stepped backward, her fingers covering her open mouth in an expression of dismay one might
use during a particularly dramatic game of charades. "Dear
heavens, you're right. It's that Gainsborough woman. How
can this possibly be happening to me?"

"No idea, I'm afraid."

Gainsborough—was that her last name? Darcy Gainsborough. Lynne didn't have the time or energy to deal with Gloria's belief that she was always at the center of whatever universe she inhabited. This poor woman was dead, and Gloria was viewing her condition as a personal inconvenience.

Now Gloria went suddenly pale and began swaying slightly. She was a rather large woman, and Lynne hastily computed the distance to the nearest chair as she took her elbow firmly. Gloria made no attempt to resist and leaned on Lynne theatrically as Lynne led her to a white Adirondack chair, releasing the swooning woman just long enough to swing the chair around so that it no longer viewed the boat ramp.

As Gloria plopped heavily into the chair, a young couple came loping toward them across a large expanse of lawn, holding hands. They looked oddly familiar. Both appeared to be in their late twenties, around Jenna's age. He was tall, lean and pale, a spill of light brown hair covering his forehead. She was a raven-haired stunner, masses of dark curls flowing down her back, dark eyes glistening and concerned.

"Something wrong?" the young man asked.

His female companion stepped to the side for an unobstructed view of the body on the boat ramp, her eyes widening. In recognition?

"There seems to have been an accident of some sort." Lynne suddenly realized where she had seen them. They'd been laughing in the hot tub when Peggy showed the Montgomery women to their cottage yesterday. "I'm afraid this woman is dead."

This was the cue for the young woman to offer identification if she knew it, but she said nothing.

"Did she drown?" Gloria put in. Her strength apparently recovered, she twisted in the chair for a better view.

"No idea," Lynne said, "but it certainly seems like a possibility." Darcy's hair was dry, however, her makeup unsmudged. Drowning would involve immersion, and only actresses in big-budget movies retained their makeup and hairstyles after spending time underwater. She thought suddenly and irrelevantly of Bo Derek striding onshore in *10*.

Just then Lynne heard the sound of an opening door and deep masculine voices. Turning in that direction, she saw the pair of fishermen who'd been coming back to the Dos Hermanas dock yesterday as she and Jenna had arrived.

"What's up?" one of them asked as his buddy stepped past him to take a look.

"It's Darcy!" the second fisherman said, rushing forward for a view of the body.

Lynne grabbed his jacket. "Wait!"

"Gotta get her out of the water," he told her irritably.

Lynne put herself between the fishermen and the dead woman. "I'm afraid she's dead. I've already checked. We need to call the police, and they'll want us to leave everything exactly as we found it." They looked unconvinced, and behind them she could see Gloria twisting her head for a better view. So much for the vapors.

Lynne looked at her watch. Six thirty. Others would be coming out soon, power failure or no. The complimentary breakfast buffet opened at seven. She addressed both the fishermen and the young couple. "If you folks could just stay here for a minute while I go call the police?" She looked directly at the fishermen, particularly the one who had recognized the victim and tried to reach her. "It's very important not to let anybody go near—" She waved an arm behind her, in the general direction of the body.

"Of course, we'll stay," the young woman said. She pushed back a section of riotously curled jet-black hair and frowned. Beside her, her male companion seemed pale, nondescript. "But are you sure she's dead? Shouldn't we be trying CPR or something? I'm certified."

Lynne shook her head. "I'm afraid she's long past CPR. But thanks for helping. I'll be right back." She turned to Gloria. "When I get back, I can walk you back to your room." This would involve negotiating a flight of stairs. She hoped Gloria would decide to go to breakfast instead.

Gloria Parker snorted. Her lips were set in a grimace, her eyes virtual slits. "I can certainly get to my own room, thank you very much."

Lynne made a mental note. The best way to avoid Gloria seemed to be to attempt to assist her. It was well worth remembering.

※

**LYNNE** hurried to the Orchid Lodge, the main resort building that held the public office and private staff areas, a laundry, an abbreviated kitchen, and the large, airy breakfast room, which Peggy had explained was used for all kinds of social activities, many involving residents of the adjacent mobile home court as well as Dos Hermanas guests.

On her way, she passed the dozen or so large cages filled with brightly colored tropical birds, many now announcing in no uncertain terms that it was morning and they could do with a little breakfast. Too bad they couldn't speak in any conventional sense. Some of the cages had an unobstructed view of the boat dock and their observations would have been useful.

Gone was any interest Lynne might have had in her own breakfast. She couldn't imagine what Darcy Gainsborough was doing on the boat dock, dead or alive, and she had a sinking feeling that her death would create problems for Peggy and Rick, who had enough problems already—what with power outages and bleached fish and vandalism, on top of all the normal challenges of running a resort.

Lynne found Peggy in the breakfast room, where small tables were set up both indoors and outside in a large screened area with a burbling fountain at its center. The room had no view of the bay, Lynne realized, or she surely wouldn't have found Peggy nonchalantly sipping coffee and reading the *Miami Herald*.

Peggy offered a broad smile as Lynne walked in. Behind her a young Latina waitress was setting out muffins and bagels on a serving table beside several large bowls of fresh fruit and an assortment of individually sized cereal boxes.

"Hey there, girl! It's really great to have you here." Peggy offered her customary sunny smile. Her white hair shone bright in the soft tropical dawn, and she wore white shorts and a lime green T-shirt that read MARGARITAVILLE.

Lynne sighed. "You may not think so after I tell you what I just found. Is Rick up?"

"You rang?" Rick came out of the office dressed in shorts and a polo shirt that said DOS HERMANAS on the breast.

"First things first. Good morning." As the Parkers nodded and offered their own morning greetings, Lynne held a hand up. "But I'm afraid there's a big problem out on the boat ramp."

Peggy and Rick listened with growing dismay, then sprang into action. "I'll call 911," Rick said, as Peggy raced toward the door. By the time Lynne caught up with her, Peggy was standing beside the body, her hands covering her cheeks in horror.

Lynne noticed that Gloria had turned her chair a bit so that she could once again view the body. The ghoul.

"Peggy, what sort of place are you running here?" Gloria asked, accusation thickening her otherwise reedy New England accent.

Peggy ignored her. "Dear God," she murmured, "What could have happened?"

❧

**LYNNE** was pleased to see how promptly the Monroe County sheriffs arrived, firmly shooing everyone away from the boat ramp while insisting with equal firmness that nobody leave the premises. They called for crime scene technicians and detectives almost immediately.

By the time those folks arrived, most of the Dos Hermanas guests were up and milling about, fussing about time confusion and the power failure even before they learned about the body. Many chose to bring their complimentary continental breakfasts out by the pool, the better to gape, albeit at a distance. The breakfast foods were, in fact, running low, due to unusually high demand, but the cops wouldn't let Rick run to the store for more cereal and Danish.

The early morning fishermen had retreated to their porch, grumbling because the police wouldn't let them take out their boat, the only craft currently docked at Dos Hermanas.

A woman from Minnesota and two kids came out of

their cottage, assessed the situation, and went right back inside. Lynne had a pretty good idea what was going on inside that unit now. The mom was getting ready to make a run for sweet rolls at the Orchid Lodge, while the dad stayed behind and found a good cartoon channel on TV for the kids. The mom had that resourceful look to her. Lynne had actually watched the woman's gears mesh as she brought her family outside, then immediately ushered them back indoors in a single fluid movement.

A sizable contingent of residents from the Little Sister Court, the immobile mobile home park next door, had also arrived. Peggy had explained last night that Darcy was a sort of informal liaison between the resort and the mobile home park, coordinating all manner of group activities.

Lynne told her story to the first cops on the scene and then again, several times more, to Detective Rafael Ruiz, a dour man with dark, hooded eyes and an unhealthy pallor. Uniformed officers kept the growing crowd at bay with crime scene tape and stern expressions.

Detective Ruiz sat at one of the umbrella-shaded tables near the shore, beneath a palm tree bending from the weight of half a dozen coconuts. There was no actual beach here, just a shoreline marked by the edge of the concrete patio areas, with dock space for boats belonging to or rented by Dos Hermanas guests. The only boat docked there now belonged to Nate Washburn of Louisville, and police had searched it thoroughly.

"So you just went for a walk and there she was," the detective said.

"Exactly."

"And you didn't call 911. You went looking for the manager."

"The owner," Lynne corrected. "And as soon as I found

her, we called. But before I went to find her and call, these other people came by."

"Mrs. Gloria Parker, the Haedrichs, and the men from Kentucky."

The young couple, it had turned out, were John and Diane Haedrich, from Battle Creek, Michigan, which was currently buried beneath a couple of feet of snow. Both were apparently involved somehow in the manufacturing of corn flakes.

And the gentlemen from Louisville, Kentucky, where there was also currently snow falling, were Nate Washburn and Bob Fendmeyer, who were probably wishing they'd gone on to Charleston with their wives.

"Anyway," Lynne went on, "I wasn't carrying my cell phone with me and I haven't even turned it on since we got here. For all I know I can't get service out here."

"Oh, you'll be able to get service all right," Detective Ruiz told her. There was an edge of resentment in his voice. "There's excellent cellular service in the Keys. Now you say you thought you recognized the victim?"

"I was introduced to her last night. My daughter and I were having dinner with the Parkers, who are old friends, and their sister-in-law, Gloria. Mrs. Gainsborough came by and left some papers for Peggy. I met her then. The next time I saw her, she was dead on the boat ramp."

"Why would she say she wanted to meet you?"

Lynne stopped, puzzled. "Say what?"

"She told a couple of people that she was looking forward to meeting you."

"I can't imagine why."

"You didn't see anybody around when you came out here?"

"I told you I didn't."

Three times she'd told him actually, or maybe four. Lynne couldn't imagine why he was trying to trip her up on details when she was so obviously an unsuspecting passerby. But if she suggested he get to work finding out what had actually happened, she'd only make him think he ought to be concentrating on her.

Talking with police officers tended to be a lose-lose situation.

*Chapter 5*

**SHERI** McManus rinsed her coffee cup, looked around to be sure everything was tidy, then picked up her tennis racket and headed for the door of her mobile home. She was running just a little late for her match with Darcy Gainsborough over on the Dos Hermanas tennis court, and Darcy was a stickler for punctuality.

Almost as soon as she came outside, however, Sheri could tell that something was wrong. Very wrong. The mobile home court was quiet, but quite a bit of noise was coming from Dos Hermanas next door. The resort was generally quiet and serene at this hour, when she and Darcy were almost certain to have the tennis court to themselves. Sheri hurried down the pathway that led along the waterfront, her heart thumping as she approached the resort.

She stopped abruptly as she came around the last stand of mangroves at the bay edge of the grounds. There were people all over the place, yellow crime scene tape draped nearby at the edge of the property, and more police officers than she'd seen together in one place since the last Police Charitable Ball back in the Atlanta suburbs.

She recognized Andi French from the Court and slipped over to her side. Andi was a trifle crusty, but she might well be the most unflappable resident of the key. Andi could generally be counted on to avoid hysteria, and she was a pretty shrewd observer of just about everything.

"What happened?" Sheri asked. She spoke softly, realizing as she did that there was certainly no reason to whisper here. The whole area was agog and a-jabber.

"It's Darcy Gainsborough," Andi reported, incredulity in her tone. "She's dead."

Sheri felt her heart plummet. "No!"

Andi nodded, her utilitarian steel-gray braid swinging slightly. "Yes. And I don't know exactly what's going on, but the police are going around asking everybody questions."

Sheri's ears rang and her heart palpitated in panic. This was not good. A lot of people were counting on Darcy. If she was dead and there was something suspicious about her demise, many folks were going to be in big trouble soon.

Sheri thought fast. She and Darcy had long ago traded keys in case of emergency, and she also knew Darcy kept a spare key under a fake rock outside her mobile home.

Sheri wasn't normally much of a risk taker, but this was important. She excused herself, walked nonchalantly back to the Court, and slipped into the screened patio area beside Darcy's coach. She found the fake rock easily and used the key to get inside.

She had been inside this mobile home countless times in the years since she had moved here, and it always felt warmly inviting. Now, however, it had a vaguely musty smell, an almost palpable difference. It seemed less friendly. But how could that be? It was just a double-wide trailer, after all. The building and its furniture couldn't know that their owner would not be coming back.

But Sheri knew. She was projecting her own anxiety on an inanimate dwelling.

Sheri also realized it was probably only a matter of minutes until the police came by. So where was the satin-covered box she needed?

Sheri had worked with Darcy in past months, laying everything out on her mirror-finish black lacquered dining table, part of a furniture grouping that always seemed a bit too large and too dark and too self-consciously modern for its sunny Florida setting. She stood in the dining room now and tried to remember what she'd ever known about where Darcy kept things.

Not much. Or maybe her mind was just too addled this morning. She couldn't think of anything. The only way to find out, she figured, was to look, and she might as well look here, where they'd worked. She started opening drawers and cabinets.

The top shelves of the china closet held china and crystal, artfully arranged behind glass with no room for anything else. The two bottom doors of the cabinet held more china, neatly labeled in quilted vinyl covers: dinner plates, soup bowls, saucers, and more.

Next she turned to the buffet, its long flat top holding a simple Oriental flower arrangement in silk. Sheri had asked Darcy about that once, why she decorated with silk flowers when she could so easily use the real thing. Incredible flowers were available in South Florida pretty much year round. Convenience, Darcy had answered, as if instructing an idiot.

The first drawer of the buffet had built-in sections to hold silverware, a very modern design that looked like it ought to be stainless, though some of it was tarnished enough to verify that it was silver.

The second drawer, however, took her breath away. It was lined with the same dark green felt as the silverware drawer, and filled with a stunning array of neatly arranged but seemingly unrelated items: key chains, earrings, little figurines, a cuff link, some Clinique samples, a large silver key, a salt shaker in the shape of a dolphin, several different styles of condom, seashells, a couple of large pieces of beach glass, and an ounce of Chanel No. 22 perfume.

But as Sheri dimly noted the drawer's contents, she found herself riveted by an item that made her gasp in dismay: a tiny ceramic covered dish, meant to decorate a fine lady's bedchamber. The fine lady in this particular instance was Sheri McManus herself, who had painted the dish more than twenty years ago in a suburban craft shop.

Surely, she told herself at first, this was a mistake. A duplicate. Anything but what it appeared.

But this was no duplicate.

She picked the dish up carefully, turned it over to see her initials on the bottom, just as she'd written them there, along with the date. She righted the dish and stared at it. A silver lightning bolt and scattering of tiny silver stars rested lightly above a deep blue background.

She remembered painting this dish in a frustrated funk, the fall when her nest was entirely emptied, all her kids finally off to college and real life. Sheri, with way too much time on her hands and no readily identifiable aspirations or talents, had plowed through a succession of various crafts:

ceramic painting, pottery, tole painting, stained glass, decoupage, counted cross-stitch, and others too stupid to remember.

She had kept this little dish, but most of the forlorn fruits of that equally forlorn period had gone as gifts to relatives those first couple years. The rest she'd given to Goodwill, which had probably tossed most of it directly into the Dumpster. But so what? Its function had been therapy and over time it had succeeded in making her feel momentarily useful and productive.

Now she slipped the ceramic dish into the pocket of her tennis dress, thoughtfully constructed with capacious pockets to hold tennis balls at the ready. No matter what else might be happening today, no matter what had happened to Darcy, Sheri was reclaiming her dish.

She had never been entirely certain when the dish went missing. It lived in a corner of her dining room hutch for many years. Then one day when she was dusting—an activity that took place only sporadically, truth be told—she noticed that the dish was gone. Gone fairly recently at that, leaving a dish print in the surrounding dust.

She had looked everywhere, a process that doesn't take all that long in a mobile home, even a double-wide. When it didn't turn up, she worried about dementia, that she might have broken the dish and forgotten all about it. Or that she had picked it up in a similar bout of dementia and tucked it somewhere. She couldn't bear to even think the "A" word—Alzheimer's.

She had finally given up, decided that worrying about the dish was worse than having lost it.

Now it was found, and she forced herself back to the job at hand. The third drawer held neatly ironed cloth napkins. The first of the three doors below held sterling silver serving platters, wrapped in plastic wrap against tarnish. The second one had the pink-satin-covered storage box that Sheri was looking for, along with a sack of empty plastic vials and the current edition of the *Physicians' Desk Reference*. She never did open the third door.

Acutely aware of the passage of time, she looked around. The place was warming up—Darcy didn't have the air conditioning on. Not surprising. This time of year, most of them ran it rarely and sporadically. There were probably records here somewhere, too, most likely on Darcy's computer, but Sheri didn't think she had time to look, and she definitely didn't want to be here when the police came.

If they came.

With luck, this was just a pointless precaution, and they'd announce that Darcy had actually had a stroke or something, had died quickly and without pain.

Her heart still racing, Sheri relocked the door and slipped down the back pathway to her own place. She'd just given some no-longer-necessary wool sweaters to the Salvation Army, which left a perfectly sized space in the back of a deep dresser drawer in her second bedroom. She put the satin box in the drawer and covered it with a scarf.

Sheri kept Darcy's key from the fake rock and laid it carefully inside the lightning bolt dish, which she then placed back in its former location in the cherry hutch. There was a certain symmetry there, she supposed, though she wasn't sure what it involved. A few minutes later, she took Darcy's key off the third hook on the porpoise-shaped key holder in her kitchen and headed back to Dos Hermanas.

What to do now?

She asked herself what Darcy might have done, took a

deep breath, and approached a policeman. As she started to speak, she found herself bursting into tears.

✌

**LYNNE** hadn't paid a lot of attention to the gathering crowd, but once she was dismissed by Detective Ruiz she began to survey them with curiosity.

Dos Hermanas Resort was a collection of cottages scattered around the central lodge, which was flanked by a pair of matching two-story buildings with half a dozen units on each floor. The porches on those buildings were wide and fully screened, with multiple, motel-style units. Some guests, indeed, were watching the show from second-story porches, which provided better vantage points than those on ground level.

Peggy sat at a table with a woman Lynne hadn't seen before, not far from where the body still lay on the boat ramp. A pair of paramedics stood waiting, heaven knows what for. Darcy had been cold and dead when Lynne first found her. Gloria had disappeared, thank goodness, and the Haedrichs were admiring a pair of magnificent blue-and-gold macaws in a cage near the Orchid Lodge.

A young female uniformed officer moved through the crowd, taking names and asking questions. Lynne could see people shaking their heads at her questions. Nobody seemed to have seen anything, and some of those questioned wore expressions of sincere regret at having missed the action.

When they got back to their chilly home towns, they'd want to report every detail of their Florida brush with death. By then, of course, the story would be fleshed out with both fact and conjecture, embroidered beyond recognition. It would continue to grow in the basements and rec rooms of Chicago and Indianapolis, the golf courses and coffee shops of Philadelphia and Syracuse, in a multi-pronged version of the old party game, Telephone.

Overall, she noticed, the crowd was remarkably sub-dued. Maybe this kind of thing happened so frequently here that nobody was surprised or alarmed. South Florida did have a rather dangerous reputation.

Lynne joined Peggy at the ringside table, where she sat with a woman in a yellow tennis dress, tears flowing down her cheeks. Peggy introduced the woman as Sheri Mc-Manus, a friend who lived in Little Sister Court.

"I can't believe this," Sheri said numbly. "I just can't believe it. We were supposed to play tennis." She seemed totally unaware of the tears that continued to flow as she looked at her watch. "Right now. And we'd decided to partner up for the tournament." Her deeply tanned face was a maze of character lines, an odd contrast to her perky little tennis dress. "But she isn't dressed for tennis." She looked around, seemingly dazed. "Where did I leave my racket?"

"Right here on the chair," Lynne told her. "Didn't I see you talking to the police?"

Sheri nodded. "I thought they might want Darcy's house key. She and I had each others' keys"—she started crying again—"in case something happened. You know?"

Lynne and Peggy nodded. They both knew.

"How long have you known Darcy?" Lynne asked.

Sheri concentrated. "Six, seven years. She was already in the Court when we moved here. That was, let me see, seven years ago last September."

"You retired here?"

Sheri nodded. "From Atlanta. That's where we knew Peggy and Rick."

"We were neighbors," Peggy explained. "And we kept in touch after she moved here. As a matter of fact, it was Sheri who first told us that Dos Hermanas was going on the market."

"I'd been here several years by then," Sheri said. "My husband passed away not long after we moved here." She shook her head sadly. "Will retired the moment he turned seventy so he could draw on his Keogh plan with no penalty. We got a nice new unit over at the court"—she pointed eastward—"and we were happy as clams."

Lynne had long wondered how the pleasure level of bivalves was measured. She kept quiet, nodded, and realized that she already knew how this story was going to play out. Peggy was silent, looking out over the bay.

"A year and a half later, Will was diagnosed with liver cancer. He was dead two months after that." Sheri stopped speaking for a moment and closed her eyes. Tears leaked out at the edges.

"I'm so sorry," Lynne responded immediately. She was all too aware how shattering the sudden death of a husband could be, the chasm dividing what was from what never again can be.

Sheri opened her eyes and smiled gently through her tears. "When I see some of the things that people endure, I really have to believe it was a blessing of sorts that Will went so quickly. And Darcy was an enormous help to me. She'd already lost her husband. I thought at first about going back to Atlanta, but I was settled into the Court and so I stayed. It's become home for me."

"So you were here when the previous owners had Dos Hermanas."

"And the owners before them, too, right at the tail end before they sold it." Sheri smiled at Peggy. "You and Rick have some tough acts to follow, but I think you're doing just fine."

Peggy shrugged. "I hope so. Everybody says that Dos Hermanas has a really loyal clientele, and we're counting on that. I just wish we'd stop having all these problems. Not Darcy, I don't mean," she hastily amended. "That's way beyond a problem. I mean the vandalism and stuff."

"Where do your guests come from?" Lynne asked. She realized as she spoke that this was a business question, information she might use to decide which of her Booked for Travel clients would enjoy a stay at the Dos Hermanas Resort on Little Sister Key in the Florida Keys. It had, she realized suddenly, a very nice ring to it.

"Lots of places. Up north, of course. There are people from up north who've come here every winter and spring for years and years. Sometimes through generations of the same family. In the fall we get Europeans, though not as many this year as we were expecting."

"So then is the place pretty empty in summer?" Lynne envisioned a steam bath rimmed with palm trees.

"Actually the summers aren't nearly as bad as you'd expect," Sheri said. She had stopped crying and seemed to be regaining her composure. "True, it's usually in the nineties, but that's only about fifteen degrees hotter than winter, and the humidity is pretty constant year-round. We get enough wind to keep it from being unbearable."

"And believe it or not," Peggy added, "the place is usually full in the summer. Floridians like to come to the Keys in the summer, for fishing and snorkeling and whatnot."

Lynne waved a hand to indicate the crowd on screened porches, the patio, and the well-manicured lawn, flanked by rows of cages of squawking birds. Where *was* the birds' breakfast? "So these folks here now, they're regulars?"

"A lot of them."

On the boat ramp there was finally some activity. The paramedics were doing something to the body. A moment later, they pushed a loaded gurney away from the water. Peggy got up and Lynne joined her, walking behind the paramedics as they headed toward the road.

❧

**JENNA** came awake slowly, unsure at first just where she was. As she stretched, she noticed she had a queen-sized bed to herself and lay beneath a ceiling fan, not currently in operation. A window beside her bed was slightly open, letting in a warm, gentle breeze. She was wearing only an oversized T-shirt, but she'd tossed aside the covers in her sleep. Was it summer already?

No, of course not. It was two weeks before Christmas, and she was in Florida.

Not a place she had ever thought about visiting, actually. Her first thoughts of Florida, on the rare occasions when she thought about it at all, were of high-rise condos and apartment buildings filled with geriatric retirees. Florida had a copycat Disney park, voracious mosquitoes, and occasional hurricanes that scoured random communities into total oblivion.

Not a travel destination she might have chosen on her own, but the company was enjoyable and the price was right

Florida.

That's where she was. Little Sister Key.

Staying at some hotel owned by Rick and Peggy Parker, people Jenna had last seen at least fifteen years ago. Jenna had been classmates with their son Lyle at Pettigrew Elementary until the Parkers moved back east during fifth grade. Jenna had never liked Lyle, who was a bigmouthed bully, and she hadn't minded a bit when the Parkers moved away. Bringing matters up to date, last night Jenna had politely admired recent pictures of Lyle and his family. Lyle still gave her the creeps, and his sons looked like thugs-in-training, growing up into a new generation of bullies, but they all lived in Orlando and with luck Jenna would never see them again.

So far Florida was disappointing. Jenna was accustomed to being around lots of people her age, folks who threw spontaneous parties and stayed out late, were either driven to succeed or trust-funders totally disinterested in conventional success. She knew aspiring film directors and screenwriters, associates at high-octane law firms, political activists—all in their twenties.

She went to movie screenings with film industry friends, explored ethnic restaurants, worked out at a twenty-four-hour gym. Los Angeles was all about options and possibilities. Florida so far seemed limited in both. Ten days here might turn out to be a lot longer than she had expected.

In addition, something seemed amiss on this balmy Florida morning. Dos Hermanas had seemed utterly deserted last night, but now Jenna could hear voices outside, lots of them. These were not the measured tones of quiet morning dialogue but the muted babble of a dozen simultaneous conversations. She looked at the clock radio blinking 12:00 beside her bed. Power failure? But this seemed like more than that.

Now one of the voices from outside came more clearly. A man with the edge of authority in his tone. "You didn't notice anything unusual last night or this morning?" He sounded like a cop. Like Jenna's brother David, actually, who had always been a bit bossy and had developed a stern, authoritarian tone once he joined the Floritas Police Department.

Jenna sat up and leaned over to the window. She pushed the curtain aside just far enough to see that a sizable crowd was gathered on the grounds of Dos Hermanas. A crowd? Several uniformed police officers moved through the crowd, including the fellow who was questioning a woman right by Jenna's window.

She got out of bed and padded to the kitchen, where the windows offered a much better view. Yep, the place was crawling with people, and a disproportionate number were oldsters. Well, disproportionate for anywhere but South Florida. She scanned the crowd for Peggy Parker's blinding white hair and found her mother's softer blonde head right beside Peggy's.

In the heart of things, things that required police attention.

Now Jenna saw a couple of men in different uniforms coming from the edge of the water, pushing a gurney that held a covered body. They moved through a suddenly silent and respectful crowd out toward the roadway. Peggy Parker followed the gurney and Lynne Montgomery followed Peggy.

You just couldn't take Mom anywhere.

## Chapter 6

"**READY** for Key West?" Lynne asked Jenna, who was eating Frosted Flakes straight from a little box, washed down by a can of Coca-Cola. The career girl diet for the twenty-first century: sugar on sugar.

"I guess," Jenna answered. "I thought you said last night we'd just hang around here today."

"That was before that unfortunate woman turned up dead on the boat ramp," Lynne answered. "Frankly, I think this is a good time to get lost."

"You seemed to be enjoying yourself earlier."

Lynne resisted the impulse to huff a denial. "I was trying to help Peggy, that's all. But she says she's fine and has all kinds of stuff to get done today, so we're free to flee."

"Not a bad idea." Jenna popped the last Frosted Flake into her mouth and pitched the box effortlessly into the trash can across the kitchenette. "Just let me shower first."

❧

**BY** the time Dan Trenton got to Dos Hermanas, he'd already heard three different versions of what was going on at the resort.

The first, from the waitress at the coffee shop where he breakfasted over on Big Pine Key, was that a raft of dead Cuban refugees had made landfall on Little Sister Key. The second, from an electrician he passed in the parking lot, was that there'd been a shooting over a beautiful Cuban girl who had then taken her own life because the man she loved lay dead. The third, from a cop stationed just off Highway 1 to keep thrill seekers away from the crime scene, was that nothing had happened and Dan should beat it.

Dan recognized the cop, a fellow his own age named Martinelli. He'd seen him around for years now, had once talked his way out of a ticket for an illegal left turn.

"Saw your sister Brenda the other day," Dan said. "Tending bar at the Blue Moon." The Blue Moon was a Key West bar frequented by locals and the occasional tourist looking for the "real" Key West.

"Uh huh." Martinelli grunted. "Don't matter who you seen. This road's off limits right now."

"What happened?" Dan kept his tone casual. If Martinelli didn't think he cared, the cop might provide some useful information.

"Somebody died at Dos Hermanas."

As confirmation, an ambulance approached from the direction of the resort, moving at a slow speed without lights or siren. Whoever was making that trip wasn't in any hurry. The ambulance passed them and turned toward Key West, a direction that would lead either to the hospital or the morgue. Dan could see a couple of Monroe County sheriffs' cars down the road, alongside the entrance to Dos Hermanas. Two guys got in one of them and headed out, giving a nod to Martinelli as they passed and turned left on Highway 1.

"Looks like the all clear," Dan said cheerfully. "So what do you say I just go on in to work? I take care of the birds at Dos Hermanas. Very expensive birds. Very valuable. And if I don't get in there and start tending to them, they're likely to croak." This wasn't true, of course. Dan was paid quite nicely to care for the birds, but they could probably go for days without food and water before they'd have any serious problems. Martinelli, however, wasn't likely to know that.

Martinelli shrugged. "Stay out of the way, you go in there. And if you get bounced, that's it. You're out for good." He stepped back before Dan could even say thanks.

Dan drove his pickup slowly down the road and passed Dos Hermanas just as another patrol car started up and headed toward the main road. He continued to the dead end, a quarter mile down the road, turned around, drove back, and parked just past the office entrance. Then he got out of the truck and ambled onto the grounds.

He found the birds a bit riled up, which wasn't all that surprising. All kinds of folks were milling around, many in close proximity to the cages. He spoke briefly with a young couple hanging out by the macaws. The birds calmed a bit with his presence. Most of them didn't mind company, but they weren't fond of crowds. Dan moved from cage to cage, said good morning to them all, then walked down to the boat ramp where Peggy Parker sat staring out into the bay.

"What's up?" Dan turned a chair to sit on it backwards,

resting his arms on the wrought-iron chair back. "Looks like some kind of excitement."

Peggy raised dull eyes to him. "Darcy Gainsborough is dead."

"Whoa! What happened? I saw the paramedics leave, thought maybe some dude was mixing Viagra with nitro-glycerine again."

"Not this time," Peggy said. Both of them recalled an incident at Little Sister Court back in August, when that particularly deadly pharmaceutical pairing had left a re-tiree in intensive care. "I don't think anybody knows what happened. She was lying right there on the boat ramp. My friend from California found her about an hour and a half ago and she was . . . well, she'd been dead a while, I guess."

"Anything I can do to help?" Dan asked. He always flirted with Peggy, just a little, because even though she was probably thirty years older than he was, she was cute and dimply and had that dynamite white hair. He liked her husband, too. Rick was an easygoing, cheerful fellow, and Peggy usually mirrored that good cheer. Not today.

"I don't think so," Peggy said. "But the birds seem upset. Can that be possible?"

"Of course. They're intelligent, living creatures. They can sense stress around them. And they like their routines same as the rest of us." He looked at his watch. "I'm a lit-tle bit late. Had to talk my way through a roadblock to get here."

"Sorry." She nodded distractedly.

"Guess I'll get to work then. You holler if you need any-thing."

He winked as he got up and began systematically ser-vicing his feathered charges. Fresh food and water, cage bottoms scrubbed, and refuse washed away down those handy little drainage channels leading to the bay. Mangrove and flowering shrubs grew in the channels, along with the occasional palm tree, helping create the notion of a free tropical habitat for the birds caged above the channels. The bird crap kept the flowers blooming, and if some of it washed into the bay, it was probably no worse than a lot of the other garbage folks dumped out there. Dan had become fatalistic about the environmental future of the Lower Keys, though it still teed him off to see obvious abuse.

Twenty minutes later, he was finishing up with a large cage holding four African gray parrots, modestly plumed but splendidly vocal, among his favorites of the Dos Hermanas flock for their brainpower and vocabulary. "See you later," Dan told them. "See you later, Dan," two of them responded. As he closed the cage door, and started down the line toward the cockatoo cage, he sensed somebody coming up behind him from one of the waterfront cottages.

"Those are amazing birds." The voice was clear and female, and he turned to find a pair of blondes at his side—both slender and lightly tanned, dressed in shorts and sandals. A strong enough resemblance that he immediately assumed they were related, probably mother and daughter. The speaker was the older and shorter of the two, a woman in her fifties who had stopped to admire the pair of blue and gold macaws in the next cage down.

"They sure are," he answered. "Those are Gus and Gertie."

It was the younger woman who caught his attention—indeed, almost caught his breath. She was not the typical Dos Hermanas guest, looked more like somebody who'd be staying with a couple of girlfriends down in Key West, hanging out at Captain Tony's or the Green Parrot on a week's vacation from some dreary job up north.

She was tall enough to look eye to eye at Dan, her long, long legs shown off nicely by hot pink shorts and a matching crop top. As she came closer to the cage, moving with the grace of a natural athlete, he caught a scent of something floral. Her tan was light but golden, not like the girls in the Lower Keys with the year-round, deepwater tans that made them so healthy looking and appealing, at least till they turned forty.

"I'm Dan," he said, addressing them both but watching the younger one. "You staying here?"

They both nodded.

"You take care of the birds?" the older one asked. "I'm Lynne, by the way, and this is my daughter, Jenna."

He'd called that one right.

He made no move to shake anybody's hand, conveniently being up to the elbow inside the cockatoo cage. "Nice to meet you both. This here is Melissa, the most spoiled bird on the premises and possibly the entire planet."

As if on cue, Melissa turned her pretty feathered head and posed. "Thank you," the bird said. "I love you."

"Very cool." It was the first time he'd heard the young one, Jenna, speak. Her voice was deeper than he'd expected, almost throaty.

"Could you hand me that bag of fruit?" he asked.

Jenna swooped down and brought the bag up. "You want something in particular?"

"Melissa likes papayas," he said, noticing that she identified and produced the papaya without further question.

"So do I."

Damn! She was being nicer than he had any reason to expect. Flirting, almost.

He offered his arm, and Melissa climbed right onto his wrist and actually seemed to duck her head as she emerged from the cage. She'd been hand-raised and she was wonderfully friendly. When she was out of the cage, he raised his wrist so that she could climb onto his shoulder. Then he closed the cage, leaving a second cockatoo inside.

"You have birds?" Dan asked.

She laughed. "Not a one. Ever. But I've always thought it would be cool to have a blue budgie."

"Really?" Lynne spoke up. "I never knew that, Jenna."

Jenna shrugged. "We had cats. No point in even suggesting it."

"Would you like to hold Melissa?" Dan suggested.

"Oh, I don't think I'd know how to do it right."

"I'll help you," he said, putting his wrist up again for the compliant Melissa, who was rubbing her feathers against his ear. "I'll put her on your shoulder to start. I'm right here if you decide to stop. Just don't scream or anything if you decide you don't want to hold her anymore. Melissa's very friendly but she's not a fan of loud noises."

She looked a bit insulted. "Melissa and I will be fine." Dan deposited the bird on her shoulder, which had just enough fabric to cover the bird's claws, which were regularly clipped but could still give a bit of a nip. "What a sweetie you are," she told Melissa softly, "my very own island girl."

Sure enough, Melissa replied, with enthusiasm, "I love you."

Dan offered the bird a piece of papaya, then handed a second piece to Jenna, who fed the bird with growing confidence.

"How old is she?" Jenna asked.

"At least fourteen," he said. "The earlier owners had her when I first started coming around to help. But you know, if you're interested in age, those blue-and-golds are celebrating their birthday this month. They're turning fifty."

"How can you know?" Lynne asked as Jenna said, "I didn't think birds lived that long."

"Oh, they do," he assured them both. "We've got a regular genealogy mapped out here, dating back to their first known owner, a guy in Palm Beach. I admit it's a guesstimate on the actual birthday, but we do know the year. Birds live a long time. You know Winston Churchill?"

A surprising number of Dos Hermanas guests, he had learned, had no idea whatsoever who Winston Churchill had been.

"Well, of course," Lynne said, sounding a trifle irritated.

"His parrot is still alive."

"You're kidding!" Jenna said.

So she knew, too.

"Not at all," he assured her.

Lynne glanced at her watch. "We ought to get going, Jenna." She turned to Dan. "Are you here all the time?"

He shook his head. "Sometimes it feels like it, but no. I usually come around mornings and take care of the birds. Sometimes I come afternoons. It depends. I work for a dive shop some days, when the water's clear, taking tourists on dives off Looe Key."

"Diving?" Jenna sounded excited. "That's one of the things I want to do while I'm here."

Bingo. Some days it really did pay to go to work.

"You certified?"

She shook her head. "Not anymore. But I used to be."

"Then I bet we can get you recertified with no trouble at

all." He dug in his back pocket, pulled out a wallet, and extricated a card. "Call and tell them you want to go on a dive with Dan. They'll set it all up. You have equipment?"

"No."

"No problem. They can fit you out."

"Thanks! Oops, I'd better get going." Jenna turned her face to Melissa, who was still sitting on her shoulder, and spoke softly to her. "You have a nice day, girl. Maybe we could do this again sometime."

"I love you," said Melissa.

Dan took that as an affirmative and offered Melissa his forearm, removing her from Jenna's shoulder. She hadn't flinched in either setting the bird down or retrieving it. He liked that.

Jenna hurried after her mother, who had been working her way along the cages toward the side parking lot. Dan won a little bet with himself when they got into a red Mustang convertible, the official rental car of Florida tourism.

A loud squawk returned his attention to the birds. He opened the bag of fruits and vegetables he'd brought for his feathered charges. Melissa had earned herself some extra papaya for behaving so nicely. Lettuce leaves for some of them, papaya chunks and grapes for others, hot peppers for Mimi the African parrot who adored chilies.

The birds were like women. If you just figured out what they wanted and provided it—or even made an effort to provide it—they'd do anything for you.

*Chapter 7*

**PEGGY** Parker felt as if she'd been slammed in the gut. She had been trying to view the events of the morning from a position of detachment, but kept failing miserably at the attempt.

In this, the first winter of the Parkers' first season as innkeepers, Dos Hermanas Resort had been the site of repeated and inexplicable problems. Once again there had been no logical explanation for the power outage. Nobody had written on the walls last night, but a couple from Maryland found four slashed tires on their SUV this morning. There was no chum in the pool, but the tropical fish were still dead.

And so was Darcy Gainsborough, a woman Peggy had genuinely enjoyed. Hers was turning into a very public death, too. Given Florida demographics, you had to expect a certain attrition, and over at Little Sister Court next door, there was a whole routine that swung into play when a resident passed on.

But this situation today was not somebody passing on. Darcy had been healthy and robust, and Peggy couldn't imagine what she had been doing out here in the middle of the night. Some kind of midnight assignation? And if so, with whom? The place wasn't exactly overrun with single men in their sunset years.

True, Darcy had a secretive side, liked to give that little smile that suggested she knew a bit more than she was revealing. Certainly she prided herself on knowing everybody's business, a trait that would have been infuriating had she not been such a cheerful and generous gossip. It was always fun to share a cup of coffee with Darcy and listen to her reports on the amusing antics and various adventures of her fellow residents at Little Sister Court.

The paramedics had worked quietly, making no comments about the cause of death. But the police had stayed busy a lot longer than seemed necessary. The detective and other police officers were acting as if they believed Darcy's death had not been natural. The implication was that somebody might have killed her.

Murder. Just what you wanted in the first season you were open for business, a carefree vacation business at that.

Here in hot-blooded South Florida, murder would make more sense if the victim had been young, ethnic, maybe involved in some kind of gangland thing. When Peggy thought of violence in this corner of the world, she generally envisioned Cubans and knives, a prejudice that had grown, as prejudice so often does, from observation, unfamiliarity, and generalization.

She had difficulty understanding the intensity of the Cuban expatriates, though few of the most vehement were expatriates in any pure sense of the word. Many of these Miami-born American citizens had never actually set foot in Cuba. Which didn't stop them from raising fanatic patriotism to an art form. Peggy was sure that if she lived out the rest of her life here she would still never come close to understanding their zealotry.

It's your English blood, Rick always told her. Your stiff-upper-lip stoicism. You can't understand because you keep trying to apply reason, and reason doesn't apply.

Well, reason certainly didn't apply to the events of the morning.

Rick was taking a much calmer attitude, as she had expected. He liked to say that nothing people did was ever really surprising, that it was all human nature once you knew what to look for. He had promised the Maryland couple that he'd buy them four new tires. She wondered what element of human nature that involved. A taste for pointless destruction?

"The police took my key to Darcy's unit," Sheri McManus said now. "I probably ought to get over there before they make a wreck out of the place."

"What did they want to get in for?"

Sheri looked at her in some confusion. "Why, to find out what happened, don't you think?"

"I don't know what I think," Peggy admitted. "But you ought to get that key back. And somebody's got to call her children, wherever they live."

"Her daughter's in Pennsylvania," Sheri said, "and her son lives in New York. I've got their numbers at my place. Darcy was always very firm about having emergency info available with friends. I had hers and she had mine."

Peggy watched Sheri hustle back to Little Sister Court, then strolled over to the boat ramp, which now seemed empty, almost forlorn. Nobody had drawn a chalk outline of Darcy's body or anything. The yellow crime scene tape lay abandoned and she set about briskly removing it, furling it into a neat roll—and why was that? Did she expect to use it again?

Actually, she realized, it was to take her mind off the ramp itself. Peggy knew she would never be able to look at the ramp again without seeing her friend lying lifeless there, her long skirt twisted in the water.

She looked up and saw Roberto Lopez sailing around the northern end of the island, heading for the Dos Hermanas dock in his skiff. Roberto lived over on Big Pine Key and often commuted by boat when he worked odd jobs around the resort and mobile home court.

The police had finally left, but a lot of the resort guests and Court tenants still were milling about aimlessly, acting as if they were just out on a boring, routine morning saunter. Rick had replenished the muffin supplies and was even now making the rounds to guests here and there, speaking reassuring words of soothing comfort. He was very good at that, with or without muffins.

She walked over to meet Roberto at the far dock where he normally tied up.

"What's going on?" he asked, in lightly accented English.

"Well, the power went out again last night. And we've had an—" She paused. What *had* they had? Not an accident, hopefully not a killing. "An incident. You know Darcy Gainsborough, from the Court?"

Roberto smiled. He was thirtyish, his toffee-colored face sculpted with flat planes and soft angles, a handsome man who moved with a chip on his shoulder that probably resulted from being barely five-foot-seven. "Of course.

Everybody knows Darcy. Why?" His expression clouded. "Did something happen to her? Is she all right?"

Peggy shook her head. "I'm afraid she . . . she's not all right. She's dead, Roberto. And I don't think anybody knows what happened."

"What do you mean?"

Peggy told him what little she knew. When she'd finished, he looked around.

"A terrible shame. She was such a nice lady. Do you want me to keep going on the air conditioners?"

Peggy felt jarred by the abrupt transition. "Um, sure. Yes, of course. How many do you have left?"

Roberto had a knack—no, a *gift*—for fixing anything mechanical, from the filtration systems on the hot tubs to the disposals in the units with kitchenettes. He could probably do equally well on electric toothbrushes and nuclear power plants, given the opportunity. This past week he'd been conducting routine maintenance on air conditioners in the units not yet occupied.

"Six or seven. That shouldn't take more than a few hours unless I find problems. Then there's the hot water heater replacement in Poinciana. Did you hear from the people who've rented it about when they're going to arrive?"

"You've got an extra two days," Peggy told him, "if you need it."

He smiled endearingly. "Well, there's a dishwasher over in the Court that's acting up. And Christmas is coming."

Roberto, like a number of the part-time workers at Dos Hermanas, was paid off the books, in cash. Peggy felt a sudden moment of panic. If the police were prowling around, could paying Roberto and others under the table turn into some kind of issue? Not likely, she knew. But you could never be sure when the charmingly loose Floridian respect for legality might suddenly snap like a giant rubber band and smack you clear into the ocean.

"Do you think it would be any problem for the birds if I put some little Christmas lights up around their cages?" she asked.

Roberto cocked his head. "That's a question you'd better save for Dan, don't you think? You'd have to be sure the birds couldn't get to the light cords and chew them, I know." Roberto had designed some clever locking arrangements for the bird cages, conversation pieces in their own right. She could have relied simply on padlocks, of course, but Roberto's locks had style, even when they actually *were* disguised padlocks. Highly intelligent parrots confined to small spaces tended to be quite adept at jail breaks.

Peggy looked around for Dan. "Shoot, I guess he's already finished and gone. I'll catch him tomorrow."

The self-designated parrot wrangler usually stopped by in the early morning to feed and water the birds. If he couldn't make it, he'd arrange for Roberto or Roberto's cousin Marta, a Dos Hermanas maid, to cover. Dan Trenton was a jewel, actually, and had found many of the Dos Hermanas flock over the years. Tropical birds often flew wild in the Keys, some naturalized after escape from civilization's cage prisons, others purely wild. Now and then she'd see one go soaring by, and she wondered what its life was like, whether she was being cruel to keep her own flock of parrots caged.

Dan had recently told Peggy that he had a line on a young scarlet macaw—a currently endangered species—that he might possibly be able to get for her. Macaws were very pricey, running to five figures, and hyacinth macaws, which were what Peggy secretly yearned for, were both endangered and exorbitant. Hyacinths were gorgeous, with rich blue plumage and bright yellow skin exposed around their eyes. In a zoo once, Peggy had seen one that was upset and had been plucking its feathers, leaving bright yellow chest skin exposed.

"Off to work," Roberto said.

As Peggy watched him pick up his toolbox and head toward the Magnolia complex, she revised her mental to-do list.

Clearly the most urgent chore de jour was to restore matters around the premises to a reasonably even keel, and she believed she was on the right track in focusing on additional Christmas decorations. This was her first winter in the Lower Keys, but already she'd noticed much less holiday decoration than there'd been back on the mainland.

A joint Dos Hermanas/Little Sister Court Christmas party was scheduled for—could it be? Oh dear Lord—tomorrow. Darcy had arranged most of the food and drink, items that Lynne had agreed to go with her to pick up this afternoon. She'd have to check and see if Sheri knew what Darcy had ordered, and where it was coming from.

She could start by heading over to Big Pine Key and getting some wreaths and a Santa hat for the manatee mailbox holder out front. A six-foot spruce hauled all the way from Maine already stood in the breakfast room, decorated with sea shells and silk tropical flowers and twinkling white lights.

Lights.

That was the ticket. It was pretty hard to have too many Christmas lights, though it could be done. She remembered a place near where they'd lived in Milwaukee with a display so extensive and garish that TV news programs had featured it each year. Not a problem here.

Time was the other variable, and it was running mighty short. She had yet to begin her Christmas gift shopping, for one thing, and putting that off was not optional. You couldn't expect young children to understand that their presents were late because Grandma was too busy.

Still, she had plenty of time to do most—maybe all—of her Christmas shopping online, paying a premium for speedy shipping. And she needed to stick around Dos Hermanas.

The party tomorrow would be—*had* to be—festive and cheerful and brimming over with holiday spirit. Not to mention holiday spirits. Peggy had a mean eggnog recipe that called for vast quantities of bourbon, brandy, and heavy cream, and she'd searched the Internet for a method to cook the egg yolks to prevent salmonella. The one she found, ironically, came from the latest edition of *Joy of Cooking,* the institution she'd relied on for most of her adult life. Her original volume, a wedding present, was in tatters.

Less than two weeks before Christmas, Dos Hermanas was filling up rapidly. Many guests had made their reservations a full year earlier, before returning to their bleak Cleveland and Pittsburgh winters after spending the holidays at Dos Hermanas. These folks wanted to bask in the sun, swill fruity rum drinks, and feel part of an in-group conspiracy while humming along to either the Andrews Sisters or the Jimmy Buffett version of "Christmas Island." The image of Santa delivering gifts by canoe was undeniably appealing and very tropically topical.

It was Rick and Peggy's mission to provide and enhance

that state of mind. And at least they had history and respectability on their side.

Dos Hermanas, as Peggy had told Lynne so proudly last night, was an institution in the Lower Keys. The place had been here nearly sixty years, growing from a humble fish camp in the 1940s to its present incarnation as a semi-upscale family-oriented resort with swimming pool, three hot tubs, a tennis court, bayside docks, and a flock of magnificent exotic birds. Caged, to be sure, but in enclosures nicely camouflaged amid the lush tropical vegetation.

Darcy's death on top of the vandalism would have been overwhelming, but Rick's instinctive calming effect on people seemed to be holding the guests into a state of blissful amnesia. *Body? What body?*

Perhaps the single most irritating component of this extremely difficult and complicated day was Gloria. Gloria Parker had never met a living creature that she didn't somehow find lacking. She maintained an intriguing, selective forgetfulness about her husband's incarceration and supersized fine for insider stock trading.

For his part, Rick believed that his brother Tom would never have committed the crimes he had pleaded guilty to, were he not eternally goaded by Gloria's quest for more, more, more. Peggy no longer cared a hoot why Tom Parker had gone astray. But if the object of his incarceration had been punishment, she thought that goal could have been more effectively achieved by having Gloria as his cellmate.

Well, screw Gloria. She was the least of Peggy's immediate problems.

"Mrs. Parker?"

Peggy jumped at the sound of her name and turned to see that grim-looking Detective Ruiz. Again. "Yes?"

"Just a few more things I need to clear up before I leave, ma'am."

Peggy sighed, fairly certain that his notion of a "few more things" differed from her own. She willed herself to be calm and congenial. There had been enough problems around here the last couple of weeks. The last thing she needed was some bumbling policeman on the loose, stirring up her remaining guests and drawing more attention to Darcy's death.

*Chapter 8*

**LYNNE** was chasing a dream as they headed into Key West, half a century after her last visit. A picture had triggered that dream—a snapshot, actually, mixed in with odds and ends in a box her mother had sent seven or eight years ago.

The picture was taken at Mallory Square at sunset, she knew. She'd been lifted onto a piling for a better view, then turned around for the camera, her sunny smile and flyaway blonde hair captured forever. She'd been dressed in a ruffled yellow polka-dotted sundress that she remembered adoring. Her parents stood on either side of her, Daddy in his crisp white uniform, Priscilla clad in a sultry hot-pink dress with halter top and a flared skirt reaching almost to mid-calf, molded against her legs by the ocean breeze.

The picture was black-and-white, but Lynne remembered it all in color, from the moment of the snapshot through the glorious pinks and golds and purples of the sunset they had watched together.

Now Lynne wondered who had taken that picture, if there had been others with them on that long ago afternoon. She had enlarged it to hang in her upstairs hall with other photos of her family and Monty's, with all the snapshots and school portraits showing David and Jenna growing up.

It was funny. Lynne had lived so many different places in her childhood that she had very few specific memories of most of them. But once she saw that picture, she remembered the day perfectly, recalled the gulls swooping down around the docks, fishing boats passing slowly past, Priscilla drinking something chartreuse with a blue paper umbrella that she solemnly presented to Lynne. Her father had lifted her to sit on his lap at the outdoor table, ordering her a Shirley Temple with six maraschino cherries, one for each year of her life.

There was a juggler, Lynne remembered, and a gymnast who did back flips and no-hands cartwheels, a man singing with his guitar case open beside him. Her father had given her a dime for each performer and she remembered feeling shy as she deposited the shiny silver coins in the singer's guitar case and the hats left upturned on the dock by the gymnast and the juggler.

But it was the laughter she remembered most emphatically, the laughter that lingered as the three of them sat through the late afternoon and then watched the sun melt into the horizon.

✿

STUCK in traffic, Jenna was finding all her preconceptions of Florida out of kilter one way or another. It had never occurred to her, however, that Key West—idyllic, romanticized home to poets and playwrights and novelists—would have a traffic jam before they even got onto the island.

Jenna had been letting her mother do the driving ever since they reached Florida, not because she didn't want to be behind the wheel of the very slick convertible, but because she wanted a full chance to experience what was going on in the landscape around them.

*You're going to love it* had been the general reaction when she announced her travel plans to friends in LA *Key West! How cool!* Given that these remarks were made by people who lived in a pretty spectacular location themselves, at least by Jenna's standards, their reactions seemed all the more intriguing.

Now they were nearly in Key West itself, and Highway 1 had expanded to four heavily traveled lanes. As they crossed the final bridge onto the island, her mother veered to the right and they were suddenly in an area filled with familiar commercial operations, the kind found in any town from Salt Lake City to Savannah. Holiday Inn and McDonald's, Home Depot and Sears. Strip malls on both sides of the highway. After just passing through a dozen miles of sparsely inhabited, lushly vegetated roadway, Jenna found the contrast stunning.

Jenna had heard, more times than she cared to recall, about the brief period that her mother and her grandparents had spent living in South Florida when her Grandpa Greg—a Navy pilot killed in a plane crash before Jenna's birth—was stationed at Key West. When you considered all the other places that the Westbrook family had lived in service of the United States Navy, it was actually remarkable that Key West had made such a strong impression. On the plane from L.A., her mother had once again spoken nostalgically about the jugglers down at Mallory Square, the six-toed cats at the Hemingway House, the tart sweetness of Key Lime pie.

The Key Lime pie had exceeded her expectations last night, had in fact been downright delicious. As they sat now, stalled at a traffic signal, Jenna wondered how her mother's other memories would fare on what seemed to be an entirely modern and relentlessly commercial island.

⚘

**LYNNE** had studied the maps before they left Dos Hermanas, had made note of a bewildering number of one-way streets and an apparent dearth of open space.

Still, she was shocked by the congestion she found on Key West. She'd disobeyed her own number one rule for traveling: pay attention to the people who have recent experience with a place. Peggy had warned her just last night that the island was likely to feel crowded and unfamiliar, that the childhood memories of a half-century earlier were certain to differ widely from the contemporary reality of an island no longer dependent on the U.S. Navy for its economy and well-being. The Navy was pretty much gone, actually, though a feisty former mayor had once protested the planned withdrawal of military forces by waterskiing to Cuba, a stunt that took him about six hours and resulted in the Navy sticking around a while longer.

Before long, she and Jenna were hopelessly lost, dodging colorful chickens meandering in the roadway as they passed through Little Bahama. The streets all seemed to be one way, headed the wrong way. Finally they reached the general vicinity of Mallory Square, parked, and hoofed it the last few blocks down Duval Street. As they walked, they passed a collection of tacky souvenir shops that seemed to all be clones, each offering the same shell jewelry, the same cigar-box purses bearing dead celebrity images, the same coconut shells painted into monkey faces, the same T-shirts announcing: I'M NOT SIXTY, I'M 18 WITH 42 YEARS EXPERIENCE.

Duval Street, the main drag, was being redeveloped to deal with the continuous onslaught of cruise ship visitors, which probably boded well for the local economy but walloped the hell out of the town's ambience. Did a street and a town that so prided themselves on character and individuality really *need* a Starbucks, a Denny's, a Walgreens? Jenna, Lynne noticed, was conspicuously silent.

Finally they reached Mallory Square, once situated openly at the northwesternmost end of the island, now accessed through a collection of souvenir shops. And then they were at land's end, facing the largest cruise ship Lynne had ever seen, the *Disney Magic,* which had disgorged some 2,500 passengers into the streets of Key West this morning.

This, at least, Lynne should have been prepared for. A client who had independently altered some Florida travel arrangements not long ago to stay at the Hilton in Key West had tossed a close-up photo of a huge white cruise ship on Lynne's desk when he returned. "This was the view from my four-hundred-dollar hotel room," he told her, and Lynne was grateful not to have booked that room for him.

The ships came in and out constantly, Peggy had said, as many as half a dozen a day, many ferrying passengers to shore by tender from offshore dockings. How could you possibly enjoy the sunset, Lynne wondered now, if you had to peek around the edges of something only slightly smaller than Mount Rushmore?

Lynne located the least obstructed view that she could find of the bay and stared out to sea for a few minutes while Jenna used a nearby restroom. It was all different from the way it had been, but she still felt a strong sense of connection.

Here was where the picture had been taken, where that golden moment from her youth had occurred. And for just a few moments, with her eyes closed, she was able to project herself back in time.

🌿

**PEGGY** Parker had been initially astonished at the number of people required to run Dos Hermanas, even without a full-scale restaurant, which apparently increased both staff and aggravation exponentially. As it was, they had a manager and assistant manager, maids, pool and spa maintenance people, the parrot wrangler, groundskeepers, laundry operator, desk clerks. The list was endless, without even allowing for somebody like Roberto Lopez, a jack-of-all-trades who generally was available when something went kaplooey.

They had been fortunate that Jim Tyler, the manager, was both competent and eager to stay under new management, and she'd left most of the personnel matters to him. Resort staff couldn't possibly handle everything, of course. Formal activities requiring equipment, boats, or certification were provided by a number of offsite fishing charter captains, dive operators, and miscellaneous sailors.

Beyond that, the resort maintained informal activity arrangements with several residents of the Little Sister Court next door. That was how Peggy had gotten to know the tireless Darcy Gainsborough so well. Darcy had served as informal liaison between the retirees and the resort, handling attendant headaches and easing the occasional friction with little input from Peggy or her staff.

It was almost impossible to think of Darcy being dead. She had been so exuberantly alive.

Darcy was a given when the Parkers arrived at Dos Hermanas, already smoothly running her end of the group activities that joined the resort and the mobile home park. Peggy had quickly grown accustomed to Darcy taking care of a whole raft of matters, things that Peggy wouldn't have even thought of in her earliest, most naïve state.

The symbiotic relationship with Little Sister Court was something she and Rick had blindly depended upon. Dos Hermanas was far enough from Key West to make impulse visits difficult. So it became doubly important to offer some local entertainment possibilities. Various retirees offered tennis lessons, manicures and pedicures, massages, and aromatherapy consultations. Dos Hermanas guests were welcome to participate in such Little Sister activities as Mah-Jongg, bridge, shuffleboard, chess, and trivia tournaments. A couple of nimble-fingered ladies offered needlework classes and sponsored the occasional quilting bee. George Wyman, a retiree from Wisconsin, ran a monthly book club, open to anyone in town long enough to read the club's current selection.

It was a splendid arrangement, all things considered: a bit of income off the books for some of the retirees and pleasurable vacation pastimes for the resort guests. Full details were provided in a frequently updated brochure left in all guest rooms—another item that Darcy had handled, along with up-to-the-minute information posted on the bulletin board in the breakfast room of the Orchid Lodge.

Who would do these things now?

JUST a moment there!"

George Wyman's booming baritone stopped Sheri Mc-Manus in her tracks. If she didn't already feel so guilty, she realized, she probably wouldn't be reacting like a four-year-old surrounded by cookie crumbs.

She ought to be used to him by now. George, who lived two units down from Darcy and another three around the corner from Sheri, was always turning up where you didn't expect him, and he was always too loud. His stentorian bellow wasn't accidental, either. He seemed to thrive on scaring the living daylights out of her. Sixty-five years ago in the Midwest, he'd probably made a habit of dropping frogs down little girls' dresses.

"What's going on?" George demanded. He rounded the corner of the Burkes' unit, which was freshly painted white and had royal blue trim and red geraniums blooming in blue-striped window boxes. Bob Burke never let anyone forget he was retired Marine Corps, and he flew the USMC colors alongside the Stars and Stripes, which he spot-lit twenty-four hours a day.

George wasn't nearly as large as his voice suggested, and he seemed to overcompensate for size with a large persona. As she watched, he trampled the tiny patch of lawn and nearly knocked over a freestanding snowman holding a smaller American flag. Watch your back, Frosty. He wore madras Bermuda shorts and a polo shirt, both neatly pressed. "I see police cars and paramedics, I try to come over and get information and I'm turned away by some snot-nosed kid in a uniform. Everything is under control, he tells me, but he forgets the part about *what's* under control."

"Darcy Gainsborough was found dead over there," Sheri told him. "On the boat ramp."

She had hoped to shut him up for a minute with her bluntness, and to her surprise, she succeeded. George had a lot of interaction with Darcy, more than most of the residents. Sheri didn't think theirs was a romantic relationship, though you could never be entirely sure what anybody would do down here. A lot of conventions that endured in the north no longer seemed so terribly important here in the tropics.

The male-to-female ratio in the Court was probably around one man for every seven or eight women, and only a handful of those men were unattached. George Wyman, if he wished, could pick and choose among a very nice selection of eligible ladies. So far as Sheri knew, he didn't. Indeed, the fact that he had remained single through seven decades suggested to Sheri that he probably was very poor husband material.

George remained deep in thought, his oversized brow furrowed. Sheri had a sudden vision of that middle drawer in Darcy's buffet table. She'd been reviewing that drawer and its contents in her mind from the very moment she had pulled the drawer open, like worrying a new sharp edge on a back tooth with an anxious tongue. Try as she might, she couldn't remember everything that had been in there. Once she had seen her own dish, everything else shifted slightly out of focus.

Still, there had been several condoms in that drawer, she was sure about that. And not all the same, either. They'd been different, four or maybe five different styles, colors, packages. Had Darcy taken them as souvenirs from sexual encounters? "Borrowed" them from a store? It was hard to imagine her purchasing them at a pharmacy, particularly anywhere local. And one of them seemed to have been neon green, which would probably call for a specialty vendor of some sort. Maybe the green ones were being marketed as tourist souvenirs, labeled Key Lime.

And face it, Darcy was long past her childbearing years. The only reason to use condoms would be as a preventive STD precaution.

She was suddenly aware that she had been deep in thought and George had been saying nothing, a rare occurrence. "Aren't you going to ask what happened, George?"

George unfurrowed the brow and straightened his trifocals on his nose. "What happened?"

"I don't know," she told him. "But the police seem to think there's something fishy about it."

"How can that be?"

"You'd have to ask them. Or maybe they'll ask you."

"Me! What on earth for?" He harrumphed for a moment, then fixed his gaze on Sheri. "What am I supposed to do with the Trivia Bee questions I've been writing?" It hadn't taken him long to return to his favorite subject—George Wyman. "I've finished Sports, with sections on Olympic Swimming and Hockey. I'm still working on Shipwrecks and Presidential Politics."

Sheri tried to shift gears, to go from the dreadful death of a dear friend—albeit one with a newly revealed and confusing secret life—to community activities that Darcy, who had organized them, would never again attend. George had all the compassion of a palmetto bug. "I'll take them when you're ready," she finally said. "Or give them to Peggy."

George routinely provided most of the questions for the monthly Trivia Bee, which was, she recalled dimly, scheduled for some time next week. The Trivia Bee had been an institution long before Sheri and Will moved into Little Sister Court, and neither one of them had paid it much attention. After Will died, however, Darcy had recruited Sheri as a judge.

Then George had arrived from Wisconsin last year and trounced the competition in all categories but Baking. His intellect so towered above his neighbors, he later announced, that he would recuse himself from further competition. It pleased him, Sheri remembered, and confirmed his sense of superiority, when he had to define "recuse" for several of the folks on the Activities Board of Little Sister Court. She personally would have gargled thumb tacks before admitting ignorance to him.

But Darcy had known just what to do. She co-opted him into providing questions, a venture he thoroughly enjoyed and devoted considerable time to. George fancied himself a historian, with a particular interest in the history of the Keys. He made some kind of historical models that Sheri had heard about but not seen, and his double-wide was reportedly crammed with books, his second bedroom fitted out as a library with extra floor support in the foundation.

George also spent hours online every day, monitoring political events and societal mores. Darcy and Sheri had decided independently that he was probably looking at porn, and had howled with joy when they shared their suspicions with each other.

Life without Darcy was going to be unspeakably empty.

*Chapter 9*

"**WELCOME** to Key West," the guide announced as she settled into the driver's seat up front and adjusted her Santa cap. A confederate moved down the right-hand side of the train, taking pictures that would be available for purchase when they returned. "You've all just become invisible. Once the Conch Train gets underway, nobody can see us. It's part of that tropical magic."

She pulled away from the curb and set off on a route that Lynne soon realized was criss-crossing the island, moving back and forth, covering territory from one angle, then swinging past it from another. After initially attempting to monitor where they were going, Lynne decided to sit back and enjoy herself. This was more of a challenge than she had expected. The orange-naugahyde-covered seats were barely twelve inches deep, the backs upright at a rigid ninety-degree angle, the leg room inadequate for anyone over the age of eight. Passengers were crammed in as tightly as possible. Lynne and Jenna shared their seat with a couple from Brooklyn, Jenna on the outside, bending her knees awkwardly out the side of the car in a futile attempt to try to stretch her legs.

"You may think," the guide said, "that this island is called Key West because it's the westernmost of the island chain called the Keys. Actually, it was anglicized after the Spanish explorers called it *Cayo Hueso,* or 'Island of Bones.' They found a lot of bones here when they first arrived. We're not real clear just whose bones they were, or what happened to them. The native Indians, the Caloosas, weren't exactly friendly, but they were wiped out by diseases like typhus or smallpox pretty soon after the Europeans arrived. Just recently some old church records showed that some of the Caloosas escaped to Cuba, but that doesn't give us any more clues about the bones."

The train moved down narrow roadways as the guide pointed out features of local architecture: tin roofs to allow the collection of rainwater in cisterns and prevent the spread of fire, porch ceilings painted blue in the Caribbean style to emulate the sky and ward off evil spirits, shotgun houses once occupied by cigar makers. Before the United States severed relations with Cuba, the cigar trade had sailed genially back and forth across the ninety-mile distance. Key West still boasted artisans who hand rolled cigars, but aficionados believed they weren't quite as special.

Not that Lynne could tell the difference, of course. Even thinking about cigar smoke made her stomach queasy.

"Where's Margaritaville?" their female seatmate asked Lynne in a piercing New York accent.

Lynne was momentarily taken aback. "I think it's a state of mind."

Mr. New York harrumphed. "It's a store, lady. Sheesh."

So much for metaphysics.

"You'll notice a lot of houses are painted white with green trim," the guide told them a moment later. "That's because those were Navy surplus paint colors. Key West has a long relationship with the Navy. There wasn't even running water here until the 1940s, when the Navy brought it in for the first time. These houses bear a resemblance to Nantucket and the New England seafaring towns, with the same gingerbread trim. There are something like a hundred and fifty different patterns of trim around town, including one that actually *is* gingerbread men."

They approached the cemetery, an above-ground affair in the manner of New Orleans, the problem here being impenetrable coral rather than the Louisiana quandary of being below sea level. A man rose suddenly from behind a mausoleum and stumbled into the roadway, nearly colliding with the train.

"He needs to be more careful," Jenna whispered, "or he'll be taking up permanent residence over there."

As they criss-crossed the town, Lynne was impressed by the Christmas decorations—simple for the most part, but almost always elegant. Freeform red poinsettias hung on street light posts. A wreath made of oversized glass balls hung on a two-story white house, an ornate white-and-silver wreath on a pink hotel. Large red balls were common, but the few pine wreaths she noticed seemed somehow out of place.

"You may be wondering what we mean when we refer to natives as Conchs," the tour guide continued, pronouncing the word "conks." "Strictly speaking, you need to be born here to call yourself a Conch. Back in 1982, Key West seceded from the Union and designated itself the Conch Republic. Which needed its own individual

form of transportation, of course. Up ahead on your right
is what's known as a 'Conch cruiser.'"

The vehicle in question was an elderly Ford painted like
a zebra. As they moved through town, Lynne had noticed a
bewildering variety of transportation methods. Bicycles,
pedicabs, scooters, mopeds, electric cars, and "Think
Pink" taxis in Barbie pink, many sporting ads for girlie
shows. She already knew that driving was tricky; but the
island was actually quite small. If you lived here, she realized now, you might not need to have a car at all, or could
make do with a Conch cruiser that didn't want a lot of attention.

Like that "old red bike" in the Jimmy Buffett song. But
this was not the Key West of Jimmy Buffett, the laid-back
tropical paradise where getting drunk was a bona fide
sport, hanging out an art form, sailing off with no destination an avocation.

This was a mercantile center with jingling cash registers
and eight hundred different ways to paint a coconut shell.

✖

**LATER,** at the Margaritaville Café, Jenna chomped her
Cheeseburger from Paradise and thought about the di-
chotomy between fantasy and reality, the blurred lines
separating the two here in this aggressively capitalistic
town. Jenna had grown up on beach music, knew the
lyrics to many Beach Boys and Buffett songs before she
ever started school.

"It's like there's a Margaritaville Empire," Jenna said,
reaching for another fry. "A Parrot Head Nation."

"I know," her mother answered. "The first time your father and I ever saw Jimmy Buffett perform was so long
ago that we didn't have any kids yet. I forget how we

knew about him in the first place, probably some surfer friend of Monty's. He did his show in a tiny room with just him and another guy, both of them playing acoustic guitars. Now he's become a big business."

"But one devoted to having a good time," Jenna pointed out, though she made no attempt to understand the Parrot Head business. A whole lot of otherwise responsible adults routinely dressed in bizarre faux-tropical attire—including the aforementioned Parrot Head prosthesis—while making every attempt to drink themselves senseless on tequila. And people said *her* generation was flighty.

"Living here would be okay," Jenna went on, "at least in the winter, I guess. But I don't understand how anybody can afford it unless they're already rich. There can't be that many jobs." Would she have viewed the town in terms of employment if her own weren't so problematic? she wondered.

Lynne nodded. "Another issue. The folks who come down from New York and buy fancy houses that they only use in the winter—those are the people that you'd have to be nice to and that you'd probably not want to."

"Rich jackasses. My favorite." Jenna took a big definitive bite out of her cheeseburger.

After lunch, they went next door to the Margaritaville store, the flagship of a growing international chain, peddling Buffettabilia by the carload. Merchandise and decorations covered every square inch of wall, including a bunch of vanity license plates from around the country: A1A—WWJBD?—SOASOAS—FINS—PRTHEAD—PHD PHD—MVILLE—KEYWST.

Jenna found herself almost more fascinated by the clientele than by the store itself. The customers were all white, all seemingly middle-class, all piling up merchandise in a shopping frenzy. In addition to CDs, there was an abundance of Parrot Head stuff—golf club covers, hats, shirts, underwear, beer ID rings, beach towels. Computer cases, mouse pads, even a working computer mouse with a floating margarita and salt shaker. Endless apparel possibilities for folks of all ages. Drinking paraphernalia, wall plaques, welcome mats, bibs, dog collars.

Somewhere under the counter, the *Coconut Telegraph* catalog promised a Parrot Head prophylactic to go along with the boxers and the coconut shell bra. No need to present proof of age.

And proof of maturity was never required.

❦

**ELLEN** Gainsborough knew when the call came that it was trouble.

Her mother had always been difficult, always prided herself on riding the edge. She wasn't exactly a scofflaw as much as an ignore-law. She did not consider herself bound by the petty rules and regulations of contemporary American society.

For this she was not entirely to blame. For whatever reasons, driven by compulsions beyond her control, Darcy Davenport Gainsborough, respectable Philadelphia suburban matron, was a kleptomaniac.

A thief, not to put too fine a point on it.

As far back as Ellen could remember—some three decades worth of her thirty-six years—her mother had thrived on getting away with things. Stealing, to be precise. She'd leave the drugstore with an extra lipstick in her purse, or the grocery store with some canned crab in her coat pocket. For purely logistical reasons, she had dozens of exotic spices—available in small, portable packages—

not that she ever cooked anything that required fenugreek, coriander, or cardamom. Once she'd boosted a whole prime rib roast when she was shopping before Christmas and carrying department store bags.

She was so respectable looking that nobody ever paid attention to her.

She'd try on expensive undergarments at very nice department stores and wear her preferred new items home, the old undies and new tags often discarded in the store's own trash.

As her mother aged, she shopped less. Ellen had worried that she had no outlets for her compulsion. These people lived in single and double-wide trailers here, no matter what they were calling them. They weren't big enough to hold a lot of contraband, particularly if one made her home open to others, which Mom clearly had.

Somewhere in Darcy Gainsborough's double-wide, there was bound to be a stash of little objects lifted from friends and neighbors, from tourist traps and newsstands, from stores up and down the Florida Keys.

What, Ellen wondered now, had her mother done that she shouldn't have?

*Chapter 10*

**DIANE** Haedrich felt alternately anxious and exhilarated, sometimes sweeping from one emotion to the other with such speed that she found herself utterly drained. They'd spent a lot of money coming down here, based on what seemed like a real pie-in-the-sky prospect. Just because John's father thought he was dying and made that astonishing revelation of *his* own father's deathbed confession, here they were, smack in the middle of a wild goose chase.

Not that she minded the trip.

To be truthful, she liked it a lot. It was such a kick to be wearing flip-flops two weeks before Christmas, to turn on the TV and see footage of a full-scale blizzard in Michigan, to go outside in that black bikini that John was so fond of. Even to be reckless about using sunscreen. To skip it altogether, really, and instead slather on tanning oil, SPF 2. She was darkening quickly, and her intention was to return to Michigan in mid winter with a deep, rich tan.

Mahogany, if she put enough time into it. All through elementary, junior, and senior high schools, she had envied her more well-to-do classmates who went to Florida for spring break and came back to Battle Creek tanned or burned or both. This was her chance to be the bronzed one, newly returned from the land of the year-round suntan.

And the birds!

Diane had yearned most of her life to own a scarlet macaw and now she was standing just inches from Angela, a magnificent specimen who was idly preening a gorgeous wing. Where was Dan, the parrot guy, anyway? Twice he'd taken Angela out and put her on Diane's shoulder while he cleaned the cage. Like the other macaws and most of the birds, Angela's feathers had been cut to prevent flight. No matter. Even short they were beautiful. She had insisted that John take pictures of her with Angela. This trip was going to seem very remote very quickly after their return, and she wanted something to put in her windowless office to remind her.

As Diane was growing up, her parents had provided a succession of canaries and budgies, which her mother had always called parakeets. Few of them ever sang or spoke and most died within the first couple of months, a syndrome she had since researched. Her birds had croaked so systematically, she discovered, because they'd always been bargain birds, from a now-defunct Battle Creek pet shop. Bargain birds, for a variety of reasons, were almost always doomed.

John had given her a pair of beautiful peach-faced lovebirds when they became engaged, solemnly introducing them as Dee and Jay, for their own first initials. These exquisite little birds had soft green body feathers deepening in hue as you moved toward their tails, which offered a surprising treat—tucked-away soft blue tail feathers. He'd also bought a charming cage with a built-in seed skirt, all white, in a pagoda style, raised on a stand so that the birds were at eye level.

Diane liked to just sit and look at them sometimes. Their beauty and devotion to one another touched her deeply.

The problem with lovebirds was . . . well, it was that they were in love, actually. They were all wrapped up in each other and spent much of each day tucked away whispering sweet nothings to each other inside the little bower Diane had set up in an upper rear corner of their cage. They had gone through nesting behavior several times without producing any eggs, as it happened, and she was starting to wonder if maybe they were actually Jim and Jay.

No matter. They were lovely and they were hers.

They were tame enough to remove from the cage, though usually both wanted out at the same time, and when she put them on her shoulder, they'd started snuggling again. She had a terrible time catching them as they flew around the apartment, from curtain rod to curtain rod. She'd stopped taking them out much, and resigned herself to being a distant observer. She was glad they seemed happy, and she didn't mind all that much that she wasn't likely to have any baby lovebirds. Still, she longed for a bit more interaction.

She'd been saving up on the side for an African parrot, a bird she thought John might like a little better, since they were so smart and easy to teach to talk. What John really wanted, however, was a cat, so unless Diane developed (or manufactured) an allergy to cats, their pet preferences seemed to be on a collision course.

"C'mon, hon." John spoke behind her, brushing aside

her hair and putting an icy cold water bottle against her neck. She jumped at the sudden chilly sensation, hadn't realized until that very moment that today was turning out to be quite warm. " 'Today's the Day,' " John quoted.

Diane recognized the phrase as a reference to treasure hunter Mel Fisher, the expression he had allegedly uttered every morning of his life when he was hunting treasure, long before he made history by finding the long-lost Spanish galleon *Atocha* and its astonishing treasures. This morning they were on their way to Mel Fisher's Treasure Museum in Key West, where half an hour later and twenty dollars lighter, they slapped gold ovals announcing I LIFTED A GOLD BAR on their left shoulders and went inside.

Diane followed dutifully, knowing that John's fascination with treasure had predated his father's remarkable— and quite possibly inaccurate—revelation. John now maintained that his long-deceased grandfather had nurtured and supported that interest, which made sense in a general sort of way.

John's mother, who pooh-poohed the whole thing and had discouraged the trip, claimed her son had dug so many boyhood holes looking for buried treasure that she'd called him the Pirate Gopher. Diane had seen corroborating pictures of John dressed as a pirate for Halloween at ages eight, nine, ten, eleven, and twelve—always with a black eye patch and scarf-draped head and a fake bird perched on his shoulder.

Hmm. Maybe there was some way she could exploit the parrot-on-shoulder as a pirate accessory, though she doubted it.

She'd listened to John talk about pirate treasure so often that her eyes glazed over. She'd even bought him the DVD of *Pirates of the Caribbean,* though she could hardly complain about having to repeatedly watch Johnny Depp in eyeliner.

He'd downloaded and printed dozens of pictures from the Mel Fisher website before the trip, so she wasn't surprised by the exhibits. Still, the size and length of the gold wedding chain, which looked about twelve feet long, were awesome; her own wedding gifts had run to Corning ware, towels, and kitchen appliances, including three crock pots and four blenders.

She spent some time contemplating a seventy-eight-carat emerald that looked like green glass, lit from below. Diane had deliberately never learned exactly what size a carat was, because it had been clear when she and John fell in love that they were bringing more passion than means to the union. They wore simple gold bands with pride.

Or so she had thought. Now she was starting to wonder a bit.

"Honey, take a heft of this." He had his hand inside a specially constructed display case where it was possible to lift a genuine gold bar. His expression was distant, foggy. He removed his hand, picked up hers, and kissed her fingertips gently. "It's like being connected to the center of the earth."

Huh? She inserted her hand, and despite the warning signs, almost twisted her wrist when she picked it up.

"It looks so . . . almost fake. You know, like old silver is tarnished, but this is all shiny."

He looked at her with disappointment in his warm brown eyes. "Gold doesn't tarnish, honey. I thought you knew that."

"I do, I do."

She decided that trying to explain would just dig herself deeper into the hole of ignorance. And so she kept quiet for the most part as they explored the museum, which was a lot smaller than she expected—much of it taken up with an exhibit of a slave ship that had been recovered somewhere.

They had lunch in downtown Key West, a meal that started with a couple of margaritas so strong that she felt herself becoming lightheaded. She didn't even mind eating shellfish, suddenly experiencing a strong desire to sample coconut shrimp. Anything to soak up the tequila, was partly what she'd been thinking, but the shrimp turned out to be pretty tasty. John was holding his liquor better than she, as was usually the case. But with the margaritas pushing her, she grew bolder.

"I just don't see how you're going to be able to find anything," she told him. "The island is a lot bigger than I thought it would be."

He smiled expansively, ate a couple of onion rings. "But there aren't that many really big banyan trees around here, and as far as I can find out, Dos Hermanas is the only place that used to be a fish camp."

They'd find it in the shade of a banyan in what was at the time a fish camp on Little Sister Key, John's father had told him, as he had promised John's grandfather he would. Back home, John had both claimed and believed it would be a slam dunk. That was before they got here, and saw how heavily vegetated Little Sister Key was.

The tequila was emboldening Diane. "I have to say"— she hesitated for a moment, then plunged ahead—"that I think this whole business seems crazy." There, she'd said it.

John tightened his facial expression. "Crazy in what way?"

"Crazy in every way. Honey, I've been humoring you

all along on this thing, but I'm just afraid you're going to end up disappointed." She offered him a sad expression, her lips pouty. "I'm just looking out for you, honey."

"And why are you telling me this now?"

"'Cause I'm afraid it's not going to work out for you and then you'll be sad." Even tipsy, she knew not to denigrate the actual mission he was on. He was so obsessed that she'd hardly complained at the expense of the top-of-the-line metal detector and the GPS unit.

John had given the metal detector a thorough break-in before leaving Battle Creek, practicing last fall around town, making its final test on the Haedrich family's backyard, where he knew he had left buried treasure twenty-some years ago. With his mother shaking her head and rolling her eyes, John had moved systematically through the yard, digging up no less than seven spots where he had left trinkets and messages in tightly capped bottles. The metal bottle caps triggered the metal detector, and he'd gotten bonus points for finding a long-missing sterling silver fork buried beside a rose bush. Nobody had any idea how it had gotten there.

"Do you really believe there's a treasure here, that if you knew exactly where to look that it would actually *be* there?"

John nodded, suddenly very serious. "My granddaddy was born in 1933, and he said it was put here when he was twenty-one. The last big hurricane that came through and totally messed with the Keys was in 1935. So whatever they put here, unless somebody's accidentally dug it up, is probably still there."

Since arriving at Dos Hermanas, traveling by car so as not to alarm airport security with their various pieces of checked equipment, John had been systematically wandering the grounds of Dos Hermanas and other accessible parts of the island with the metal detector, looking for banyans. He'd also routinely worked grids as well, not wanting to inadvertently miss anything. He'd found some pocket change and bottle caps, a trowel with a pink plastic handle, and a metal compact with a badly molded powder puff still inside. He worked as nonchalantly as possible, usually late at night. They'd been in town four days now and he had pretty much eliminated large expanses of the property.

"It doesn't belong to you."

He grinned. "If it's there, and I find it, it does. Finders keepers."

⚘

**SHERI** had stewed all afternoon about how to handle Darcy's unfinished business. The two of them had split some of the responsibilities for this venture, but Darcy was the point woman, the one who met with the delivery people. She had intentionally kept this information from Sheri.

"Deniability," Darcy had said, sitting at the black lacquer dining table as they counted and packaged and labeled. "If you're asked about this, God forbid, you can honestly say you have no idea."

The problem was that Sheri did have a pretty good idea, and she also knew that people were counting on regular delivery. Already today three folks had slipped up to her, asked about Darcy, murmured platitudes, then gotten right to the point.

"I don't know," she'd told them all. "But I'll find out."

⚘

**THIS** wasn't, Jenna told herself, any kind of big deal. She'd met a guy on vacation and was going to hang out with him a bit.

More than a bit, though, if she was paying him to take her diving. But it would be worth every penny. She'd already decided to fund her diving out of the dwindling life insurance policy money that her dad had left her. The cost of living lately had been far beyond Jenna's income, and she knew she needed some kind of stability. Come the first of the year, she'd go out and find herself a real job, complete with benefits package: health insurance, paid vacations, honest-to-God sick leave. Just the thought of it made her feel giddy.

She had no idea what that job might be. That was not an issue with which she concerned herself just now. She was, after all, on vacation.

When they returned to Dos Hermanas from Key West, her mother took a book out and lay in the sun, something that Jenna couldn't recall ever previously witnessing. Mom was sufficiently tan to suggest that this wasn't a shocking new habit, though Jenna wasn't sure how she got that color. Probably puttering around the yard in a swimsuit, she decided. Her mother was too organized and too efficient to merely sunbathe. She'd want to be doing something productive at the same time.

Jenna took a saunter around the bird cages. Dan the parrot wrangler, as Peggy called him, was nowhere in sight. Phooey. She made a systematic swing around the cages, noting the occupants. There'd been a big coffee table book on parrots at Peggy and Rick's place, and she could check that out later. In the meantime, labels on the cages identified species and familiar names. That was good enough for now.

She cruised, counting fifteen cages. This would be a great setting for a full-blown aviary, she realized. Enclose a big enough area—the way they did at the San Diego Zoo and the Wild Animal Park—with double sets of doors to prevent escape, leave some of the shrubs inside, and then select a dozen or more birds that would coexist nicely. This might take a little fine tuning. Some birds, she remembered from a friend whose family owned an ill-tempered green parrot named Pedro, did not play well with others.

A half dozen lorikeets were as brightly colored as a child's drawing, their cage large enough to allow some brief flight. The blue-and-gold macaws were dignified and mature, their cage nestled in a hibiscus bush just beginning to bloom, its rosy pink flowers fluffy as tissue paper.

Four African Grey parrots shared a large cage surrounded by mangrove. The stuff was so ubiquitous in this area that even Jenna, who never paid attention to the names of plants, could now recognize it immediately. As best she could tell, the only reason these islands down here existed at all was that over millennia, the jagged, knife-edged coral atolls had mellowed, crumbled a bit, and allowed mangrove the toehold that would one day make the Lower Keys both shaded and habitable.

Even now, out there in the bay, it was happening. One day those little specks of green might have human habitation—not that this necessarily represented progress. Of course there was also the possibility of a hurricane, which could just as easily scrape everything from Key West to Key Largo right into the ocean. It had happened before and it would happen again. Hurricane Charley had come close, had swept through Cuba and been one course correction away from scouring the Lower Keys. Peggy had talked about this in wonder, noting that even though they had been spared direct hurricane landfall, the area had been through one serious tropical storm. Whatever survived—and this included just about everything at Dos Hermanas, which had plenty of experience battening down over the decades—was tough.

It was, in a way, like earthquakes back home.

You knew there were going to be earthquakes. You understood that every now and then those earthquakes would be really bad—pancaking apartment buildings, collapsing freeways, shattering lifelong crystal collections and family heirloom china. But you didn't think about them, or at least Jenna didn't. She had even used a course on earthquakes to fulfill part of her science requirement at UCLA.

Maybe if she found herself smack at the epicenter of an 8.4 she would feel differently about the subject.

Maybe not.

**HE'D** given her a business card, but when Jenna punched the numbers into her cell phone, he merely answered, "Hello."

What had she been expecting? An actual business with some perky little divette holding down the front counter while Dan and the other dudes ferried tourists down to Looe Key?

Dan Trenton was a really good-looking guy, the somewhat disheveled type she always found intriguing, often because such fellows were so into what they did that they didn't care about conventional grooming and dress. Not a slob, she amended hurriedly. That he wasn't. Just casual, easy going, laid-back. Deepwater tan. No extra meat on him, his slender body moving gracefully as he interacted with the birds. No discernable tattoos, though this issue bothered her mother much more than it bothered Jenna.

She caught herself. How much was she trying to read into this? Over a brief period she had watched a guy change water, offer food, and hose away bird shit, all in an easy and relaxed style. No extra movements, no lazy short-cuts. Just a good-looking guy in faded blue jean cutoffs and a gray T-shirt from a dive shop.

"I was wondering if I could set something up for div-ing," she told him. "I talked to you this morning when you were working with the birds. I'm Jenna Montgomery."

"Well, sure." The voice was slow and easy. "You want to get recertified first? That'll take some time in the shop and a couple of multiple guess tests, then a practical."

"Well, I . . ."

"Or if you want to skip that part right now, we could do a quick check out and go down together."

"Sounds good," Jenna said, realizing that indeed it did. "With a group?"

"I was thinking more without one," he answered slowly. "It's been kind of windy and that churns up the water some. We could go tomorrow, but I can't promise real fine diving. I was thinking we'd go to the *Adolphus Busch,* but that's at fifty feet and I thought we'd start a little closer to the surface."

"Is that the one they sank to make an artificial reef?" She was proud to know that, had actually researched Keys diving quite a bit once her mother made the offer of the trip.

"One and the same."

They talked about money briefly and matter-of-factly. From her research, Jenna knew his fee was on the low end of the local price range. She decided to think he was cutting her a deal, and agreed immediately.

"If you want," he said, "I can come and do the birds early, then pick you up and bring you back to the boat."

Jenna told him that would be just fine. As she hung up the phone, she surprised herself by wondering what Dan Trenton was doing when she reached him, how he spent his time. Had he been coming on to her this morning, just a little bit? Did she want him to?

Or was her imagination working overtime?

*Chapter 11*

**JOHN** was outside with the big picture book on pirates that he'd borrowed from the Battle Creek library. Here, by the side of the water, he could look out across the bay, squinting his eyes a bit, imagining that a pirate sloop was about to suddenly emerge from behind one of the islands. The *Jolly Roger* would be flying, a white skull against a black background, and heavily armed pirates would swarm on deck, knives between their teeth, ready for action. For all the time that John had spent studying and imagining pirates, this was the first time he'd ever been in a setting where pirates might actually have been. It was a heady, exhilarating experience.

Diane had passed out in the car coming back from Key West and had roused just long enough to stumble back to their room, where he left her sprawled on the bed. He was a little bit buzzed himself, actually.

He was giving her concerns some thought, however, He couldn't tell if there were banyan trees in some of the southern parts of the key because they were fenced off and posted. He had been really hopeful when he saw that banyan tree just beyond the owners' house, because he knew that Dos Hermanas had been a fish camp back in the fifties, and he had managed to check back there surreptitiously. But he had found nothing. It was an enormous disappointment, as he had fruitlessly circled the thick aerial roots of that tree with his metal detector. No response at all. His determination to find the treasure he believed was there wasn't shaken, but Diane had tickled him with just a touch of doubt.

"Fine book you've got there," a male voice boomed beside him.

Startled, John looked up. A knobby-kneed older man in plaid shorts was standing by his chaise, keyed in on *The History of Pirates.*

"It's a good one," John agreed. "I've had it out of the library back home so many times the librarian was teasing about giving it to me for Christmas."

"It'd make a good gift," the man said. "I own a copy myself. Excellent illustrations, though a mite sketchy on prose."

In John's state of mild inebriation, this matter-of-fact statement stunned him. "You're kidding," he said. "You own this book?"

Looking up at the man was putting a crick in his neck. He rose awkwardly to his feet and extended a hand. "I'm John Haedrich."

The man was probably around seventy, thin and sinewy. He wore a ball cap with the logo of the Green Bay Packers and very dark, wire-rimmed sunglasses. His skin was pale and it wasn't possible to see his hair, if he had any, or the color of his eyes. He was shorter than John, not much taller than Diane. He probably didn't weigh much more than Diane, for that matter, though she was far from overweight. While thin, however, the man gave no sign of frailty.

"George Wyman," the man told him, offering a firm handshake. "Haedrich. That's an interesting name."

"It's German."

"So it is. Where are you from, John?"

"Michigan, sir. Battle Creek."

"Ah. Mind if I join you for a moment? I don't often run across young people interested in piracy. Oh, there are children who like *Peter Pan,* but that's Disney. I mean the real thing." He pulled over a chair and motioned for John to sit back down.

"That's me," John told him. "The real thing. Pirates just have always, I don't know, fascinated me. That's one of the reasons my wife and I came to the Keys. And you, sir?"

The man pulled over a chair and motioned for John to sit down again.

"Call me George, son," he said settling into his chair. "Same as you, I expect. Though there wasn't all that much action here because of the reefs. Caribbean piracy was concentrated more to the east. Not that the Keys lacked for plunder. Do you know that in the middle of the nineteenth century, Key West was the wealthiest city in America?"

John nodded. This was going to be a quiz, and he was ready. "Those wreckers were really something, weren't they?"

Wyman raised his eyebrows, just a quarter of an inch. "Tremendous fortunes were made in these parts."

"True, but that was largely opportunism, wasn't it? People grabbing whatever might have foundered on the reef.

And for a while there, all the European powers were looting the resources of the New World. Spain in particular."

John heard himself and realized that he was speaking in the formalized language of books he'd read on piracy, the studied prose of the nineteenth century and before. "But the more serious pirates, they were something else altogether. Captain Kidd. Blackbeard, that nasty son of a gun. And Jean Lafitte later, after the Golden Age had ended." Despite centuries of piracy around the globe, most of the pirate activity that had made its way into contemporary folklore had occurred in four decades, ending around 1730. The Caribbean was a happening place for pirates, wasn't it?" He listened to what he had said, regretted the "happening place" reference. He was afraid he'd be treated like a kid.

"For hundreds of years," Wyman said. He removed a pack of Marlboro Red cigarettes from a pocket, extracted one, and flicked a lighter, inhaling deeply, then giving a dry, hacking cough. "You're absolutely right. But the first pirates weren't really pirates at all, of course. They were emissaries from the governments of Europe."

"Privateers," John put in.

Wyman raised an eyebrow. "Indeed. Privateers. Exploiting letters de marque, for the most part. By most definitions, Christopher Columbus himself was a pirate before he set out heading west, looking for India."

This was news to John. "Really?" Maybe he'd just stumbled on a local nutcase.

"Really. Like many of the sailing men of that era, Columbus worked for whatever country would support him. He was on a French vessel when they fought a fierce battle off the coast of Portugal, taking plunder from Venetian galleys bound for London. European piracy was a specialized art. The area covered was really quite small, off-shore from countries that were well-populated. Most of the action was in the Mediterranean, which just isn't that large a body of water. But then men like Columbus moved into the unknown. That's when the *real* era of piracy began."

George Wyman offered a wide, satisfied grin. His teeth were dark yellow.

"I had no idea," John told him truthfully.

Christopher Columbus a pirate? Or even a privateer?

Without even thinking it through, John realized that this was possible, even logical. He felt his awareness of that entire historical period move to a new level. There was something intoxicating about being around somebody who actually seemed to know more than John did about all of this.

For a long, long time, John's obsession with pirates had been a solitary pleasure, cautiously revealed to others, rarely shared by anyone. Certainly not shared with anyone who had a comparable level of knowledge. There'd been some guys from his childhood who thought pirates were pretty cool for a while, but they tended to drift off to things like baseball, or drug abuse, or bagging groceries at the A&P.

One of the things that John had enjoyed about ten years of independent pirate study was his confidence that he *owned* this knowledge, that it was his and irrefutable. He also loved the awareness that his consciousness of piracy seemed to expand in rich, billowing clouds of knowledge every time he came across a fact or concept that was entirely new.

This was, John thought, the essence of knowledge. The core of discovery.

George Wyman raised a finger. "History is rich with

contradictions. You mentioned William Kidd. Were you aware that before he become known as Captain Kidd, the pirate, he was a respectable sea captain?"

John did, in fact, know this and a great deal more about Captain Kidd. "Yes, sir. I read a really good book about him last year. *The Pirate Hunter*, it was called."

Wyman nodded, looking a bit surprised. "By Richard Zacks. Always credit the author, son. Yes, Kidd was a complex man, one of the best illustrations of that thin line dividing loyalties on the high seas in that era. An ignominious end for such a man, to be hanged at Executioner's Dock and left to rot in the gibbet at Tilbury for years to come."

"So many of them were hanged." This detail had always felt inexorably sad to John.

Wyman nodded. "It wasn't a position with a lot of job security, being a pirate. You didn't know from one day to the next if you were likely to be killed for no particular reason, or fall into a fatal illness from something you ate or breathed. Medicine on the world's pirate fleet was always rudimentary. They even had a sort of worker's comp scale for compensation when you lost a limb or an eye."

"Excuse me?" This was truly news to John.

George Wyman nodded. "If you happened to lose an eye, or an arm, or a leg in the course of battle, you had your choice of pieces-of-eight or slaves. There were standard compensations, just like you might get today if you had an industrial accident and lost a limb. It was quite specialized, actually. You got more gold for losing a right arm than a left, for instance."

"I guess that makes sense," John said slowly. He was starting to get really sleepy. Midday margaritas packed a wallop. "I'd better go check on my wife. Are you staying here?"

"For the rest of my life, son. I live just over there in the Little Sister Court. You'll have to come visit me sometime. Check out my library. And I've got some other things I think you'll find of interest as well."

✿

**SHERI** had observed the police moving around Little Sister Court through the morning, interviewing folks from unit to unit. So she wasn't surprised to hear a knock on her door in the early afternoon. On the other side of the carefully latched screen door, she could see Detective Rafael Ruiz shifting his weight as she went to greet him.

"Come in," she offered immediately.

She wasn't sure how she was supposed to be acting, but she figured that since her good friend had died under strange circumstances, she ought to be concerned and eager to help. As a point of fact, this was all true. Half an hour ago, she'd indulged herself in a good cry, and she was relieved to have that out of the way and her makeup refreshed. Silly, she supposed, but habits were habits. For the last fifty-five years, until today, in fact, when she'd lost her composure and dissolved into tears over at Dos Hermanas, Sheri had never appeared in public without makeup. The day of Darcy's death was no time to break that tradition.

Detective Ruiz had looked tired earlier this morning, and in the bright midday light the sallow bags beneath his limpid brown eyes seemed more pronounced, his countenance congenitally unhappy. Even his suit looked dispirited.

It must be an awful job, Sheri thought, dealing with sudden death. Everybody would be so emotionally overwrought, except of course for the poor dead person. And in the midst of all that sorrow, the policeman would have to try to figure out who killed the person and why. Nobody had said in so many words that Darcy had been murdered, but the longer the police spent snooping around Little Sister Court, the more likely it seemed that they believed this to be the case.

"Would you like a glass of limeade, Detective? It's fresh, from the tree down by the office."

She expected him to decline and was rather surprised when he smiled. Even his smile looked sad.

"That would be very nice," he said. "Thank you."

She fussed a bit in the kitchen with ice and the limeade and decided after a moment's hesitation that it couldn't possibly hurt to put out some cookies. She'd thawed the last box of Girl Scout Thin Mints just a few days ago.

"Now, what can I help you with?" she asked, sitting across from him in the La-Z-Boy recliner. It had been Will's, and she had never realized how comfy it was until after he died. Now she wished she'd had one of her own all along, wondered why she had never considered it before, why she had always limited herself to a much less comfortable wing chair, even for relaxing to watch TV.

"You had a spare key for Mrs. Gainsborough's trailer," he began.

"Her coach," Sheri corrected politely. "There are only a handful of trailers here, all down on the far end. Nobody in this section calls them trailers." She hoped he'd understand the connotation without having to hear it spelled out. The unspoken word *trash* hung in the air for a moment.

"You had a spare key for Mrs. Gainsborough's *coach*," he said. "The one you gave me. How long ago did she give you that key?"

Sheri stopped to think. "It's been years, but you know, I really don't remember. It was after my husband passed away, I do know, and that's been six years. So maybe five?"

As best she knew, nobody else was aware of the key Darcy kept in the fake rock in her overgrown entryway, the key now moved to Sheri's own key ring. The area was littered with rocks of all sizes. Of course if anybody *did* know, and told the police, they'd be watching to see who used it. Then Sheri wouldn't be able to get back in later, to get the records. And she needed those records.

"And she had a key to your place?"

Sheri nodded.

She took a deep breath, conscious of her racing heart. Keep calm, that was the ticket.

"We exchanged them at the same time. I think that Darcy had a key for Lucia Miller's place, but then Lucia passed away. That happens, of course, though this isn't the kind of place where you have to put a sign out each morning to show that you're still alive. Most of the folks here are extremely active and relatively healthy." She realized the conversation was moving into dangerous territory and redirected it quickly. "That's why we're so lucky to have Dos Hermanas right next door, with the pool and the tennis court. Darcy and I played several times a week. We were planning to enter the tournament as doubles partners."

Detective Ruiz frowned slightly. "What tournament was that?"

As Sheri offered the details, he listened thoughtfully.

Then he threw a sudden question that made her almost drop her glass of limeade. "Are you familiar with the contents of her coach?"

Sheri nodded, her heart suddenly racing again.

"Would you mind coming over and looking around to see if anything seems out of place or is missing?"

Sheri flushed, thinking of her hand-painted covered dish. Thinking even more anxiously about the materials in her own dresser drawer, not ten feet from where Detective Ruiz sat sipping his limeade. The police probably didn't know anything, she told herself, fighting back panic. If they *did* know, then surely he'd be asking different questions.

"Anything I can do to help," she answered sweetly. "Though wouldn't you want to wait for her children?" She had shared the names and phone numbers of Darcy's grown children with the detective earlier this morning, making a special trip over to Dos Hermanas to give him the slip of paper she had filled out so neatly.

"Her daughter won't be able to get here till late today," he said, "and her son's in Europe on a business trip. I imagine it may take him a day or two. But more to the point, neither of them would have the day-to-day familiarity with Mrs. Gainsborough's home that somebody here— you, for instance—probably does. Do you have a few minutes now to come with me to check it?"

"Of course."

❧

**DARCY'S** place was already stuffy and hot, much more so than it had been just a few hours ago. Sheri stood just inside the doorway, wondering what the detective had in mind for her to do.

"Just look around," he told her, reading her mind, "and see if everything is the way you'd expect it to be."

"Well, it wouldn't be this hot," she said tentatively. "Darcy liked her place cool, almost chilly." She remembered coming in this morning, recalled that the A/C hadn't been on then. Who had shut it off? When? "I can't believe she'd have the air off."

Detective Ruiz nodded but didn't speak.

Sheri moved into the kitchen. "Is it all right for me to touch things?"

"I'd prefer that you don't," he told her. He removed a pair of surgical gloves from his pocket and handed them to her, pulling a second pair onto his own hands.

"If this is to avoid getting my fingerprints on things," she said carefully, "you ought to know that I've been in here a lot over the years. My prints are probably all over the place already."

Until this very moment, it had never occurred to her to worry about fingerprints. What a dunce she was! She'd seen all those TV shows where detectives and crime scene investigators were always slipping on a fresh pair of gloves. They sold those gloves everywhere now, it seemed. So why hadn't she been smart enough to get some before she came grubbing around Darcy's coach? She didn't need special latex, even. She could have dug out her up-north black leather gloves. Even the heavy blue Playtex rubber gloves she used to scrub the toilet would have been preferable to coming in here with ten stupid, unprotected fingers.

Sure, she could say she was there often. But no casual guest would leave her marks everywhere. That dining room suite was so bright and shiny that they could probably just snap photographs of her fingerprints. Never mind dusting and superglue and all that crime-scene-show rigmarole.

Detective Ruiz led her through the rooms.

Darcy's bedroom with its Mondrian-style bedspread and curtains, all geometric primary colors. A second bedroom with the daybed and Darcy's desk, this one done in sunflowers. The kitchen where herbs on the windowsill were already looking a bit droopy. The carport. The jungly entrance area. The tiny laundry room.

They finished their rounds back in the living room, adjacent to the tiny dining room full of shiny black furniture. She remembered Darcy once stating, with no particular regret, that she had never served a meal in there. No wonder she didn't bother with live flowers.

"I wish I could be more help," Sheri told the detective as he opened the front door and held it for her to leave, pulling off the gloves as he did so.

"Every little bit helps," Detective Ruiz said, in a tone that suggested that nothing ever helped anything. He said goodbye and started off in the opposite direction as Sheri walked slowly toward her own unit.

Tonight, if they didn't arrest her first—a thought she had initially intended to be light before realizing with a severe stomach plummet that they actually *might* arrest her—she'd have to get back in there. As soon as the sun set and the police left, in whichever order those things happened.

She had taken a hasty look at the contents of the satin box she'd pulled out of Darcy's buffet. First, there wasn't nearly as much as she was expecting, and second, she had no idea who it belonged to. She had the packaging materials but no labels. She was stuck, not even entirely sure what was her own.

Folks would be coming around soon, she could count on that. Darcy's daughter was on the way as well. Somewhere in Darcy's place, probably on the computer, there would be a master list. If the police were going to be hanging around, which was starting to feel probable, she needed that info.

Fast. She considered. Darcy's entryway was so overgrown that it would be easy to slip in there. She still had the key Darcy had kept in the fake rock, and Detective Ruiz had left a couple of lights on inside her coach, whether by accident or design.

She had a thought then that literally stopped her in her tracks.

Maybe what had happened to Darcy had occurred because of the package now in Sheri's former sweater drawer. And if that was the case, had Sheri put herself in danger by removing it?

**TWELVE** or so hours before Darcy Gainsborough turned up dead on the boat ramp, Lynne and Jenna had eagerly promised to take their hosts to dinner at a Cuban restaurant the Parkers liked the next night. Now, after returning from Key West, Lynne asked Peggy if she should also invite Gloria. She watched her friend shiver in revulsion.

"Gloria can get her own damn dinner," Peggy stated emphatically. "I'm tired of having her attached to us like some snotty upper-class leech. I didn't realize how good we had it when she considered us beneath her and left us alone. She's always been a bitch."

They were sitting on the patio outside the Parkers' place, which seemed so tropical and isolated that Lynne realized with a start that their voices might be carrying beyond the bougainvillea. She waved a hand in the general direction of the rest of Dos Hermanas. In the distance, she could hear kids shouting "Marco Polo" in the pool. "Is it okay to talk here?"

"Not a problem," Peggy said, though she did drop her voice. "Gloria's unit is too far off to hear us, and I know for a fact that her hearing is bad. She's just too vain to get a hearing aid."

"Maybe they have one in celery," Lynne suggested, recalling Gloria's ensemble from the night before, "and also in mauve and taupe. I picture her in muted noncolors, though I could be way off base."

"You're actually dead on," Peggy told her.

Lynne hesitated. "I was wondering, what are those lumps on Gloria's cheeks?"

Expecting news of some unpleasant diagnosis, Lynne was taken aback by Peggy's chuckle. This time she did look around hastily and then lowered her voice. "I think of them as divine justice. You and I are still wearing the faces we were issued at birth, and however physically fit we still manage to be, it's because we work at it. Gloria's too lazy for any of that. She's been fiddling with surgical improvement for decades. She's had her face lifted and her tummy tucked, her butt liposuctioned, her eyelids trimmed, and her chin de-creped. Plus Botox and collagen. Collagen made those lumps and the facelifts tightened her skin so they're even more obvious. She's been frantic to fix it, but there doesn't seem to be anything she can do about the bumps even if she could afford it, which she claims she can't. In a way, she's got the appearance she always deserved."

"A pity," Lynne murmured.

## Chapter 12

AS soon as Lynne heard Peggy's cell phone play "Silver Bells" as its holiday ring, she resolved to find something equally appropriate, even to download it if necessary, however you'd do that. Jenna would know. Maybe "Pretty Paper" or "White Christmas."

"Hello." Peggy was frowning as she listened. "I'll be right there. Thanks, Jim."

She flipped the phone shut. "That was Jim in the office. Darcy's daughter is here. You want to come along and meet her?

"You bet."

In the office they found manager Jim Tyler conversing with a woman in her mid-thirties who wore a pale gray silk dress, a navy blazer, and Darcy Gainsborough's face. She was imperceptibly shaking as she clutched the counter. Tyler looked relieved to see Peggy and Lynne. "This is Ellen Gainsborough," he told Peggy. "Mrs. Gainsborough's daughter."

"I'm Peggy Parker," Peggy said, extending a hand. "I'm so sorry to meet you under these circumstances."

Ellen Gainsborough looked as if she were about to faint.

"Come on into my office," Peggy said. "Jim, could you find some iced tea, please?"

As Jim Tyler headed off to the breakfast room, Peggy led Ellen Gainsborough into her small office at the end of a short hall. A tidy desk filled most of the space, leaving just enough room for a visitor's chair and a wastebasket. Peggy helped the young woman into the visitor's chair, all but cooing as she tried to calm and settle her. Lynne stood in the doorway, the only space that remained.

Inside the small office, the young woman sank into a chair. "What happened?" she asked.

"We don't really know," Peggy told her. "I'm so terribly sorry about your mother. She was a fascinating and energetic lady. None of us understand this."

"The police officer who called me said that her death was suspicious, but he wouldn't say anything else. Do you know anything about what happened?"

Lynne and Peggy both shook their heads.

"I wish we did," Peggy said quickly. "We all just feel so horribly helpless."

Jim Tyler reappeared with a glass of iced tea, handing it to Ellen.

"Thank you," Ellen said, looking up at Tyler. "I appreciate your kindness." She turned to Peggy. "The detective on the phone told me that Mother's trailer is closed off as a crime scene. So I can't even get in there to stay. I don't quite understand why they won't let me in. It's my mother's home, for heaven's sake." A cloud crossed her face. "I guess it's mine, now, technically. Not that

*that* matters. And I thought that the policeman who called told me she was found in the bay."

"That's true," Lynne said. "I'm the one who found her, actually. She was right at the shore, here on the Dos Hermanas boat ramp." She nodded her head vaguely behind her. If Ellen Gainsborough wanted to visit the site, she'd say so. "I'm Lynne Montgomery, by the way, a guest here and an old friend of Peggy's. I'm also very sorry about your loss."

"I just don't understand," Ellen said again.

As Lynne and Peggy shared what little they knew, Lynne watched Ellen, who seemed to be in shock. She had the soft white complexion and smooth grooming typical of women in the upper echelons of the labor force. Sheri McManus had said that Darcy's daughter was a lawyer, and divorced.

"Are you here by yourself?" Lynne asked carefully, leaving the door open for as much or as little information as Ellen chose to share.

"Yes."

"Well, don't hesitate to ask us for help with anything," Lynne said. "The worst that will happen is we won't be able to help."

Peggy smiled gently. "There's one thing I think we can help with right now, and that's a place to stay. I can't bring back your mother, and I can't tell you what happened to her, but I can offer you a room here for as long as you need or want. No charge, of course. Darcy was a good friend."

Lynne thought something passed over Ellen's face just then.

"How long did you know her?" Ellen asked.

"Less than a year," Peggy admitted. "We just bought

this place last spring, and I know your mom was here a long time before that."

Ellen nodded. "She and my father moved down here when he retired."

"Did they come because they knew somebody here?"

Ellen shrugged. "Not that I ever knew about. My dad was a born salesman, so he never met anybody he didn't like. He might have heard about it from somebody. I was kind of relieved, actually. I wanted to stay in Philadelphia and . . . well, it was easier to get along with my mother at a distance."

Lynne, whose own mother had been born under the zodiac sign "Big Trouble" and was presently somewhere between New Hampshire and Southern California, chuckled. "I know what you're talking about."

Peggy stood. "Let me get a room for you. Do you have luggage?"

"Just a carry-on. It's out in my rental car."

Lynne stayed with Ellen as Peggy went out into the lobby and murmured with Jim Tyler. Peggy returned with a room key and a soft smile. "I've got you all set, in Gumbo Limbo. And there's a second bedroom for when your brother arrives."

"Gumbo Limbo?" Ellen stood and they all went out front to her rental car, parked by the office.

Lynne explained as Ellen pulled her luggage out of the car. "Gumbo Limbo is the name of the tree. It's also called 'Tourist Tree' and 'Sunburn Tree.' There's one over here."

Peggy had taken Ellen's suitcase and was leading the way to a cottage right beside a prime specimen. As she set down the bag and unlocked the door, she nodded toward the tree, pointing at the bark. "See how it peels, and that rich golden red color?"

Ellen Gainsborough nodded, but Lynne could see that her thoughts were elsewhere.

Nearby, most likely, in her mother's mobile home, now a Monroe County crime scene.

☙

**JENNA** loved Cuban food and tried to make it to Versailles, her favorite Cuban restaurant in LA, at least once a month. She sat now with her mother and the Parkers, drinking icy beer and munching on Cuban bread while they waited for their entrees in a charmingly casual wooden building with the omnipresent nautical motifs of the Keys. She studied a large mounted fish hanging on the wall above their table.

"How do they do that?" Jenna asked, pointing.

"Do what?" Rick Parker asked. "Catch fish?"

"No, I mean how do they mount it? Mom and I stayed in a place in Vermont where they had all kinds of animal heads hanging on the walls, even a buffalo, and I have a kind of vague idea what goes into preserving them. But mammals have skin and fur. Fish has scales. It spoils. Fish gets funky real fast, and the ones with interesting color usually lose that color as soon as they die. So how can all these fish be real?"

"Easy enough," Rick answered. "They're not. But they're approximations of what the fish actually looked like while they were alive. Taxidermy is an art, really. And part of that art is to reproduce the actual fish in fiberglass and acrylic."

The waitress brought their food then—platters of roast pork and black beans and rice, with extra fried plantains, Jenna's favorite.

"So when are you going to dive?" Peggy asked Jenna a few minutes later.

"Tomorrow, I think. Dan Trenton's going to take me."

"Are you going with a group?" Rick asked.

Jenna shook her head. "I don't think so. He said the water's not very clear because it's been windy, so I guess there aren't a lot of people willing to go under those circumstances. Me, I just want to get back in the water again."

It was, indeed, the prospect of diving that had finally snared Jenna into taking this trip. She'd already taken a chunk of time away in October to visit New England with her mother, and the notion of another trip so soon seemed downright decadent.

Jenna had grown up in a household with a strong work ethic. Her father had surfed early most mornings, but after that he was generally in his insurance office every weekday, save for an occasional "Mental Health Friday" and the week between Christmas and New Year's. Other vacations were limited to a week. And while her mother had been a stay-at-home mom for most of Jenna's childhood, Lynne also took responsibility seriously, whether it was serving as Girl Scout cookie mom, scrounging donations for Grad Night, or doing repeated stints as PTA president.

But Jenna's work ethic was only part of the issue here, and her boss Larry's insistence that she take this trip had actually surprised her. "Enjoy every minute of your life," he'd counseled. "Remember that old saying, Nobody ever got to their deathbed saying, 'I wish I'd spent more time at the office.' And Jenna, if you come across some kind of chance to do something that looks promising, go for it. I probably should have pressured you to move on before this, but I enjoyed having you around. And face it, you can't work in a store that doesn't exist, can you?"

Larry didn't know about her secret cushion, the dwindling fifty-thousand-dollar life insurance policy that her father had left her. She'd already tapped into those funds several times in her underemployed post-college years. But Larry was right. With Booker T closing in January, she needed to figure out something to do soon. What better way to contemplate those changes than to go diving in the Caribbean?

**LYNNE** wasn't really concentrating on anything but her meal when she heard Rick Parker ask a question that froze her fork on its way to her mouth, leaving a slice of fried plantain hanging suspended.

"What ever happened to Monty's woody?" Rick asked. "If you don't mind my asking," he added hastily.

"Not at all," Lynne answered with a smile. Yes, she'd been startled, but she didn't mind these questions so much anymore. A couple of years ago, the question would have reduced her to tears. "I sold it a few years ago. Neither of the kids wanted it, and it seemed a shame not to let it go to somebody who'd really appreciate it."

"Didn't it have a name?" Rick went on. "Big Blue, something like that?"

"Big Red, actually."

"Big Red." Rick leaned back expansively. "That was one fine vehicle. I remember going to that car show up at Moonlight Beach, walking around with him, hearing him talking car trash with the other guys who had woodies."

"I remember how cool it was having him pick us up from stuff," Jenna put in. "I just loved that car."

"So did he," Lynne said now, pleased that she could matter-of-factly discuss this with people who cared, who weren't afraid to bring up her dead husband and his possessions. She did some fast math. "You know, Jenna, Big Red is twice your age right now." She watched Jenna's eyes as she performed the computation.

"You're right, Mom. Somehow that seems very weird."

"What year was it?" Peggy asked.

"Fifty-one." Lynne could picture the Woody clearly: a 1951 Ford station wagon, a deep, rich shade of burgundy with ash and cherry woodwork. "A very good year."

"I was in second or third grade before I realized there was anything unusual about it," Jenna said now. "It was just my dad's car."

"What I liked about Big Red," Rick said, clearly savoring the memory, "was that Monty actually drove it around town, used it as his car. So many of those cars at the Moonlight Beach show looked like the owners were afraid to take them out of the garage. I kept thinking, what's the point?"

"Aficionados' cars," Lynne agreed. "But incredible restorations."

She hadn't thought about it in ages, but Big Red had, in fact, provided solace of sorts in the early weeks and months after Monty's death. When Lynne was so overcome by raw emotion that she could barely breathe, she sometimes had gone out to the garage and simply sat in Big Red, letting the flash floods of grief roll over her as she struggled with the never-answered question, *Why?*

Three years after Monty's death, she had been contacted by an acquaintance who also exhibited at the Wavecrest show held at Moonlight Beach in Encinitas every fall. She remembered meeting this fellow, and liking him. If she ever considered selling Big Red, the man told her, he hoped to be allowed to make a bid. As it happened, a number of people had expressed interest, but this offer came at a time when Lynne was cautiously divesting herself of some of the outer trappings of her marriage. What would Monty have wanted? she asked herself. As clearly as if he had spoken aloud, she had his answer. Big Red should go to somebody who'd love him.

Her son David had taken Monty's surfboards but didn't want Big Red. Jenna had been so indifferent that the enthusiasm she had just now voiced surprised Lynne.

Lynne had gone online, done some research, and come back with a counter offer to the guy who wanted Big Red. He accepted the offer so quickly that she thought maybe she'd set the price too low, but she only allowed herself a few moments of doubt before telling him that he had a deal.

Wavecrest was too painful an event, however. Years had passed. It was only last fall that she'd summoned the energy and nerve to visit Moonlight Beach while the show was going on.

In the second row she walked along, she spotted Big Red.

She didn't cry. That was the first thing she noticed.

Big Red was in great shape. That was the second thing she noticed. His woodwork was burnished to a warm glow, his metal surfaces polished to a dazzling sheen. He was, indeed, more lovingly cared for than he'd ever been as Monty's around-town car.

"As a matter of fact," she said now, "I saw Big Red just a little while ago." She laughed at Jenna's surprised expression. "Get used to it, kiddo. I have a life of my own."

And she told the story.

✀

**GLORIA** Parker had been suffering from insomnia for several years now, unable to fall asleep at a respectable hour or to remain asleep until morning. This unfortunate problem had started some time back when Tom's legal problems began to escalate, but she had managed for a while to keep it under control with the help of various pills that her Greenwich doctor had prescribed.

The doctor had been sympathetic about Tom's situation, had indeed been the beneficiary of Tom's investment advice at various times over the years, though fortunately not during the recent unpleasantness. He had assured Gloria that the medication would allow her to drift into the arms of Morpheus, but Morpheus refused to cooperate.

Still she continued to take the pills, staring sleeplessly at the shadowed ceiling in her darkened Lake Avenue master bedroom, calm and sepulchral with its four-poster bed and heavy brocade draperies closed tightly against daylight. Sometimes she would fall asleep just before sunrise, awakening midday with a disoriented sense of having missed out on something important. But the only important things happening in her life were utterly beyond her control.

Gloria had truly believed that wintering in Florida would cure the insomnia, but so far nothing was working as she'd planned. Dos Hermanas was downright shabby, occupied by middle-class burghers and their mousy wives and unpalatable children. The trailer park was beneath contempt. Rick couldn't be bothered with her, despite what he had promised Tom. And as for Peggy—well, she'd been a snippy little wench when they first met and now was absolutely intolerable, apparently proud to be running this third-rate dive.

She sighed, turned on a light and got out of bed, crossing to the window where the curtains never entirely closed, letting in morning sun too early, often just after Gloria had finally drifted to sleep. She pulled the curtain aside and gazed down onto the grounds in puzzlement. The grounds were reasonably well lit at night, but still . . .

Was she really seeing what she thought she was?

She went back to the bedside table and retrieved her blended trifocals. As she stood by the window again, the unexpected scene more clearly defined, she became even more confused. She leaned forward to get a better view and accidentally banged her elbow into the window frame with a dishearteningly loud *thwap*.

The noise carried across the silent night, drew attention to her. Fearful and bewildered, she tightened her satin dressing gown around her waist and shrank back into the room—but not, she was quite sure, before she was observed.

## Chapter 13

**SHERI** had decided to wait until after midnight to return to Darcy's coach in search of the missing records. She was becoming more and more anxious, and the appearance of Darcy's daughter Ellen that afternoon had really thrown her. Sheri had no idea how much of her mother's life Ellen knew about, and she did not want to be the one who explained that Darcy was a sneak thief who had also been running a smuggling ring.

Not for the first time, Sheri wished she had made the time to take a couple of computer courses. Everybody always assured her that they adored surfing the net, and they chattered on about listservs and news groups and bookmarks. A lot of them sent her forwarded jokes and links to political groups they thought she should embrace. On top of that there was a bewildering proliferation of spam—suggestions on improving the function of organs she didn't possess; pleas for money from people she didn't know; solicitations for services she didn't need, including all manner of pharmaceuticals. Every now and then she did check one of those, but it was never as inexpensive or convenient as the opportunity she had right in her own home court. But for the most part, Sheri quietly pushed her DELETE button.

Darcy had played this whole import business so close to her chest that nobody else—at least nobody that Sheri was aware of—really knew the entire picture. Sheri had a pretty good idea where the merchandise came from, and who brought it. Beyond that she knew only how her own small consumer end of the process was carried out.

Darcy's computer was newer than Sheri's, but they both used Windows and Darcy had once commented that apart from the Internet, which she navigated confidently and embraced with great enthusiasm, she had no use for the various bells and whistles bundled into the unit. Microsoft Word was all she needed, Darcy had claimed, and Sheri hoped that was true, because Word was the only program beyond email that Sheri knew how to operate.

Apparently Darcy had not feared exposure. It was laughably easy to get to Darcy's records, so simple that Sheri wondered anxiously if the police had already downloaded them. She went into My Documents and immediately found a folder called Pharmaceuticals. She opened the most recent file, labeled "December Orders" and turned on the printer. It was all there: names, dates, drugs, dosages, costs, charges.

Sheri first went to her own entry. Prinivil, Premarin, Pravachol, her three P's. She generally tried to get at least three months' worth at a time for simple convenience. But something was wrong here. The price Sheri paid for her drugs was significantly higher than what they were costing Darcy, even allowing for a profit to the actual smugglers.

And surely their fees would be included in whatever Darcy paid.

"The acquisition costs include the fee for my delivery people," Darcy had explained more than once, "and I take expenses right off the top, a straight five percent. I wouldn't dream of marking anything up beyond that. The satisfaction I receive in helping folks on fixed incomes is all the reward I need."

Not quite. Sheri did some fast computations, grateful to have been educated in a pre-calculator era when long division was an elementary school standard.

Sheri had been paying twenty percent more for her prescriptions than what they actually cost Darcy. Fifteen percent higher than what Darcy claimed they cost her. And if this was the way Darcy treated an allegedly close friend, how much more had she been tacking on to others?

No time to find out now. Sheri turned on the printer and began printing out all the records she could find—the entire contents of the Pharmaceuticals folder, dating back four years. The printer was slow, and every page seemed to take an eternity. After a while, she noticed that the ink was fading. She had no idea how to fix that. She'd been proud enough to figure out how to turn the fool thing on and use it.

Later on she'd try to make sense of these records, to determine who had ordered what. She'd seen dozens of acquaintances from Little Sister Court on the December list, had scanned several lists looking for Rick and Peggy Parker, who weren't listed.

She wondered who would carry on the operation with Darcy gone. She knew that it wasn't something she would be able to do herself. It wasn't precisely against the law, but it skirted issues of morality and legality in ways that felt surprisingly uncomfortable.

After spending the entire day mourning her friend, Sheri realized, this past half hour had turned her feelings all the way around. She was startled to find herself downright furious.

※

ONCE again up at dawn, her internal clock totally out of kilter, Lynne dressed and headed outside. She found Peggy and Rick by the bird cages, several of which sat empty, their doors wide open. Rick was trying to coax Angela, the scarlet macaw, down from a mangrove branch above her cage. Angela was having none of it.

"What happened?" Lynne asked in dismay.

"Somebody cut the locks off these cages," Peggy told her. "I just can't believe it." She had Melissa the cockatoo on her shoulder, eating green grapes as she moved cautiously toward Melissa's cage. She offered the bird a hand. "I love you," Melissa said between grapes, and she allowed herself to be returned to the cage.

Peggy then quickly closed the door and wrapped a couple twirls of duct tape around the bars as a temporary lock.

Rick momentarily abandoned Angela. "Dan swears that with their wings clipped, they can't fly," he told Lynne. "I sure hope he's right."

"Where *is* he, anyway? It has to be at least half an hour since I called. He said he'd be right over."

"You looking for me?" Dan Trenton asked, approaching Gus and Gertie, the blue-and-gold macaws, who were sitting atop their cage. "Hey, guys," he crooned. "What have you been up to? Lock picking in the first degree?"

"Not really," Rick said, as the birds hopped to a mangrove branch over the cage. "All those fancy lock disguises that Roberto made are still intact. These locks were cut with a regular old bolt cutter."

Dan looked perplexed. "And the birds are all still here? None of them were stolen?"

This was the first time it had occurred to Lynne that birds were a stealable item. But it was perfectly reasonable, given what Peggy had told her about how expensive birds like these could be.

"I don't think any are gone," Peggy said, "except for the little ones, and I'm guessing they just flew away. If you're going to steal a bird, wouldn't you take one of the macaws?"

Dan looked around. "So where are the others?"

"The African grays are over there in the mimosa, playing hide and seek. And a couple of the green parrots are chasing each other across the lawn. So far I haven't seen any of the big birds actually fly. And I don't think any of them are missing."

Dan pulled a chili pepper out of a bag and held it out toward the blue-and-gold macaws. "Hey, Gus. Hey, Gertie," he told them in a soft, seductive voice. "Chilis for breakfast. Huevos rancheros, hold the huevos." He looked sideways at Peggy. "Seems too much like cannibalism."

After a moment or two, one of them hopped down low enough to take the pepper from his right hand. He brought his left up smoothly then and grabbed the bird, returning it swiftly to the cage. The other blue-and-gold hopped to a higher branch as Peggy produced a spring-clip clothespin and used it to secure the cage door.

Half an hour later, they'd located all the larger parrots. A cage that had held a group of finches remained empty, and Dan didn't hold much hope for their return. He'd taped all the cages shut and promised to return quickly with new locks.

"And after that," he told Lynne with an ingratiating smile, "I have a diving session with your daughter."

*⁒*

**THE** morning papers had arrived by the time the bird crisis was remedied, bringing genuine news for once.

Darcy Gainsborough's death had been officially declared a homicide.

Lynne scanned the page one story and read aloud. "'The cause of death was a blunt trauma head injury.'" She considered. "I don't remember seeing anything like that, but I didn't touch her head. I was trying to avoid it, actually. But I'm pretty sure there wasn't any blood."

"It couldn't have been washed off, could it?"

"Her hair wasn't wet. It was kind of in a 'do. And she was wearing makeup. But what do you make about this? A 'foreign object' lodged in her throat?"

Peggy grimaced. "I didn't see anything. Did you?"

"No, and her mouth was closed. Could it be something that got into her mouth accidentally?"

"Maybe. I just wish we didn't have to find these things out from the newspaper. Not that we could do anything anyway."

"It's tough," Lynne agreed. "Now, what's up for today? That party and Craft Fair?"

"Yep. But that doesn't start till four. They'll start setting up in here once breakfast is over. Some women from Little Sister Court are in charge of the Craft Fair end of things. They assured me that they'd handle everything—setup, sales, breakdown."

"What'll they be selling?"

"No idea," Peggy admitted. "This is my maiden voyage. I'm guessing ornaments, gee-gaws, cute little thingies. I figure it'll be pretty standard Christmas bazaar stuff, though who knows? Nothing in the Keys is really standard."

"Was Darcy supposed to help with this? Did she do some of the crafts?"

Peggy shook her head. "No and no. Darcy coordinated lots of things, but not this kind. And she wasn't artsy herself. Just athletic, and highly organized."

"What about the decorations?"

Peggy pointed to the Christmas tree hung with seashells. "Partly done and partly ready to go. I'm going to run out later this morning and get some more lights and stuff. I meant to do that yesterday, but time got away from me."

"I'll help you get things set. How about the food?" Assisting with somebody else's party, Lynne had noticed, was almost always easier and more fun than working on your own. The responsibility ultimately rested elsewhere.

"A couple of the staff here will take care of that, and a bunch of the women in the Court bake cookies. It's all pretty basic. Cookies, punch, some hors d'oeuvres. And my infamous eggnog, but the base for that is ready. All we need to do is whip the cream and add the booze."

Marta Lopez, a pretty young woman in jeans and a red shell, came into the room with a box of muffins. Peggy exchanged greetings and spoke to her briefly about the morning's plans.

"I've got an idea," Lynne said, after helping herself to a lemon poppy seed muffin. "If everything's as well organized as you say, why don't you and I slip out later this morning and go somewhere?"

As Peggy shook her head, Lynne could see waves of

panic flooding over her friend. "The Christmas party and Craft Fair are institutions at Dos Hermanas," Peggy said. "Everything I know is hearsay, but even before this awful business about Darcy, I was nervous about getting it right. I couldn't possibly leave today."

"Of course you could. We can keep it simple. What about Crane Point? That sounds pretty interesting and not too far away. Didn't you say it's just over on Marathon?"

Peggy had sworn, before events blew up, that Lynne would love Crane Point, had indeed been singing its praises when the two of them discussed possible side trips.

"You know you want to," Lynne said. "It'll do you good to take a break. And when we get back, I'll work like a galley slave to make your party a success."

❦

**GEORGE** Wyman carefully pulled a volume from the bookshelf and returned to the desk where he was surrounded by neat piles of books and papers.

He was fascinated and intrigued by the chance encounter with young John Haedrich from Michigan, and with the boy's interest in piracy. This couldn't be coincidence, could it? He'd have to wait and see where the boy's interests were aimed, let him take the lead.

Meanwhile, he continued to compile trivia questions. There was no reason to believe that the Trivia Bee wouldn't take place as scheduled, though without Darcy Gainsborough coordinating matters it was possible that the entire affair would go up in smoke. That would be a shame, and he hoped that wouldn't be the case. He derived great pleasure from constructing these questions.

Had his life taken a different path, George could picture himself as a long-term *Jeopardy!* champion, exulting in both the accomplishment and the financial rewards. He had no doubt whatsoever that he could wipe up the competition. He had watched the show faithfully for years, taping it when unavoidable conflicts made it impossible to watch during the scheduled broadcast time. He nearly always knew as many correct answers as the actual contestants, and when they had the Celebrity Moron programs, he wiped the floor with their laughably simple responses.

The Little Sister Key Trivia Bee was structured so that teams of three contestants worked together to answer specific questions on ten different categories, which varied from one bee to the next. George tried to keep the categories fair and varied, though they leaned a bit toward history, science, and sports. Each category had ten questions, and the teams conferred quietly and wrote down answers, which were collected and graded after each round, so that a cumulative score could be announced. To keep interest and enthusiasm high, each team paid a ten dollar entry fee and the proceeds were apportioned among the three teams with the highest scores.

For this Trivia Bee, George had been particularly enjoying the category "Piracy & Shipwrecks," which drew so heavily on his own knowledge. Piracy, as he had discussed with the Haedrich boy, was a matter of semantics. During the centuries when sailing ships roamed the globe scooping up whatever natural resources—gold, silver, salt, sugar, emeralds, slaves—they could find to haul to the European nations that sponsored them, sovereign nations had commissioned privateers to harass and disrupt ships belonging to other countries. Privateering was differentiated from out-and-out piracy largely by the fact that pirates kept their booty rather than turning it over to any government.

Some of these questions were ridiculously easy.

*What was the wealthiest city in America in the mid–nineteenth century?*

Key West, of course, where aggressive "wreckers" took advantage of the treacherous reefs around the keys and the shortage of lighthouses. A ship gone aground on the reef was considered fair game, and the Key West wreckers would quickly salvage any wealth or negotiable materials on board. Some of the crew from those wrecked ships sized up their options and settled in Key West themselves, ready to go after the next group of unlucky sailors.

*What is the local name for widow's walks?*

Wreckers' walks, constructed atop the clapboard houses so that natives could witness wrecks that required liberation. Finally the U.S. government had intervened, first building lightships that were pretty universally unsuccessful and were themselves inclined to founder on the reefs. Later, finally, they'd constructed wrought-iron lighthouses with skeletal bases to allow water flow, and many of these survived today.

*What was the ill-fated whaler foundered by a furious whale, sending its crew into the Pacific in boats where some of them resorted to cannibalism to survive?*

The *Essex*.

*And the literary work based on that incident?*

Herman Melville's *Moby Dick*, of course.

George took some pride in the tougher questions.

*What was the doomed passenger liner named for the famed Christian Admiral who had taken on the Moslem Barbary Pirates?*

*Andrea Doria*.

And finally, the toughest of all:

*What was the names of the two pirates who said, "Milord, we plead our bellies" to avoid hanging, and the reason they were spared?*

Anne Bonny and Mary Read, the only two documented female pirates of the eighteenth century, both pregnant at the time they were apprehended and brought to trial. He doubted that anybody would know the identity of the sixteenth century Irish Pirate Queen, Grace O'Malley, so he had regretfully omitted her from the Bee.

A sharp rapping on his door brought George back to the twenty-first century. He glanced at his watch, then opened the door to Detective Ruiz, whom George had called half an hour earlier.

"Good morning, Detective," George said. "I have information that I believe is germane to your investigation of the unfortunate death of Mrs. Gainsborough."

❧

**THE** first thing Dan Trenton noticed, even before he registered the orange bikini underneath the loose white T-shirt, was that Jenna was carrying her own wetsuit. A girl with her own wetsuit would be just fine.

Diving with Jenna shouldn't be any trouble; it was simply a matter of getting her back up to speed. And by the time he got all the birds returned to their cages with new padlocks in place, it was time for the dive. Roberto had taken the damaged locks away in hope of reconstructing them.

"So, you ready to see the reef?" he asked.

"Absolutely. Where are we going to go?"

"The reef off Looe Key. There's a lot of good diving there, though like I told you yesterday, it won't be perfect.

There's been too much wind, chopping up the water, messing up visibility."

"Are you saying it isn't worth going today?" Her hair was blonde, lightly curled, just long enough that she could pull it back off her face with a clip. No makeup, a smidgen of tan. It might even be that all-over spray tan that was popular these days, though if she lived in Southern California that probably wasn't necessary. In any event, her skin was softer and smoother than the girls who lived here year-round, whose tans called to mind that other definition of tanning: treating hides for preservation. Folks who lived a long time in the Keys nearly always developed, without realizing it was happening, leathery skin that would never soften again.

"Not at all. And we're not likely to have many other divers around."

She climbed into the front seat of the pickup. How women reacted to the interior, which was undeniably raunchy and always in need of cleaning and organization, told him a lot about how they were reacting to him. She glanced around and said nothing. A good start. He realized, belatedly, that he should have removed his various jackets, shirts, and miscellaneous clothing, some chunks of wood for the birds to chew on, and the lengths of PVC pipe. And it wouldn't be a bad idea to get rid of the beer and soda cans, bagged to go in for recycling and then forgotten.

"So how'd you end up here?" she asked. "Or were you always here?"

He laughed. "Damn near nobody was always here, Jenna. Most of us came for one reason or another and just never went back."

"And where was 'back'?"

"Upstate New York."

"You mean like Albany?"

He shook his head. "I mean like almost in Canada. A little town near a little lake. I worked as a lifeguard and fished, but you could only do that a few months of the year. Then I came down to Florida. No snow. End of story."

"Well, hardly," she said, leaning back as he turned onto the highway. But she didn't ask any more questions, and he liked that, too.

"What about you?" he asked after a while. Not that he was all that interested, really, but women wanted you to at least make an effort.

"I grew up in a Southern California beach town, which is where I learned how to swim and surf. I haven't done much of that for a while, actually. I went to college in LA and stayed there, but it's a major production to get to a surf beach from where I live."

Interesting. You didn't run into a lot of girl surfers.

"Not any real surfing near here," he said. "But I guess you already know that."

"Well, yeah." She waved a hand at the placid blue water off to the right of the bridge they were currently crossing. "It may be chopping up underwater for diving, but you sure couldn't catch a wave here. I haven't seen anything that even resembles a wave since we got here."

"It's a different kind of ocean, the Atlantic. Except for hurricane season it's pretty mellow. And the Gulf here is even milder. Your Pacific, now, that's a badass ocean. I bet you weren't diving there."

"Nope. I learned to dive in Mexico and Hawaii. But there's nothing quite like surfing. I kinda miss it, actually. I was never as gung ho about surfing as my father or my brother, but I've had some good times out there. I saw some signs on the way down here for places where you can swim with the dolphins. Well, sometimes the dolphins would come and surf with *us*—just hang out and body surf. It wasn't anything you could count on, but when it happened it was just awesome."

This was turning out even better than he had expected.

*Chapter 14*

SHERI'S dining table was covered with plastic bags and jars full of brightly colored pills in miscellaneous shapes, accompanied by dozens of little vials and several sheets of blank adhesive labels. She had just finished labeling Lorraine Grant's Premarin when she heard an insistent knocking on her door.

Panic time.

She looked around frantically, then capped or sealed everything that was open, swept it all into a brown paper grocery sack, and turned off the dining room light.

"Just a minute," she called, as the knocking resumed, more insistent this time. Maybe, she thought hopefully, it was somebody looking for a slightly overdue December order. People in the Court were antsy, some of them running low. But in her heart she knew otherwise.

The jig was up. Her goose was cooked. There'd be hell to pay. Her brain flooded with clichés as she wiped her hands on her shorts and went to open the door.

Detective Ruiz stood there, looking accusatory. "Mrs. McManus? I need to speak with you." Another man stood behind him, younger and vaguely familiar from the dockside crowd the previous morning. A cop, undoubtedly.

"Come in," she said, suddenly lightheaded. It wouldn't do to faint just now, she realized, so she took a couple of deep breaths and led them into her living room. Today Detective Ruiz declined her offer of limeade and cookies. Another bad sign.

"This is Detective Jackson," he told her. But before she could even offer a pleased-to-meet-you, Detective Ruiz continued. "You've been holding back on our investigation, and I'd like to know why."

Why? Because she was scared witless, that was why. She didn't know how she could ever make the police understand how charming and benign Darcy's operation had seemed. She offered a mental amendment. Darcy's *unexpectedly profitable* operation.

"I don't understand," she said meekly.

"The drug running." His tone was low and harsh.

"Drug running?" That made it sound like something nasty and illicit. Heroin, perhaps.

"Mrs. Gainsborough's smuggling operation."

She shook her head. "It wasn't smuggling. She just imported some medicines for people who couldn't afford them otherwise."

There, she'd said it. It was out on the table, just like the drugs themselves had been out on the dining table moments ago. That brown paper sack was probably glowing right now, beckoning these detectives. Why hadn't she taken care of all this last night when nobody was around?

"You're in a lot of trouble, Mrs. McManus," Detective

Ruiz told her. "The smartest thing you can do right now is to tell us everything."

She found herself suddenly speechless.

"Mrs. Gainsborough's drug operation," he prompted. The other detective hadn't yet opened his mouth.

"I don't know what to tell you," she said, faltering.

"Start at the beginning then," Detective Jackson, the newcomer, suggested. His tone was gentle and understanding. Did they think she'd never watched television, that she couldn't recognize a good cop/bad cop situation when it happened under her own nose? Even so, she couldn't fight the urge to explain.

"I don't know how it started," she said. "Darcy never told me. But after my husband passed away, she told me that she could help me save some money on the medications I was taking. They're dreadfully expensive, you know."

"Costs my folks plenty," Detective Jackson agreed. "I hear them complaining all the time."

He looked to be in his mid-thirties. His parents would be of an age when systems start to falter, when active people begin to need chemical adjustments to control creaky joints, irritable bowels, escalating blood pressure, horrendous heartburn, soaring cholesterol, and a dozen other ailments. Seeing Darcy's complete list of drug orders had been a sobering and eye-opening experience. And not just because she now knew who used Viagra and Cialis—Darcy had always handled those orders herself.

Sheri composed herself. "The government keeps saying that Medicare will start to help out more with these costs, but it's so complicated that almost nobody understands how to use their systems. If you don't have private insurance, and a lot of us who are retired don't, or if you have coverage that doesn't include pharmacy costs, then almost anything is too expensive."

"That's rough," Detective Jackson agreed. "How about you? Do you have a lot of personal pharmaceutical costs?"

Sheri shook her head. "Actually, compared to some of the others, I get off pretty easy. I have blood pressure medication and cholesterol medicine. And, er, hormone replacement. I used to use a prescription antihistamine because there are so many kinds of weird pollens down here that I was sneezing all the time. Then I lucked out and it went over the counter right after I started taking it. But just these three prescriptions cost me over five hundred dollars a month at the drugstore. I could afford it, barely, but some of the others here are desperate. And even those of us who can afford to pay the high prices don't have any money left over for anything else."

"So it was Mrs. Gainsborough's idea to import Mexican drugs?" Detective Ruiz sounded skeptical.

"I really couldn't tell you. I know that some of us had been getting our prescriptions filled in Canada and mailed down here. The government doesn't like that, I guess, but every little bit helps. Although Canada was still pretty expensive."

"So you all looked to Mexico?" The skepticism remained.

"It's closer, and cheaper. The thing is, the big pharmaceutical companies ship the same things overseas that we get here, but at a fraction of the cost. Sometimes the drugs aren't even made here in the U.S. Prilosec is made in Sweden, for instance. Anyway, whatever you could get cheaper than the U.S. in Canada, would be even cheaper from Mexico. Some of the people here were nervous about Mexico—concerned about quality control—but I haven't heard of anybody who's had trouble."

"We've been examining Mrs. Gainsborough's computer," Detective Ruiz said abruptly, "and somebody was using her drug files late last night. Would you know anything about that?"

Sheri was starting to wonder if she needed a lawyer. But if she asked the police that, they'd just tell her not to worry if she was innocent. The problem was, she didn't know what constituted being "innocent" here.

Not that she could afford a lawyer anyway. She wouldn't know where to start to find one. To her knowledge, there were no attorneys, active or retired, living in the Court. Betty Bronson had been a paralegal in Atlanta, but that was about it.

The only lawyer Sheri could think of was Darcy's daughter Ellen, who was staying over at Dos Hermanas. Sheri had yet to meet Ellen, but she remembered Darcy speaking with pride of Ellen's work, which had something to do with securities. Not, Sheri was sure, criminal law. Besides, Darcy's death might be related to the drug operation. Ellen Gainsborough was hardly a disinterested party.

She took a deep breath. "I knew that Darcy had just gotten the December shipment in a couple of days ago, and that it hadn't been distributed yet. I wanted to help the people who were waiting for their medications, so I went in and printed the files."

"The files wouldn't help much without the drugs," Detective Jackson said. "We haven't been able to locate those in Mrs. Gainsborough's trailer."

Sheri let the trailer reference pass as another flood of

clichés coursed through her brain. She was in deep doo-doo, up the creek without a paddle, in the soup.

"That's because I have them here," she said, deciding to stop making any pretense of ignorance. "After her body was found yesterday, I used my key to go take them out of her coach. Then last night I went back and printed out the records. I was hoping I could get everything to the people who'd ordered it without having to"—she hesitated—"without having to go through this."

"And where are the drugs now? And the records you printed?"

"They're in my dining room," Sheri told them in a very small voice.

"We need to take them with us," Detective Ruiz told her. "And I'd like you to come with us so we can straighten things out as quickly as possible."

"Am I under arrest? Do I need a lawyer?"

"Not at the moment, as long as you continue to cooperate with us."

Sheri sighed, then stood and led them into the dining room. Detective Jackson put on gloves before handling anything, and that almost totally unnerved her.

"There's something else," Sheri said, watching the young man gather up the big bottles and little vials she had so recently scrambled to hide. She was sitting in one of the dining room chairs, where she had set herself down as she became dizzy with alarm and confusion.

Detective Ruiz looked down at her. "Yes?" Suddenly his tone was just as sweet as it could be. No need to be nasty anymore, she figured. He had what he'd come for.

She chose her words carefully. "First of all, you're probably going to find my fingerprints all over Darcy's place. But I found something else while I was looking for the pills, and I don't know what it means, exactly."

"Uh huh." Detective Ruiz was sitting now, too, in one of the dining room chairs, leaning forward to encourage her. His tired eyes regarded her steadily, his head nodding at intervals.

"The middle drawer of Darcy's buffet has a collection of odd little things in it. If you've been searching over there, I'm sure you noticed it." How best to put this, without having to reveal her own ceramic dish? She looked at her hands as she told him of the contents of the drawer. "I think those are things she pilfered from people around here. They didn't seem to have any useful purpose."

"Then why would she take them?"

"I don't know."

"What did you find of yours in there?"

The question blindsided her, and before she thought, her gaze moved to the hutch where the ceramic dish was back in place. Too late. She told him about the dish—where it had come from and how she had recognized it. Detective Ruiz put it into a plastic evidence bag and she opened her mouth to ask him to handle it carefully, then realized that that would give more importance to the stupid dish than it warranted, and said nothing.

Detective Jackson was wrapping up his collecting and cataloguing. She felt dizzy with fear at the prospect of leaving her home in police custody. In all her life, Sheri had never had so much as a speeding ticket. Now she was being arrested in connection with the murder of a friend. Not *arrested*, they kept saying, but it sure seemed that way to her. She had to let somebody know what was happening, where she was going.

Where *was* she going, anyway? She asked and Detective Ruiz answered matter-of-factly.

"I want to make a phone call before we leave," she said. "I'm expected to take care of some things for a party this afternoon over at Dos Hermanas." It was true, sort of. She'd told Darcy she would help with the Craft Fair, but so had everybody else. Sheri had no specific assignment and probably wouldn't even be missed. She had to get word to somebody, though. But who would care? Her only hope would be to reach Peggy.

Detective Ruiz stood at her elbow as she punched in Peggy Parker's cell phone number. It was too much of a hassle trying to call through the switchboard at Dos Hermanas. But Peggy didn't answer. Sheri left a terse message, apologizing for being unavailable and explaining that she would be at police headquarters.

As she hung up the phone, she felt tears slipping out of the corners of her eyes.

**AS** Jenna slid below the surface of the warm blue water, she felt exuberant. It had been years now since she'd been diving, and she was starting to remember just how much she had enjoyed it. There was something about suiting up, in her short suit, that pulled a lever in Jenna's mind. She was *there* again, in the reefs off Mexico and Hawaii, exploring the eerie and often magnificent underwater worlds that existed all the while as she went about other business above the surface, unaware. They had decided to worry about recertification later, but they had done a short pool session. Then he had carefully reviewed all the equipment with her, and they had practiced the hand signals that would provide their only underwater communication.

The reef was so stunningly beautiful that she didn't at all mind missing the *Adolphus Busch* artificial reef today. The 210-foot freighter had been deliberately sunk by the Anheuser Busch family in 1998, settling upright to create what had developed into an artificial reef. But that was deeper than she wanted to go, and dead ships didn't interest her nearly as much as live fish and coral, which were present at other, closer, locations.

She had forgotten the languor of underwater exploration, the distortion of time, the feeling of suspension in this strange and mysterious world.

The coral was incredible—star, brain, and elkhorn coral extending toward the surface. Lacy purple sea fans seemed to wave in the turquoise light. This was the only living reef in North America, and she was here, moving smoothly through the water, breathing easily in her scuba gear, in the company of a pretty handsome guy who knew his way around the water.

These reefs were home to some of the most unusual and spectacular fish she'd ever seen, a riotous collection of fabulous yellow and crimson and rich turquoise blue. Anemones undulated, their pastel arms swaying gently in the underwater currents. She was comfortable with the scuba apparatus, had slipped back into diving mode so easily it had surprised her. Not exactly like riding a bicycle, she supposed, but plenty similar.

She wasn't sure what to make of Dan Trenton. He was great with the birds, had apparently single-handedly retrieved most of the briefly liberated Dos Hermanas flock before she even woke up this morning. He was a capable sailor and a supremely confident diver—she could tell that right away—but there were odd silences around him, moments when he seemed to cut himself off altogether. Probably he was just shy, or maybe he had a girlfriend or a wife that he'd neglected to mention.

But here, thirty feet beneath the ocean surface, he was a splendid ally and a great tour guide, moving her from one breathtaking underwater vista to another, pointing out particularly interesting or vivid forms of marine life.

This was, she realized, a life she could grow to love.

*Chapter 15*

LYNNE was relieved when Rick Parker deputized himself to assume Peggy's hostess duties and to take Lynne to visit Crane Point. With this afternoon's party looming, even though the ladies from Little Sister Court were taking care of almost everything, Peggy felt she just couldn't leave. Rick, on the other hand, was delighted to go, though their departure was delayed so that he could arrange assistance for the Kentucky fishermen, whose truck had three flat tires. Fortunately they were good sports, once Rick notified the police and promised to pick up the tab.

"Are you sure it's okay to sneak out and leave all this stuff for Peggy to do?" Lynne asked.

Rick laughed. "She's got a platoon of helpers from the trailer park. I think we could probably stay out till sundown and she'd never miss us. Well, maybe she'd miss you. I sometimes think that both of us working on the same job is a little too much togetherness."

They headed off from Dos Hermanas in Rick's restored white '68 Mustang convertible, with the top down and the Rolling Stones blasting out of a very sophisticated, aftermarket sound system. Once they were on Highway 1, he turned to Lynne. "I'm glad you're here, but everything is going to hell around the place."

"None of it seems to be your fault, Rick. And it doesn't make sense."

Rick nodded grimly. "All of a sudden somebody seems to have it in for Dos Hermanas, and I can't figure out why. And Darcy—I just don't understand it. Peggy's taking her death hard. I hadn't realized they were such good friends."

"It can happen that way," Lynne agreed. Her true friends, people like Betsy Danforth or Peggy herself, were folks with whom she could connect instantly and automatically, no matter how long their separation. "You guys seem like you've been having fun doing this. Running Dos Hermanas, I mean."

Rick turned to face her and grinned, turning down the music just a bit. "Until this last month or so, it's been an amazing amount of fun. Lots of work, too, of course. But all those years I spent on the road gave me a chance to see a lot of different places, and South Florida was my favorite. In some kind of weird masochistic way, I think. There's an element of danger, the chance that some hurricane could come through and scrape these keys back to coral bedrock. And a larger share of nutcases than you get most places, but not necessarily dangerous ones."

"There's at least one dangerous one," Lynne reminded him. "Somebody killed Darcy Gainsborough."

Rick turned his attention back to the road. They were moving north along the Overseas Highway, with traffic light in both directions. He slowed a bit as they passed a huge brush heap being burned by convicts, with a collection of police cars reinforcing the custody issue, along with signs that announced STATE PRISONERS WORKING.

"The place we're going, Crane Point, is actually what I always fantasized Florida would be like," Rick said. "I got most of my beliefs about Florida from reading John D. MacDonald when I was younger. I can remember sitting in a hotel room in Duluth, Minnesota, in January one time, reading about Travis McGee and looking out the window at a blizzard that was going to keep me in town at least twenty-four hours longer than I'd planned. Gave me time to read more McGee, and for some reason, it happened that the ones I had along with me were all set in winter in South Florida. Made an impression that's never gone away."

"And is it what you wanted?"

"Actually, I think it is. Though MacDonald's Florida is gone for good, I'm afraid. There are too many people here, with all the problems overpopulation brings. The environment is trashed and big business doesn't seem to care. They've killed most of the Everglades. People who retire here are living a lot longer than they used to, and they can't afford it."

"Don't you think that's true of most places in the sunbelt, Rick?"

"I guess so. Maybe. But that would mean we're pretty much all doomed, wouldn't it?" Rick slowed for a particularly uninspiring stretch of Marathon Key, all strip malls and fishing charter signs and tacky souvenir shops. They were almost at the entrance to Crown Point. "Close your eyes, Lynne."

She obeyed. They drove for a few moments like this.

"Now open them. This may just be the last truly unspoiled spot in the Keys, and I'm glad I'm the one who gets to show it to you. I think you're going to like this."

Lynne was amazed at the stunning change in environment. The moment they left the road, they had catapulted into an entirely different world, on a narrow, winding roadway with a lush tropical canopy closing overhead. She turned her head from side to side. "Wow!"

Rick stopped and considered as he parked the car. "I ought to clarify what I just said. I think it's the last unspoiled spot in the Keys that's available to the public. I'm sure there are people with a gazillion bucks who have property that's just as nice."

"Peggy really raved about the gardens here," Lynne said.

"She always says she's never known anybody who knew so much about gardening and made it seem as effortless as you do."

"I just enjoy it, that's all. The trick is to hide your mistakes. Something dies, fill in the hole with something else. But back then when the kids were young, I was too busy to do much. I just had tomatoes and some flowers."

"But it was summer all the time, Lynne. It was the first place that Peggy and I had ever lived where it didn't freeze in the winter. Blew us both away. So to speak," Rick said.

Lynne knew her garden had always had a reputation for magic, though she didn't claim any special secrets or expertise. A stay-at-home mom at the time, Lynne had tended a stupendous garden, a yearlong festival of flowers, with dozens of different species blooming at any given moment. There were just enough seasonable vegetables to prove she wasn't entirely frivolous, and to share with friends who were interested. Peggy and Rick had always been interested.

"So tell me about this place," Lynne said, getting out of the car.

"Well, this piece of land was owned by one family for over fifty years. The Cranes used to divide their time between here and Maine, I think it was. They had eighty acres here and kept the hammock pretty much as it was when they arrived. But before that, there was a settlement of black Bahamians here. They were sponge divers and charcoal makers around the turn of the twentieth century. The nonprofit that owns this place now is recreating a home built by one of the Bahamians, a guy named George Adderley. We'll pass by his place on the trail."

They paid their admission fees and cruised through the museum without stopping. On the far side of the building, they were quickly swallowed by the Rain Forest trail, wonderfully moist and green and unspoiled.

Lynne felt her breath slow and she moved slowly, almost as if she were in a trance.

Ferns with delicate five-foot-long fans of pale green fronds swept across the trail. Unfamiliar plants bore shiny leaves the size of throw pillows and sofa cushions, some as long as four feet from tip to stem. Vines grew straight up tree trunks, neatly stopping at twelve-inch intervals to wind an anchor around the host tree. Staghorn ferns and other epiphytes seemed utterly at home here in the crooks of tall, thirsty trees. The rich smell of humus hovered in the moist tropical air.

"I suppose it sounds silly or naïve, now, but this is how I visualized living in Florida," Rick admitted. "Flowers spilling out of palm trees, picking oranges for morning juice, wild parrots squawking overhead, all around a private little cove suitable for skinny dipping."

"What you have now isn't too far removed from that,"

Lynne pointed out. "This morning you had all those parrots up in the trees, remember? And I do think a key lime tree has more cachet than an ordinary old orange tree. I'm considering potting one in when I get home. I just need to figure out a place to put it."

She moved in closer to an orchid spilling fragile pink blossoms out of the crook of a tree branch. "I can't get over the way these orchids and bromeliads are just casually growing on tree trunks and in the crooks of branches. Even though I know that somebody must have put them there."

"And what if they did?" Rick asked. "Isn't that how they grow in the wild?"

"Good point. It *is* supposed to be a tropical garden."

"Not all of it," he said. "We're about to come to the Adderley house." He led her down a side path into the clearing where George Adderley's house was slowly being rebuilt. The walls were made of something called "tabby," a blend of cement and shells. A sloped roof on the separate kitchen was covered with palm fronds, while the newly rebuilt house was roofed with tin. "Whoosh!" he said after a few minutes. "It's hot out here today."

Lynne was already headed for the shaded trail leading out toward the tip of the property. She stopped abruptly in front of a gargantuan stand of something that looked like eight-foot green swords. Had they walked right into the Little Shop of Horrors?

"Good Lord," Lynne said, gaping at the blades. "It's sanseveria. Mother-in-law's tongue."

"Really? Get my picture by it, will you? I'll send it to Peggy's mom up in Maryland. She's got a great sense of humor, amen."

Rick posed while Lynne snapped several pictures by the

sanseveria. "You know," he said, "I actually recognize this, now that you told me what it is. We had one of these as a house plant when we were first married. It was called cast-iron plant because it was supposed to be so hardy that even the blackest-thumbed couldn't kill it. We proved them wrong. But that was a long time ago."

They continued moving down the trail, stopping now and then while Lynne examined various shrubs and trees. Rick seemed pleased to be able to identify a couple of things she wasn't sure of, like sea grape, which actually had a couple of different looks, with deep, rich maroon leaves and bright red ones on the same branch.

"There's one really nasty tree that I've never seen," Rick said. "Or at least I never realized I saw it. It's called manchineel, and around these islands it's got a well-deserved reputation for being deadly."

Lynne frowned. "You know, they're always saying that about plants and then half the time it turns out they weren't right after all. Like poinsettias. When my kids were young, we were told to never have them around little children and then it turned out they aren't really poisonous after all."

She felt entirely at ease here with Rick, she realized. Though Peggy had been her friend and to a lesser degree Rick, Monty's friend, the four of them had always been comfortable in any combination. In khaki shorts and a tennis shirt, Rick seemed young and vibrant, rejuvenated by the Dos Hermanas experience. She could only imagine how peppy and upbeat he would have been without the resort's litany of problems.

"The manchineel is the real deal," Rick said. "It does all kinds of miscellaneous damage. The fruit is deadly when it's eaten, and they say that's how zombies were created. Somebody'd eat the poison apple and then recover enough to come forth out of the grave. But that's not the half of it. The tree has really caustic sap, and a lot of it. Keys folklore says that the Caloosa Indians would torture captives by tying them to the tree, slashing the bark above, and letting the sap drip on them. And Ponce de Leon actually died of the effects of being hit by an arrow dipped in manchineel juice."

"This is sounding familiar. They talked about it on the Everglades boat tour. That you can even get poisoned taking shelter under the tree in a rainstorm. That it's an alkaloid like Drano." Lynne wiped her sweaty brow with the back of her hand. "I don't know how these early settlers managed. This place would be pretty much uninhabitable in the summer without screens and air conditioning. The bugs are everywhere."

"Well, one thing the early settlers did was keep smudge pots burning all summer long to try to keep the mosquitoes at bay."

"What a mess *that* would be," Lynne said, "and I bet you'd get bitten anyway. Maybe not quite as much, but how do you make the decision about what a manageable number of bites would be?"

They continued walking, past a large cage of recuperating birds of all sizes, invalids recovering under veterinary guidance to be re-released into the wild. A detailed diagram offered instruction on how to remove a fishhook from an inadvertently caught bird. It was essentially the same technique as used on mammals: push it through and cut it off. Lynne shuddered at the notion.

"If you survived yellow fever?" Rick asked.

Lynne laughed. "That would do it. Everything would be solid, gunky black, but you'd be alive. Not that I think that's much of what I'd consider living."

"Well, there'd be none of that nice white overstuffed furniture that the New Yorkers like to have in their Key West pied-à-terres."

"Well, if living covered with creosote was the only life you knew . . ."

"Yeah, I know," Rick said. "Like we didn't realize you didn't have to be cold in the winter till we moved to Floritas. But this isn't even a quality-of-life issue. It would be a matter of survival. And survival here had to be a never-ending challenge. You'd have some pretty serious Darwinian natural selection going on. No wilting-flower belles in crinolines, no useless willowy dilettante males in white linen suits. Everybody'd be fighting just to stay alive."

Lynne stole a glance at Rick and pictured him in a white linen suit. Not half bad.

They reached the Crane House—a Frank Lloyd Wright knockoff from the 1950s, pink with turquoise trim, now housing government officials. Beyond the house they found a spectacular bay view with a choice of benches donated by local individuals and organizations. They sat on one donated by "Marathon Zonta Club," some kind of women's organization.

Lynne felt wonderfully restored after a few minutes of companionable silence. It was nice to be away from the resort, alive and in the company of friends.

"I may be stepping in something I shouldn't here," Rick said slowly, "but I feel bad that we never did more for you when Monty died."

"You couldn't," Lynne reminded him. "You lived on the other side of the country. And by the time I told you about it, it was long over." Lynne had written personal notes, on plain ecru cards, telling faraway friends about Monty's fatal heart attack. He had died in January, and it was July before she was able to bring herself to write the notes. But she knew that she didn't want the news going out with Christmas cards and greetings.

"Not for you, certainly."

Lynne spoke softly. "No, you're right. Not for me. And I don't think that you ever really do get over losing a spouse that way. It's not even a one-day-at-a-time situation. For a long time it felt like I could only get through one hour at a time. Jenna was off at school and David was working. The house seemed so incredibly empty, and that was even before I could bear to do anything with Monty's stuff."

"But you have so many friends."

Lynne shook her head sadly. "Yes, but you know what, Rick? A lot of them gradually disappeared. Not everybody, of course, but some folks just don't know what to do or say so they drift away. Although this may be more true when the person who dies is young." Monty had been fifty-four when he died, and she always thought of him as young, even after he was snatched by an old man's disease.

"You didn't have any warning? He wasn't sick or anything?"

"Nope. He'd just had a physical a couple months earlier, actually, and he came away with a clean bill of health. After he died, I forced myself to talk to his doctor, and he swore that there was nothing that could have prevented it. Sometimes people just up and die from heart attacks, he told me, and even if Monty had actually been in the ER when it happened, it still wouldn't have made a difference."

She shook herself out of the past. "Rick, I appreciate you talking to me this way. It's hard. And I hope you never have to go through this."

*Chapter 16*

**ELLEN** Gainsborough was talking with her brother Ed for the third time since she had gotten the call about their mother at work yesterday. Ed had been in Brussels on business when she finally got hold of him yesterday. Now he was at JFK airport, waiting for his flight to Miami. "So what was she mixed up in? I can't see anybody caring much about importing prescription drugs. For Pete's sake, there are some state and local *governments* who are filling their employee prescriptions out of Canada."

"But this wasn't Canada. It was Mexico, and it all has this dramatic tropical flourish. The thing is, I figure she was probably being cute about it. Overcharging people, or playing favorites, or doing something that would upset folks." Ellen didn't need to remind Ed of the obvious—that their mother was an expert at duplicity.

"How did she get drugs from Mexico, anyway?" Ed asked. "It's not like she lived in San Diego or El Paso, where she could walk across the border and stock up."

"They're not telling me. Maybe they don't even know. But I assume that somebody was bringing it in by boat. The Keys have always had a reputation as a smuggler's haven. Even the cops kind of shrug their shoulders, like smuggling's just another local industry."

"I can't see anybody getting upset enough to kill her over a prescription for beta-blockers," Ed said. "There must be something else going on. You know Mom always was up to something." He paused delicately.

"You mean the stealing."

"Well, yes. Has anybody said anything about that? If she took the wrong thing from somebody . . ."

"Oh, please, Ed. These are old people. They retired from places in the Midwest and Northeast and they live in a trailer park. What could anybody there possibly have that would get Mom in trouble?"

"Have they said anything about the Social Security?"

"No, why would they?" The Social Security Administration probably didn't send hit squads to punish women who continued to receive payments for a deceased husband.

"Then it must be some kind of awful, random crime. Standard senseless violence. Which is what I'd have thought immediately if she didn't have that—Ellen, I need to go. They're calling my flight. I'll call you when I hit Miami."

"Hurry. I keep thinking something is going to blow up here."

"It already has, Ellen. Somebody killed Mom. You be careful, little sis."

As she hung up, Ellen realized that the dispassionate conversation she had just concluded was about the death of her mother. The apparent *murder* of her mother. Outside the window of her cottage she could see big puffy pink drifts of flowers on some exotic shrub. Beyond that lay Florida Bay, its waters warm and blue and inviting.

She knew nobody on Little Sister Key beyond perfunctory self-introductions to the staff. Her mother was dead and her brother was still in New York. Right now she would have loved another sibling, or a husband or a daughter. A whole complicated brood of relatives. But she had nobody, only Ed.

She sat in the chair looking out onto the Bay until she noticed that her tears had run down onto the front of her dress, puckering the silk. Mom would have had some instructions for what to do to prevent permanent damage to the fabric.

But Mom herself had been permanently damaged.

✷

**BACK** in the sunshine above the Looe Key reef, shedding equipment in the boat and feeling the balmy warmth of the midday sun washing over her, Jenna felt terrific.

Excited, engrossed, refreshed, intrigued.

Funny how a brief interlude in the ocean deeps could cast everything in a different light. Offhand, Jenna couldn't recall a recent time when she had feel so exuberant. She wanted to jump up and down, hug Dan Trenton for taking her down to the reef, holler to the heavens that life was wonderful everywhere.

There was something almost mystical about being underwater, surrounded by extraordinarily beautiful fish. Schools of them, brilliantly colored in hues that could only feel real underwater. Like magic they would approach, gliding past in slow, almost melodic rhythms. Many of the most stunning of these underwater creatures had a beauty that nobody above water could ever really appreciate. She remembered watching Jacques Cousteau specials as a child, mesmerized by the worlds that Cousteau and his *Calypso* crew explored. She also remembered the first time she had gone snorkeling with her family in Hawaii. There she was, essentially just lying on top of the water, suddenly witnessing incredible new worlds opened simply because she was able to see below the surface.

In the pickup on the way back to Dos Hermanas, Dan looked over at her. "How do you feel about stone crabs?"

"As an underwater phenomenon? Or as a meal?"

"Well, both, I guess. But I was thinking of as a meal, actually."

"Don't know about stone crabs," Jenna admitted, "though I think that's what was in the dip that Peggy served the other night, and that was delicious. I have to admit, however, that I have yet to try a crab I haven't adored. Soft shell. Dungeness. Snow. Alaskan King. I'm a sucker for them all."

He was looking right at her now, and he looked pretty good. "I've got a friend who brought in a whole mess of them," he said. "Offered me a bunch and I said yeah. Interested?"

Was he asking her for a date?

"I probably could be," she said. "When would this be?"

He smiled and little lines crinkled around his chocolate eyes. "I'd suggest tonight. Seafood's best fresh."

Was this what Larry, back in West LA presiding over the demise of his moribund bookstore, had been hinting at when he told her to be open to possibilities? She wasn't sure, and she didn't care.

"Then tonight it is," she told him. "I'll need some time to clean up and all that. And I need to check in with my mom. There's some kind of party this afternoon that she's involved with. Tell me where and when to meet you."

"I could come by and get you. It's kind of tricky finding the place."

She considered. This wasn't LA, where you never knew what kind of wacko you were arranging to see alone. It was a community where everybody seemed to know everybody else, maybe too well.

Peggy and Rick seemed to like Dan, which was a plus, though as far as Jenna could see, Peggy liked everybody and Rick was even less discriminating. Undoubtedly why he had done so well in sales.

Old habits and ingrained caution won out. "Let me meet you," she repeated. "I need to be able to cut out in a hurry if something happens and my mom needs me."

Dan cocked his head. "Something like what?"

Good question. Nobody at Dos Hermanas was likely to require anything at all from Jenna Montgomery. The car, maybe, but that was clearly the wrong answer here. And she was surprised, even after spending so much time underwater with Dan, that she still felt she needed her own transportation, the ability to leave whenever she wanted.

"Oh, I don't know. But I just want it that way."

He capitulated easily as they arrived at Dos Hermanas. "Let me give you directions then. But you'd better figure on getting there before dark, or you might have trouble finding the place. Say by six?"

"Six it is," she told him as she wrote the directions on the back of a dive shop brochure. She hopped out of the pickup and waved goodbye.

Back in their cottage, she found a note from her mother asking Jenna to come by the Orchid Lodge when she got back. She rinsed her wetsuit and set it to dry on the porch, then jumped at the sound of her cell phone, which hadn't rung since she left LA. She grinned as she recognized the number, her soon-to-be-former workplace. "Hey."

It was Larry Bradford, her soon-to-be-former boss.

"Jenna! Tell me you're under a palm tree, sipping a margarita."

She told him about their various adventures and as he filled her in on the final sale's progress, she felt an overwhelming sense of loss. In the three years that Jenna had worked at the West LA independent bookstore, Booker T had maintained a steady and apparently unstoppable downward spiral.

They talked for half an hour, Larry stopping now and then to ring up a customer. "Call me from the Hemingway House," he reminded, when the conversation ended, and she promised she would. After she hung up, she took a long hot shower, washing off the salt, savoring the needles of fresh water running down her back.

She also felt a sudden urge to go shopping. She'd been uncertain what to pack for the Keys in December, and her mother's vague statement, "It'll be warmer than home," hadn't helped much.

As a Southern California native, Jenna was accustomed to balmy winters, massive outdoor poinsettia arrangements, Christmases with blue skies and warm breezes. She, David, and Dad had even gone surfing one Christmas, on the spur of the moment when an Alaskan storm front had sent huge waves toward the Floritas beaches. Her mother hadn't joined them in the water, but she'd sat on the beach reading, with a thermos of hot mulled cider waiting when they emerged from the water, exhilarated.

But how warm was warm? Nothing too fancy, Lynne had told her, but there again the definition of "fancy" was problematic. No strappy high heels? No slinky black dresses? No fringed silk shawls?

In the end, she brought jeans and T-shirts, shorts and swimsuits, sandals and her wetsuit. If what she'd chosen was all wrong, she decided, there would probably be stores in Florida.

And, of course, there were.

Perennially underemployed in a very expensive city, Jenna had developed antennae that could search out almost any kind of genuine bargain. In particular, she was an aficionado of thrift and consignment shops, which in better Los Angeles neighborhoods were a treasure trove of couture, both haut and recently haut, items sometimes discarded before a style had even passed, often unworn, still bearing tags. Wrong color, maybe, or a size just a bit off the expectation.

Jenna had automatically noticed a plethora of Salvation Army Thrift Shops in her travels up and down the Overseas Highway. She had a couple of hours free now before she was supposed to meet up again with Dan Trenton, and the thought of going to a Christmas bazaar held little appeal. She ducked into the Orchid Lodge to tell her mother where she was going, looked up the various thrift shop locations in the phone book, then headed for the parking lot.

As she passed by the bird cages, Melissa the cockatoo gave a little squawk, then turned her head sideways in an appealing pose.

"Hello," said Melissa. "I love you."

"I love you, too," Jenna told her, and hit the road, musing on her new habit of conversing with birds. And enjoying it.

*Chapter 17*

**LYNNE** felt pretty much superfluous in the breakfast room of the Orchid Lodge, where half a dozen sprightly women fussed and fiddled with tables full of homemade tschotskes. She had been allowed to spread a few of the holiday motif tablecloths, but that was about it.

All told, it was a dazzling display for something put together by a bunch of budget-conscious retirees with too much time on their hands. The inveterate needlecrafters seemed unable to shake their holiday habits, even in this land where ice never ventured. They knit and crocheted afghans and scarves and bed socks and adorable little booties for grandchildren and great-grandchildren. Paint-by-number as a viable craft seemed to have finally dropped off the face of the earth, but as Lynne looked at a display of acrylic-painted plaster figures, she knew what had replaced it.

Wreaths and swags in both holiday and year-round selections of silk, dried flowers, and foliage took up two tables pushed together under a particularly long cloth of solid evergreen. Lynne, who had repeatedly warned herself that she was on vacation without room for extra items in her suitcase, was also keenly aware that she and Jenna could each check an additional bag or box on the flight home.

She was pleased that Jenna had gone diving, had indeed managed to hook up with a guy who looked both interesting and capable. A South Florida boat-and-bird bum certainly wasn't her first choice for a daughter's life mate, but it was good to see Jenna diving, an activity she had always enjoyed. Lynne reminded herself that speculation about any kind of permanent relationship for Jenna was strictly verboten. Speculation itself wasn't prohibited; it was verbalizing that speculation. And so far she was clean on that account. She grinned as she headed over to peruse a display of starched lace snowflake ornaments.

❧

**PEGGY** was liking Detective Ruiz less and less by the minute. He had descended on her with that Gloomy Gus persona, wearing another rumpled suit—this one gray—almost immediately after Rick and Lynne returned from Crane Point. Lynne had discreetly slipped away and Peggy envied her the vacationer's freedom to drift off to another activity.

"And you're saying that you only recently learned of Mrs. Gainsborough's drug smuggling activities?" Detective Ruiz sounded quite doubtful.

"I've only lived here since February," Peggy reminded him. She knew she'd shared that information at least twice before. "Before I moved here I'd never met her. She did kind of sound me out at one point, fairly early on, but we have good insurance and neither of us uses anything very exotic or expensive."

"Who do you know of who *did* use Mrs. Gainsborough's services?"

"I really couldn't say for the people over at Little Sister Court, though I have the impression that a lot of them bought their drugs through Darcy. Here, most of the guests are transient and they don't stay long enough to need drug refills. The people who work at Dos Hermanas are young and healthy, for the most part. My manager's wife has a seizure disorder, and I think that one of the maids gets something for her parents. They live in Miami. And my bookkeeper is a breast cancer survivor. I know she takes tamoxifen, but I don't know if she's able to get it through Mexico."

Peggy smiled sweetly, watching the detective jotting down notes. She felt a bit like Lieutenant Columbo, holding her one-more-thing for last. "And of course there's my sister-in-law, Gloria Parker, who's living here all winter. She glommed onto Darcy's service as soon as she heard about it. I'm not sure what all Gloria takes, but I saw her bathroom counter one time and there were at least half a dozen prescription bottles there."

※

**GEORGE** Wyman had lived the majority of his adult years as a cautious and relatively productive member of society. After an extremely misspent youth, he had awakened one day in the hospital, sole survivor of a single-car automobile accident that had killed his girlfriend Lois and his best friend Walt, who had been at the wheel under the influence of large quantities of Seagram's Seven.

By the time he regained consciousness, both Lois and

Walt were buried in the local cemetery. He had no memories of the evening's activities that preceded the accident, and as he later pieced matters together, he decided that this was probably something he was just as happy to forget.

While still in the hospital, arm and leg suspended in huge white casts, fractured pelvis knitting at a snail's pace, he made three vows. The first was to move to a new town, where he and his history would be unknown; the second was to find a career in which he would be happy for many decades to come; and the third and most difficult was to leave alcohol behind him forevermore. He kept all three vows. There had been another piece of unfinished business, but he had had no way to check on that for a while, until he was ambulatory. He visited the graves of Lois and Walt in opposite ends of the cemetery, their graves now covered with soft green grass, the dirt mounds almost level with their markers and the rest of the smooth, memorial park lawn.

Then he left town and George Wyman began life anew in Appleton, Wisconsin, where he found work as a lab assistant for a large paper company. He discovered that he liked the precision of chemistry, the certainty that if you combined A and B and C in exactly the same way, you would always get ABC. He studied for a degree in chemistry at Lawrence College. George flourished at his job, and by the time he retired forty years later, he was a vice president. He had never married and had no children.

Not that anybody cared about that down here, which alternately pleased and irritated him. When you crossed the Florida border, a lot of playing fields automatically leveled. He was not one of those Midwesterners who had ruminated about warmer climes in the dead of winter. He'd been quite content where he was, and might never have visited the state at all were it not for the disquieting information from his doctor and a heightened sense of curiosity.

Curiosity had opened the possibilities of artichokes, sea urchins, and tripe as foodstuffs. Had developed modern telecommunication, produced musical instruments and the melodies that flowed through them, created patterns and styles to both mimic nature and expand beyond it.

Curiosity had led to the ends of the earth, the bottom of the deepest oceanic trenches, the tops of the highest mountains. It had found undersea wrecks and jungle-hidden pyramids, recreating history based on them.

And curiosity had brought George Wyman to the Florida Keys in the sunset of his life.

**GEORGE** encountered a gaggle of women from the Court when he entered the Orchid Lodge, transformed into a bastardized winter wonderland with large white snowflakes suspended in midair, wreathes and garland strung about and a Christmas tree covered in seashells and marine life, presumably all dead.

"Afternoon, George!" Andi French greeted him. Andi was one of the widows in the Court who brought by homemade soup and cookies at regular intervals, in a none-too-subtle attempt at courtship. She was tall and spare and no-nonsense, with a steel-gray braid running down her back, the type of woman George might once have found attractive. She wore her customary denim jumper and crisply ironed white long-sleeved shirt, with a small glass holiday wreath pin.

"Don't hog that handsome devil now, Andi." Donna Lawson beamed hello from behind the entry table, where she was writing names in red calligraphy on gummed tags with a holiday border of tiny Christmas trees. Donna was Andi's physical opposite, short and plump with billowy white hair. She was all a-Christmas, from the red velvet ribbon in her hair to the green elf slippers on her feet. Her shirtwaist dress was a busy print of cheerful Santas.

"Everything looks lovely as usual, ladies," George told them, accepting his name badge and carefully peeling away the shiny backing.

"Why thank you, George!" Donna was always perky. "We can meet all your holiday gift-giving needs."

George didn't really have any gift-giving needs, but he nodded agreeably. "I think I'd like to wet my whistle first."

"Then you want the beverage table over by the aquarium." Donna's eyes widened as she realized that she'd stumbled into non-festive territory with mention of the aquarium, which at the moment was entirely covered by a large, white tablecloth. Everybody at Dos Hermanas and the Court knew about the recent demise of the resort's saltwater fish. "I mean, what used to be—"

"A doggone shame what happened to those fish," George interrupted fervently. He had found the tiny schools of gorgeous, vibrantly colored saltwater fish quite captivating, always providing entertainment in that back corner of the Orchid Lodge. "But I do believe I see a punchbowl, so I'll be on my way, if you'll excuse me."

As he moved out into the room, where a dozen or so early-bird guests from the Court were holding punch cups and little plates of cookies and hors d'oeuvres, he heard Donna Lawson say, "Such lovely manners, that George."

He smiled as he approached the punch table, which appeared to be self-service, with little cards identifying the four options: Holiday Crangria, Eggnog Extraordinaire,

Keys Juice Jubilee (nonalcoholic), and Warm Wintry Cider (ditto).

Peggy Parker stood by the table greeting visitors. She wore black slacks, a royal blue sweater patterned with snowflakes, and large dangly snowflake earrings. Her best accessory, however, had to be her holiday-bright, white hair.

Her face lit up when she saw him. "George! I got your questions, thank you so much. Right now I don't know if we're going to go ahead with the Trivia Bee on schedule, or postpone it, or what. It's been so upsetting, Darcy's death and"—she waved her hand in a circular motion to indicate the room in general—"I've been kind of busy. So I'm trying to streamline things for the moment."

Now that she mentioned it, George noticed that Peggy looked both terribly earnest and understandably upset. George hadn't realized that Peggy and Darcy were so close, but it seemed a logical friendship, built on a foundation of overlapping activities.

"I felt I had to follow through on this party because of the bazaar part of it," Peggy went on. "People have been making these things all year for this. But maybe we'll skip the Trivia Bee this month."

George frowned and willed himself not to glower. There was no reason whatsoever not to go ahead with the Trivia Bee, particularly since Peggy had specifically asked him to work up some holiday questions. "The History of Christmas" wasn't really a category you could postpone and slide into an April competition.

"Let's talk about it later," he said, and she agreed without further discussion. As she moved away to greet someone else, he sampled the various choices, then used a stainless steel ladle to fill a Styrofoam cup with warm cider from a crockpot. Cloves and cinnamon sticks sent a wonderfully Midwestern aroma into air much more accustomed to Florida's tantalizing citruses.

George sipped his cider with satisfaction. It had just the right cinnamony flavor. Then he moved along to a table loaded with hors d'oeuvres. He paid no attention to the platters of appealingly arranged vegetables and tropical fruits but homed in on the comfortably familiar: onion dip in a red poinsettia-shaped bowl, centered on a green ceramic holly platter full of potato chips.

He sampled a few items and found them a bit too exotic for his taste. Curry in deviled eggs? No thank you. And he was more than willing to leave the mushroom pâté for those who could better appreciate it. Eventually, he assembled a ham and cheese sandwich, got a cider refill, and moved toward the doors leading onto the Dos Hermanas central bayside lawn.

He checked to be sure there was no dirt or moisture on a dark green resin chair, then used his holiday paper napkin to perform a fast wipe-down before taking a seat looking out at Florida Bay. Was this the spot, he wondered? Would he ever know?

From somewhere out in the cages, he heard a wolf whistle.

*Chapter 18*

RICK Parker was lounging on his private patio in his green Lafuma recliner, quite possibly the most comfortable piece of outdoor furniture ever invented. He was flipping through *Sports Illustrated* and wishing it were time for the swimsuit issue when he heard Gloria's staccato knock coming from inside the house. Shave and a haircut. She had always been unoriginal.

"Come in," he called, knowing that she'd already be halfway through the door.

He had given her a key in an early unguarded moment, though it probably didn't matter since most of the time when he or Peggy was here, the door was unlocked anyway. In some ways, Little Sister Key seemed a thousand miles from the crime-riddled streets of Miami.

She bustled through the house. Considering that Gloria never seemed to actually accomplish anything, she always gave the impression of being in a remarkable hurry. He once had wondered about this, but now simply accepted it.

"You'll get yourself a melanoma, sitting out there," she greeted him, coming onto the patio but making a big deal out of remaining in the shade.

Time had not been kind to Gloria. She'd been pretty long ago, but the ill-fated collagen treatments had oddly complicated her facial contours. Her once-voluptuous curves had settled into a configuration not unlike a municipal trash barrel. Her personality had always been iffy, but now she seemed incredibly soured, not unlike those damned Singapore Slings that Peggy mixed up in job lots, all but the alcohol, which Gloria preferred to add herself. He had seen his sister-in-law in action. She had a heavy hand with the booze bottle.

Today she appeared to be decked out for the DAR convention, in an ensemble of navy blue trimmed in red and white, complete to large rhinestone American flag earrings. At least he assumed they were rhinestones, though anything was possible as a souvenir from Gloria and Tom's go-go years. Gloria certainly wouldn't mind if folks thought they were made of genuine rubies, sapphires, and diamonds, he knew.

"Are you ready for this silly little party?" she asked. "I can't believe you want me to attend. It sounds so incredibly déclassé."

"I just want you to show up and raise the flag for Peggy, who's done a lot to put this thing together under some pretty adverse conditions." Too late he caught his flag reference and he held his breath for a moment, fearing an onslaught of Gloria's neoconservative proselytizing.

Mercifully, she kept her tongue. "Then let's get it over with."

"Oh, c'mon," he told her. "It's just a regular old Christmas bazaar, Glo." She disliked being called Glo, and he liked to watch her hackles rise. He didn't do it often, and he didn't do it around others. "Surely you've been to one before." Over the years, even without any personal enthusiasm for the events, Rick had attended any number of these functions, often in a church basement or veterans' hall. Peggy was usually in charge of something.

Gloria shuddered. "Not when there was a way to avoid it. Over in Palm Beach we have a charity auction of some magnificently decorated trees. But this sounds to me like needlepoint coasters and cut-rate potpourri burners."

Rick had long ago stopped wondering what his brother Tom saw in this woman, though he had no difficulty understanding why Tom had developed into such a workaholic, logging brutal hours, working weekends, accumulating wealth and toys he didn't have time to enjoy. Now that Tom *did* have time to spare, being a full-time guest of the government, Rick wondered how much his brother regretted the choices that had led to his maximum dollar fine and minimum security cell.

Gloria chose not to discuss the matter and on Rick's only visit to his incarcerated brother, Tom had been philosophic. "I know you and Gloria haven't always seen eye to eye," Tom had told him, "but I'd appreciate it if you could watch out for her. She's not used to taking care of herself." It was the closest thing to begging that Rick had ever observed in his brother, and he agreed automatically.

Fraternal loyalty, he'd found, was a lot more appealing in the abstract.

"You can probably do a lot of your Christmas shopping," Rick told her now. "I bet there's stuff you could send the grandkids. Or your daughters-in-law."

"Tawdry trinkets." Gloria sniffed and cocked her head sideways, like a robin sounding out a worm. Rick couldn't remember her ever saying anything positive about her daughters-in-law. "But at least they won't be expensive."

Tom and Gloria had miraculously managed to raise four well-adjusted sons, all comfortably settled in various northeastern cities, doing respectable work. Gloria wore blinders where her youngest son Jamie, a Boston interior designer, was concerned, and Rick was taking a perverse anticipatory pleasure in Jamie's planned Christmas visit to Key West with his partner. The boy was smart and witty and self-deprecating, and Rick had always enjoyed him the most of his Parker nephews.

Rick stood and came inside, picking a red velvet Santa hat up off the breakfast bar in the kitchen, stopping at a mirror just inside the door to adjust it. He made a fine figure of a Santa, the Ponce de Leon version. "Shall we?"

Gloria sighed. "If we must."

⚜

**LYNNE** was sitting in a balmy breeze with Peggy and Rick out on the lawn, drinking eggnog. It exceeded her expectations and contained enough hard liquor to pickle a platoon of Marines.

Peggy had allowed—begged, actually—Lynne to whip the cream that provided the eggnog's thick, rich finish, and while Lynne had initially questioned the vast quantities of rum and bourbon and brandy that the recipe called for, she found the resulting combination quite splendid. It helped that she didn't have to drive anywhere, or move any farther than her cottage, which was in clear view of where she sat. She could crawl if necessary.

At the bazaar she'd purchased a nautically themed wreath and a couple of stuffed manatees wearing Santa hats for her grandchildren, and arranged to ship home a box of homemade orange marmalade to give as hostess gifts throughout the holiday season. She was also seriously considering submitting a sealed bid for an exquisite pastel quilt that her mother, currently in the process of relocating from New England to Southern California, would probably like. All that was holding her back was the awareness that her mother had, in the course of outfitting a proposed New Hampshire bed-and-breakfast, already accumulated more quilts than she could ever use.

Peggy was also drinking eggnog, and was a couple of cups ahead of Lynne. She had ushered Rick and Gloria inside when they first arrived, returning a few minutes later with Rick in tow and a fresh cup of eggnog in hand. Gloria had reappeared shortly thereafter, carrying no purchases and allowing as how she'd prefer to go to her own quarters and have a Singapore Sling or two.

Rick sipped his crangria. "This is great stuff, Lynne. I'd forgotten all about this. How come we never have this, Peg?"

Crangria was a staple of Montgomery family holiday functions—a delicious and easily prepared combo of red wine, cranberry juice, and 7-Up, with orange slices and fresh cranberries floating in it.

"Because you're an eggnog junkie, that's why," Peggy answered.

Rick nodded. "A solid reason. And I almost hate to bring this up, but what do we know about Darcy?"

Peggy made a face of mock concentration. "Well, I believe she's dead." She heard herself with shock and raised her eyebrows. "Whoops."

"Time to cut *you* off," Rick said easily. "Hasn't that detective been back here today?"

Peggy nodded. "All morning. Some of the folks from

the Court said they saw him leaving with Sheri Mc-Manus."

"Sheri!? You mean as in taking her away in custody?" He raised his voice and sounded alarmed.

"Oh hell," Peggy said, contrition washing over her expression. "It was while you and Lynne were gone. I probably should have been more worried about her, but I was just so frazzled getting this party set up. But I'm sure it's just some kind of misunderstanding about the medicine business."

She pulled a cell phone from her pocket, punched in a number, and waited, her face growing anxious. "Dammit," she muttered, then a moment later left a cheery message. "Sheri, this is Peggy. We're over here at the Christmas party and I was wondering where you might be. Call me."

⚘

**SHERI** McManus was exhausted.

She'd spent most of the afternoon in the same small, stuffy room, waiting patiently between bouts of questioning. Detective Ruiz and Detective Jackson talked to her separately, then left her alone for as long as half an hour before returning. She felt remarkably exposed and oddly violated. Somebody was probably watching or recording her every move, not that they were going to learn anything that way. They had let her use the restroom a couple of times and brought her a Coca-Cola and some crackers at one point, when she threatened to faint from hunger and thirst.

If she hadn't been wearing a reasonably accurate watch, she'd have sworn that she had been stuck in this wretched little room for nine or ten hours. It had, in fact, been only half that.

Early on, right around the time she'd discovered her little dish in Darcy's drawer, she had decided that there was no reason to try to protect Darcy or her reputation. And to their credit, the cops had followed up reasonably well.

"Why do you think she had all those things, Mrs. McManus?" Detective Ruiz asked her.

Sheri had been giving this a lot of thought. "Because she's a sneak thief, I assume. Obviously they weren't things she needed, and for the most part, they don't seem particularly valuable. My dish has sentimental value, but it's not worth anything to anybody but me."

"Did you recognize anything other than your dish in that drawer?"

She hesitated, wishing she had a clearer recall of the drawer's odd contents. "There was a little brass ashtray that I remember seeing on somebody's patio once, but I don't remember whose. It was shaped like one of those Mexican sombreros."

"Are there many smokers in the Court?"

"Not at all. But most folks keep ashtrays outside as a courtesy."

"Who do you know who smokes?"

She stared at them. "Why?"

Detective Ruiz looked almost annoyed. "If Mrs. Gainsborough took things that belonged to other people, she might have inadvertently taken something that made someone angry."

Oh. Sheri hadn't thought of that, but it made perfect sense. She named a dozen or so smokers that she could recall. Tom Lanahan, Will Noren, Dave Hepburn, Susan Halligan, Judy Malinovsky, George Wyman, Kay Stringer. There were probably others, but her concentration was going.

"What else did you recognize in the drawer?"

Sheri frowned. "You know, this would be a lot easier if you could just show me those things. This way it's like that stupid party game where you put a bunch of stuff on a tray, give people thirty seconds to memorize it, then cover the tray and make them write down what they remember."

"Well, let's just start with what you *do* remember."

To her embarrassment, the items that she thought of immediately were the condoms. Oh, what the hell. "She had a number of condoms in there. Not like a package, but a bunch of different brands and styles."

"Styles?"

"I think one of them was neon green. But the point is that I think Darcy has been . . . well, a bit promiscuous."

Silence.

More silence. Detective Jackson left the room.

"Did she ever discuss any relationships that she might have had?" Detective Ruiz asked.

Sheri shook her head. "Darcy wasn't like that. She wouldn't come right out and say she was sleeping with somebody. But she might make kind of sly little references. Not about specific men," she added hurriedly. "More like that she'd been up really late. With a little wink."

"Would these be people in the Court?"

"Not necessarily. I think that she spent some time with guests at Dos Hermanas. You know, sometimes guys who come down to go fishing and they leave their wives at home. Once there was a really nice-looking fellow who stayed for a month over there, and I know Darcy was involved with him. They went out to dinner and stuff. I seem to remember her saying that he was a recent widower."

"Was she looking for a husband, do you think?"

Sheri shook her head and laughed. "That I pretty much know for sure. Darcy *loved* living by herself. She always said that she loved her independence." One of the things Darcy frequently said was that she didn't intend to ever share a bathroom with a man again. Of course that could be interpreted as meaning she would only marry someone well enough off to provide her with her own powder room. Somehow Sheri doubted that. Though if the right billionaire had happened along, she was pretty sure Darcy might have opened her bathroom to him without complaining.

Detective Jackson entered the room then, carrying a cafeteria tray with a lot of small plastic bags on it. When he set it down, Sheri had to stifle a chuckle. It *was* the party game. These were the items from Darcy's dining room drawer.

"May I move them around?" she asked.

"So long as you don't open the evidence bags."

She pulled the tray toward her and looked at it thoughtfully for a moment. There were more things here than she remembered. Would they try to trick her by putting in items that hadn't actually come out of Darcy's drawer? No reason they wouldn't, she decided quickly.

She separated out the condoms and moved them off the tray. There were some books of matches from Key West hotels and restaurants and she moved those off as well. She picked up a bag holding several brightly colored feathers.

"These must be from the birds over at Dos Hermanas," she said. "I don't know anybody in the court who has fancy parrots." A glass ashtray she didn't remember seeing had a Marine Corps logo on it. "I don't recall seeing that before, but it's probably from Bob Burke. He lives near Darcy and he's a very gung-ho retired Marine."

"He smoke?"

She shook her head. "No, but I think I remember seeing an ashtray on their patio. And—oh, my!—this pen! I'm pretty sure it's a Mont Blanc." She paused, then went on when the detective said nothing. "That's a very expensive pen. Somebody's missed that, I'm sure."

A hardwood crab mallet might belong to anybody. Other bags held single earrings, a Lucite paperweight filled with small seashells, and what appeared to be a refrigerator magnet of a spatula holding a pancake. "No idea about these."

She picked up a bag with a small silver picture frame holding a picture of an elderly couple gazing fondly at one another. "This is the Rutledges! I can't believe they didn't miss it. Though now that I think about it, they have a ton of little pictures sitting on a couple of shelves. It could be that she took one that wouldn't be missed, kind of like my ceramic dish." A laughing Buddha of rosewood stood only two inches tall, and a Precious Moments figurine wasn't much larger.

Sheri leaned back. "You know, this looks like she systematically looted every place she went. Was she a kleptomaniac or something?"

Detective Ruiz said, "Or something."

"But don't those people usually get caught? They take bigger and bigger things and then they get arrested for shoplifting or something."

"We're looking into that, both here and in Philadelphia. We've spoken with her daughter, and her son is supposed to be arriving tonight from Europe."

"You know," Sheri said, "seeing these things makes me look at Darcy a whole different way. It's as if I never really knew her at all."

*Chapter 19*

**JOHN** Haedrich was shy by nature.

He had never been very fond of parties, where he usually found himself checking his watch and backing into corners, watching Diane chatter merrily with people he knew she didn't even like. He envied her easy public charm, which made her so popular both at work and in the community. He didn't admit this to anybody, but Diane had actually initiated their first date. Before that, John had watched her from a distance, without ever considering that she might find anything of interest in him. After four years of marriage, he still marveled at his luck at wooing and winning her.

She was decked out in her holiday finery, a bright red velvet miniskirt, a white angora sweater with sequined ornaments all over its front, and very red, very high heels. It was really too hot to wear *any* sweater, but she had her heart set on it.

Diane had worried just now, getting ready, that the outfit

was too dressy for Florida. His reassuring smooch had turned into more, and her cheeks now bore the telltale flush that always followed their lovemaking. The unruly black curls that she despaired of ever controlling cascaded down her back and her dark eyes glittered. She was already well on the road to a respectable suntan, while John had only achieved a vaguely uncomfortable light sunburn.

She no longer seemed concerned about any sort of Florida-casual dress code, and he was quite certain she'd be the biggest knockout at the party.

On his own he would never have even considered attending this gathering of strangers. But because Diane so wanted to attend, and because he enjoyed watching her pleasure at just about anything, he had allowed her to believe he shared her enthusiasm. As they walked past the bird cages on their way to the Orchid Lodge, he regarded her with frank adoration.

She lingered in front of the macaw cage, the brilliant red of the birds' feathers a perfect match for her sexy, scarlet skirt. Before Florida, John had considered Diane's interest in birds to be relatively minor and inconsequential. He'd indulged her with the lovebirds, thinking that would be enough, but watching her this past week around the cockatoos and macaws, the parrots and lorikeets, he realized he had underestimated her desire.

Who knows? Maybe this trip would turn out to be the jackpot that would allow him to spend twenty-five grand on a hyacinth macaw for her birthday in January.

Not likely, he knew. And nothing was going to happen unless he started to show a bit of initiative. If only he could figure out what to do next. He'd pretty much finished covering the obvious spots on Little Sister Key with his metal detector. The Mel Fisher museum had energized

John, reminding him of his own hidden agenda and how little he had done to further it.

A number of small tables and chairs were set up out on the lawn near the screened portion of the breakfast area, and the sounds of "Rockin' Around the Christmas Tree" greeted them as they approached. They exchanged hellos with the Parkers, that nice older couple who owned the place, and a couple of other guests they had encountered around the grounds, then headed indoors.

Behind him as they talked, while Diane made easy chatter, John could hear the clear Midwestern tones of a familiar deep and gravelly male voice.

"It would take a government or a billionaire to solve the mystery of Oak Island," the voice said.

Oak Island? John knew it well, knew its legend and its curse. And he knew the voice, too. It was George Wyman, who was so familiar with piracy.

John hurried indoors, snatched up a nametag from the insistent woman at the door, then made one dutiful sweep around the room in Diane's company. Obligation met, he kissed her lightly, got himself some refreshments, and headed outside.

✳

"MIND if I join you?"

John held his plate of little sandwiches and his glass of thick, potent eggnog in his left hand. He was fervently relieved to find George Wyman alone.

"May I?" John indicated the chair.

George Wyman nodded as he settled himself again. "I saw you arrive with a beautiful young lady, son. Why aren't you in there with her?"

John offered a conspiratorial grin and rolled his eyes.

"She's gotten all involved with shopping. She's in there jabbering away about stuff like knitting and crochet."

"Ah, needlework." Wyman smiled. "There's a reason they call it 'crewel.' "

He expected a response, John realized suddenly, even though John had no idea what he had just said. He smiled and nodded, noncommittally and not too enthusiastically, in case the remark was somehow offensive and he'd be accused of joining in.

John allowed a moment of comfortable silence, then leaned back and turned toward George. "I couldn't help but overhear your mention of Oak Island a few minutes ago."

"And?" The tone grew cautious.

John, especially after the previous conversation, figured he'd just plunge ahead. It happened that he knew quite a lot about Oak Island, a tiny speck off the coast of Nova Scotia rumored for over a century to have been the site of buried treasure.

"And I would've loved to get to Oak Island first, but once those tunnels were opened to the sea, I think that pretty much ended the possibility of recovering whatever was hidden there."

"You think something was hidden there?" George pulled a hard pack of Marlboro Reds out of his shorts pocket and removed a cigarette.

"No doubt at all," John answered immediately. "This was one case where somebody was too smart and clever for their own good."

Wyman produced a silver lighter and lit the cigarette. "So, treasure hunting really bring you to the Keys, John?"

"Not really. Like I told you, I always had a lot of interest in pirates."

"Weren't any of them burying treasure on the Keys. These islands are solid coral. Only a couple places that dug out any land, and those were big projects. That Hemingway House over in Key West is one. Built by a fellow who had chunks of coral dug out of the ground, ended up with a basement Hemingway used as a wine cellar."

"Interesting," John said, and he actually thought so.

Then he saw Diane stagger out onto the lawn, calling his name. "John! John!"

He was shocked by the change in her color. When he had left her inside, her cheeks were flushed and her eyes sparkled. Now her skin was sallow, her eyes wide in fear.

"I don't feel so . . ."

She turned aside quickly, then lurched into a bush and threw up.

**WHEN** Jenna returned from her Salvation Army shopping spree, she expected to drop by and grab a fast cup of punch before showering, sprucing up, and heading out to Dan Trenton's place for stone crabs. She'd found some really fun clothing, the first store whetting her appetite for some serious bargain shopping in the second. All that had kept her from a bargain hunter's trifecta was the fact that the third store closed as she was pulling into the lot.

Three dresses, a sweater, several pairs of shorts, and a bunch of little tops. Jenna had a whole new Florida wardrobe.

But when she came around the corner from parking the Mustang, she found chaos on the lawn outside the Orchid Lodge.

People were barfing into bushes. The lawn smelled like a particularly unruly fraternity party. An old lady sat at a table alone, tears pouring down her face. That cute black-haired girl from Michigan was sprawled in a chaise longue, wearing a darling little Christmasy outfit, a trifle tarty but not too much. The skirt was red and her face was green.

It occurred to Jenna that her mother was probably up to her elbows in something, and she hoped it wasn't vomit. She took the coward's way out and slipped back to their cottage. This was something she could put off hearing about.

Indefinitely.

*Chapter 20*

**LYNNE** had her first clue that something was seriously wrong with the afternoon's festivities when she went inside to use the restroom. She'd been taking it easy, hanging out on the lawn with the Parkers, super-sizing her last eggnog to avoid having to make so many trips back to the punchbowl.

Just inside the door, at the table where folks had picked up nametags, a fluffy little woman whose nametag identified her as DONNA sat alone, looking ashen.

"Are you all right?" Lynne asked, though the answer seemed pretty obvious.

"My stomach . . . queasy . . ."

Suddenly Donna stood and bolted toward the public restrooms, located in a small hallway off the breakfast room. Lynne followed close behind, catching up abruptly and growing alarmed as she turned the corner and discovered a line of three people waiting to use the Ladies. Donna's erstwhile helper at check-in, Andi, was emerging from the

Gents, looking distressed. A distinct smell of vomit came from either Andi, the restroom, or both. Nobody seemed to notice or mind Andi's social lapse, and the first person in the Ladies line immediately leapt to take her place inside the Gents.

Lynne hadn't been feeling the least bit nauseated when she came inside, but there were few things as socially contagious as vomiting. As her own stomach grew queasy, she recalled, with some embarrassment, the difficulty she had experienced maintaining her digestive equanimity when her children had stomach flu.

Before she could do or say anything, however, the woman who was now first in line at the Ladies banged several times at the door, turned away, and upchucked in a nearby corner.

This was not looking good.

Reinforcements were required. Rick and Peggy needed to get involved here, and fast. Lynne looked around hastily for some kind of receptacle to leave in the hall for the afflicted. Nothing. She hurried into the front office. Facing the street outside, the desk clerk was playing solitaire on his computer monitor. As he heard the door open and hastily hit a button to return the screen to a serious, work-oriented screen, Lynne looked around and grabbed two trash cans.

"You need to go out back right now and get Peggy," she told the clerk. "Tell her that people are getting sick and we need her help."

The manager, whose name she couldn't remember—Jack? Jeff? Jim?—appeared at the open door of his office as the desk clerk hurried through the door to the breakfast room. "Is there a problem?"

Lynne nodded. "A big one. I'm not sure what's happening, but several people at the party are violently ill."

Hotel management people usually were pretty unflappable. This one was no exception. What *was* his name?

"Did I hear you send Derek to get Peggy?" he asked. Derek must be the solitaire-playing desk clerk.

"Yeah. She's just outside on the lawn with Rick. There's half a dozen people waiting for the johns inside here, and somebody just barfed in a corner by the men's room. I'm taking the trash cans for . . . well, you know."

Jim, that was it. Jim Tyler. He stepped back inside his office and emerged with a third can. "Let's go."

The party room had emptied pretty quickly, with only a few somewhat confused-looking merrymakers remaining inside. Platters of cookies and hors d'oeuvres lay abandoned and forlorn on the serving table. The three punch-bowls and hot cider crock pot hadn't moved and continued to hold quite a lot of libations. This was a party that could have and should have gone on a good deal longer.

Through the windows and screens, Lynne could see folks milling about and others who appeared to be heaving into the shrubbery. As she watched, she saw that cute little girl from Michigan, dressed to the nines, stumble into a hibiscus bush and hurl. Her husband, seated nearby, looked on in horror and then approached cautiously. Men were such wusses.

What could be causing this? She thought immediately of salmonella, and the eggs that had gone into the eggnog. Salmonella was practically a guaranteed ingredient in today's egg market. But Lynne had watched Peggy strain three separate batches of cooked eggnog base, following directions from the latest edition of *Joy of Cooking*. And if you couldn't trust *Joy of Cooking,* what could you trust? In any case, she'd put away plenty of eggnog without being affected.

Maintaining a prudent distance from the nauseated, many of the guests outside seemed unaffected but uncertain what to do. Others were drifting away. One of the unaffected couples loudly discussed their need to find a place to stay that didn't endanger the guests. "This is just too much," a woman said loudly. Another couple near them joined in agreement.

Lynne stepped aside as Peggy passed into the Orchid Lodge, looking horrified as she headed for the restrooms. Outside she saw Rick Parker loping away across the lawn, apparently headed for the privacy of his own home and bathroom. As she watched, he stopped abruptly, stepped off the lawn, and bent at the waist over one of the drainage canals beneath the bird cages.

Looked like he wasn't going to be much help.

Jim Tyler stood on the periphery, taking stock. He seemed calmer than the situation warranted, but Lynne figured that was probably a valuable management trait in action.

"Were all these people at the party?" he asked Lynne.

"I believe so. It must be some kind of food poisoning, except that food poisoning usually isn't quite this immediate." Lynne's mind returned to a long, unhappy night in California's Gold Rush country—though as it turned out, that hadn't been food poisoning at all. "I can't tell if any of these people need to go to the hospital or not, but you probably ought to figure some of them will, just to be on the safe side."

"What safe side might that be?" Peggy appeared at Lynne's side. "This looks like a full-blown disaster to me. Where's Rick?"

Lynne pointed across the lawn. Rick was holding onto a mangrove with one hand and a bird cage with the other. "I don't think he's going to be much help right now. Are you okay?"

Peggy nodded, with a wan smile. "Apart from wanting to urp each time I'm near somebody who's sick, I think I'm fine. And whatever the problem is, I think you and I have proven that it can't be the eggnog."

Lynne gave her friend a hug. "It'll be fine. And you're probably right about us." She noticed that while she was slightly slurring her speech, she didn't really feel drunk. Nor did she feel nauseated, beyond the normal reaction when somebody else has puked. There must be some kind of emergency reflex kicking in to give her this period of artificial and accelerated sobriety.

She hoped it would last.

※

**HOURS** later, Peggy surveyed the wreckage of her Christmas party and Craft Fair, holding back tears.

Seven people had been transported to the hospital. She had sent Roberto Lopez, who was installing a new water heater in one of the empty units during the party, to check on how they were and report back. The ever-reliable Roberto had some relative who worked at the hospital and he assured her this connection would help cut through bureaucratic red tape.

His latest call had been comforting, kind of. As best he could determine, Roberto told her, none of the people who'd taken ill at the party was likely to be admitted. The hospital had notified the Health Department, and Peggy should expect an imminent visit from their representatives. As if she didn't have enough to worry about. Still, the

Health Department had the means to figure out what had caused this, and with a little luck it would be something purchased off-site and brought by one of the ladies from the Court.

Make that a lot of luck. And she wasn't feeling especially lucky today.

Most people had gone back to their residences at the Court or their rooms at Dos Hermanas. Six sets of guests had checked out, including the family renting the pricey, two-bedroom Poinciana house for three weeks. She'd probably be able to rent those newly empty units in the weeks to come as folks arrived in the Keys on impulse. She hoped. Was there some kind of truth-in-advertising requirement that would require her to post a warning in the lobby? STAYING AT THIS RESORT MAY BE HAZARDOUS TO YOUR DIGESTION, AND KEEP AN EYE ON YOUR TIRES, TOO.

The thought was only partly facetious. Bad news spread quickly. It was unavoidable.

Peggy had no idea how many resort and Court residents had quietly gone home, keeping their upset stomachs to themselves. Jim Tyler had swung into action, systematically interviewing the guests who lingered, noting the items they had eaten and drank, as well as the current state of their digestive tracts. Peggy hadn't had time yet to look at his lists, but she'd told him to make a copy before turning anything over to the Health Department. She didn't allow herself to even think about the possible litigation that could arise from this ill-fated gathering, the *Lusitania* of Christmas Bazaars.

Unsold craft items lay in disarray on the sale tables, waiting to be picked up or packed up, depending on what the ladies from the Court decided to do. Somebody had removed the fishing-tackle cash boxes, presumably for safekeeping. It certainly wasn't worth the chaos and inconvenience of creating mass nausea to steal their meager contents, which were mostly checks anyway. She picked up a birdhouse painted in charming pastel flowers, an item that would probably have traveled back to somebody's yard in the Midwest had the party not been interrupted so early.

Peggy's first impulse had been to throw away all the food and pour all the drinks down the drain. Lynne had stopped her, pointing out that if there were any kind of residual problems, it would probably be necessary to trace the cause. Neither one of them mentioned the term "lawsuit," which continued to linger unspoken in the air.

Lynne was a rock, even tipsy. While Peggy moved helplessly from one trouble site to another, Lynne had systematically bagged samples of all the cookies and hors d'oeuvres, labeling them and covering what remained on the trays with plastic wrap. She had also taken cupfuls of the four beverages, put them into small Mason jars, then refrigerated the remaining liquids in the large refrigerator behind the breakfast room. The sample foods sat in a cooler on what had recently been the punch table.

Like Lynne, Peggy had been unaffected by whatever evil wind had blown through the Christmas party, and the last time she'd looked in on Rick he said he thought he was better, but preferred to wait it out near his own bathroom. Gloria had swept through like the Queen of England, retreating to her room. That, at least, was something to be grateful for.

So, the one thing she was fairly sure of was that there'd been nothing wrong with the eggnog. She and Lynne had put away staggering quantities of eggnog with no ill effects. In the midst of chaos, that was the only thing she knew with certainty.

So what on earth was happening? And why?

**LATER** that evening, Jenna made two wrong turns requiring backtracking on her way to Dan Trenton's place, located on a cow path—or, more probably, a gator trail—that didn't show up on any map she had, not even the extremely detailed AAA one. She was starting to think she should have left a trail of breadcrumbs, or brought along a GPS.

Just about the time she was ready to give up and go back to Dos Hermanas, she finally caught sight of his truck, tucked into the shrubbery at the side of the road. She exhaled in relief. She still had no real idea where she was, but it was less worrisome now that she had found him.

It was all very jungly back here, and his place seemed to be the last little house on a very secondary road, with a small skiff tied to an equally small dock. If she'd tried to find the place after dark, it would have been difficult. If she'd let him bring her here and then decided she wanted to leave, getting back on her own would have been hopeless.

He lay outside in a hammock, the very picture of tropical languor, with Emmylou Harris singing from the treetops or, more probably, from some waterproof outdoor speakers. A bright green parrot sat on the wooden headboard of the hammock.

"Good to see you," he said, swinging up onto his feet in a single graceful movement. "I was just about to start worrying that you were lost."

"Well, I was, actually. But I'm here now."

She took it all in: the simple square house made of cinderblocks painted pink long ago, the ancient scarred picnic table, the familiar truck, a rusty bicycle with two flat tires, all sorts of dense vegetation. A propane tank stood just past the house, and beyond that gray tarps covered something large and shapeless. It was the kind of place where she wouldn't have been surprised to find a couple of cars up on blocks, a dead refrigerator in the front yard, maybe a washer that even Maytag had given up on.

Still, the night air smelled of flowers—a sweet scent, unfamiliar and enticing. The vegetation was lushly tropical, the night air warm and moist. Dan was as appealing as he'd been both above and under water, maybe even more so. The sun was setting behind the mangroves. And she loved crab.

Dan offered his hand to the parrot, who obligingly climbed on. An empty cage stood near the door to the house.

"Crab claws?" the bird inquired.

Jenna laughed. "Reading my mind. Is this your cook? And won't he fly away if you have him out of the cage?"

"No to both questions," Dan said, moving to greet her. "His wings are clipped, just like the birds that got out this morning at Dos Hermanas."

"I seem to have slept through that," Jenna admitted, though of course he knew she hadn't been there. "Seems like there's a lot of trouble over there."

Dan nodded. "But let's not worry about that tonight. Meet Luigi. Luigi, this is Jenna."

"Pleased to meet you," Luigi said. It wasn't exactly a squawk, and it wouldn't have passed for human delivery, but the diction was surprisingly good.

"Likewise, I'm sure," Jenna said. Once again, she was

conversing with a bird. Good thing her LA friends couldn't see this.

"Crab claws," Luigi repeated.

"An excellent idea," she told the parrot.

Apparently so. But on to more important matters. Dan had a couple of torches burning and Jenna hoped they were citronella, though the insects she could see flying in the dusk air didn't seem repelled. And there were plenty of them.

"I'd better break out the bug spray," she said, digging in her bag. She'd brought along that smelly bottle from the Everglades, as anxious to be prepared as she was to remain unchewed. Everglades Everyday, it was called, and she suspected that she'd have to bathe in the stuff if she ever lived in South Florida. She'd also covered up, wearing jeans, socks, and sneakers, with a long-sleeved shirt still in the car. Maybe she should have bought that mosquito net headgear after all.

"Couldn't hurt, I suppose. But there's not much biting tonight."

She slapped at a mosquito settling in for dinner on her forearm. "Maybe not for you." She resisted making the kind of stupid remark about being sweet that folks always trotted out when they were being devoured by mosquitoes. Sweet had nothing to do with it. It was biochemistry and bad luck. She fished the repellent out of her bag and slathered up. "I suppose next you're going to tell me that you never get bit."

He shook his head, smiling. He was in cutoffs and a T-shirt, wearing sandals. Lots of exposed brown skin. Not a mosquito in sight. "Not really. But I've got a theory on that, actually. Seems to me that the folks who stay here are the ones who aren't bothered too much. Kind of Darwinian. You come down here and you're getting chawed to pieces, you're likely to go back wherever you came from. Or at least to move on somewhere else."

"Makes sense."

He gave a little chuckle. "I've gotta admit though, the folks who first settled this area must have had hides like rhinoceroses. Summers, the skeeters are pretty nasty, particularly out here in the boonies. Even I get bit now and again."

He offered beer and went inside to fetch it, returning with a bottle from an unfamiliar microbrewery that she accepted appreciatively. She knocked back a pretty good slug to start, and liked it. Now that she had found the house, met up with Dan again, and determined that she was probably safe, she could appreciate just how nervous she had been.

"Crab claws?" the parrot asked again.

"In a minute, Luigi," Dan told him. "You don't even like crab claws." He disappeared into the house again and returned with a cluster of grapes. He put the grapes into the parrot's cage and Luigi followed willingly. Dan closed and locked the cage door.

"The crab'll be ready in a couple minutes. I just need to steam it to reheat it."

"You won't believe what happened this afternoon at Dos Hermanas," Jenna told him.

His eyes widened as she filled in what she had learned, when her mother returned to their cottage as Jenna prepared to leave. When she finished, he shook his head.

"I've never heard of anything like that happening around here."

"Or anywhere else," Jenna added.

"What do you suppose it was?"

"No idea. But I did notice that the people who got sick seemed to be all right once they barfed."

"Food poisoning, probably," Dan said.

"Yeah, I suppose, but my mom said that most of the time it takes a while before food poisoning hits you. She told me that the party was just barely underway when people started getting sick."

"Was your mom sick?"

"No, and neither was Peggy Parker. They were trying to track down what everybody had eaten and drunk when I was getting ready to leave."

"Sounds like a good party to have missed," Dan Trenton said.

*Chapter 21*

**ELLEN** Gainsborough had taken a nap, waking to the chirp of her cell phone and her brother Ed's announcement that he was just starting to cross the Seven Mile Bridge and should be at Dos Hermanas within half an hour. She stretched, got up, and decided that since she was in the Keys in December, and had noticed a warm breeze blowing earlier, she might as well put on shorts. She'd grabbed a couple of warm weather outfits from the closet in her second bedroom where she kept out-of-season apparel before packing.

Showered and dressed, she stepped outdoors, and found chaos.

She had intended to leave word at the front desk and have Ed directed back to her cottage, which featured a nice little porch overlooking the bay. There they would talk, figure out what to do. But after seeing what was happening outdoors, she decided a change of plans was in order. This place was crazy. She locked the door and headed for the office.

People were wandering about, a very unpleasant and unmistakable odor was wafting down across the lawns, and the damn birds were squawking. She began consciously breathing through her mouth to avoid the odor as she picked her way around the periphery of the property, ignoring the milling groups of people. She found the office empty and it seemed more prudent to wait for Ed out front, which had the additional advantage of being upwind. When Ed arrived, she didn't even let him out of the car. She jumped into the front seat and told him to head into Key West. They could have dinner and regroup there. One of the things she had always admired in her brother was his ability to move quickly and without hesitation when necessary. He didn't question, but simply nodded and started to turn around.

As he began the three-point turn, however, an SUV with Indiana plates nearly took off the back end of his rental car, blasting its horn as it did so. The front was crowded with passengers, the back-end loaded with luggage. As the SUV passed them, at least three of its passengers offered the Gainsboroughs their middle digits.

※

**AFTER** about an hour, the detectives called Sheri's attention to initials on the matchbooks and condom wrappers. W.N. D.H. B.B. G.W. N.W. J.J.K. Some of them seemed to correspond to men in the Court, while others were entirely unfamiliar. At least one set of initials, B.B., seemed to belong to Bob Burke, who was married and ought to have known better.

"Are you planning to release this information to the public?" Sheri asked. "It's one thing to tarnish Darcy's reputation, since Darcy was responsible for that herself.

But these others . . . it seems like making needless trouble for a lot of people. I'm willing to give folks the benefit of the doubt. Darcy could be . . . well, I guess coquettish is the best description. If she set out to seduce somebody, even one of the old guys at Little Sister Court, I think he'd be pretty much a sitting duck." She allowed herself a brief, ironic smile. "And don't forget, she knew who was taking Viagra and Cialis."

Sheri was starting to think that perhaps she had blundered in not asking for an attorney. Before they even left Little Sister Court, Detective Jackson had given her that warning they always have on the TV cop shows, about the right to remain silent and an attorney being provided if she couldn't afford one. It had sounded silly at the time, and she had pooh-poohed the need for an attorney. Too late she comprehended that part of her rationale for not asking for counsel was a self-righteous belief that of course she could afford a lawyer—when in fact she probably couldn't.

In any case, the innocent shouldn't need legal representation, though she might be off-track a little believing that. Except for the pseudo-cooperative venture of examining the contents of Darcy's "loot drawer," nothing in the questioning she had undergone suggested that the police considered her innocent, or even just stupid or naïve. The way they spoke to her, over and over again, made it pretty clear that they were expecting her to break.

Enough, already.

It was all starting to blur, endless rounds of the same questions.

Yes, she had helped Darcy package the pills before. Many times. The pills arrived, as best Sheri knew, the first week of each month. Each medication was packaged in a large bottle, and Darcy and Sheri would count and separate out the various orders. Most people ordered a couple of months' worth at a time, just so they wouldn't be bothered so often.

Darcy had handled all orders and payments, including Sheri's own. The pharmacy operation was cash only, and Sheri had no idea whether Darcy declared this income to the IRS. The two had not been in the habit of discussing their personal finances. She acknowledged being surprised to learn that Darcy's profit was larger than her friend had claimed, though she was quick to add that this didn't really matter, since the pills were still significantly less expensive than they would have been otherwise.

No, she had never had anything to do with the smuggler or smugglers, and no, she had no idea at all who that might be. Surely they didn't believe she could keep track of all the boats that came and went around Little Sister Key and the surrounding waters. She didn't own a boat herself and had no idea how to operate one.

Boats were nearly as common as cars in these parts. As for who owned a boat with enough range to go to Mexico and back, that was way outside Sheri's field of knowledge. All she knew about salt-water travel was the pithy saying that her father, who had served in the Navy between World War I and World War II, had taught her: *You can put a boat on a ship, but you can't put a ship on a boat.*

The cops repeated their questions about the bottles and vials that Darcy used to package the pills. Those Sheri knew a little more about. Darcy ordered them from a plastics company in Texas. She had experimented with having people bring their used vials back for refills, but the logistics in this process had made it more trouble than it was worth. Darcy had also worried about thoroughly cleaning the recyclable vials, so as not to mix medications or taint one with the residue of another. She printed the labels on standard-sized Avery labels on her own printer, and always had them printed up in advance when Sheri helped with the packaging. A vial or bottle wasn't filled until after its label was attached.

Finally Detective Ruiz brought one of the small cylindrical vials in, set it in the middle of the table, and left without saying a word. Apparently Sheri was expected to either screech in guilty horror or blanch with remorse and faint dead away.

No such luck, guys. She wasn't smart enough to shut up, she was realizing too late, but she wasn't dumb enough to act guilty when she wasn't. Eventually, during one of the many awkward silences of the afternoon, she asked about the vial.

"You don't know?" Detective Jackson asked, his young brow furrowed in confusion. When had the policemen all become children?

"Know what?"

"Know why this vial is so important."

Sheri inhaled deeply at that. "If I knew, now why would I ask?" He said nothing. "Oh, never mind. It can't matter. You guys are just trying to trick me."

"How could we trick you if you have nothing to hide?"

They'd been down *this* merry path before.

"Because it seems to me that you people are in the business of trickery. You ought to be out trying to find who killed poor Darcy, and here are you just badgering me." At this point she started to cry. Detective Jackson offered a box of Kleenex, then sat back and watched her.

Suddenly Sheri remembered one of the rumors that had been floating through Little Sister Court prior to her . . . well, you couldn't call it an arrest, she supposed, because she was theoretically free to go. Prior to her nightmare, that summed it up pretty well. Some kind of foreign object had been found in Darcy's throat. Sheri picked up the vial and turned it around in her fingers. This size would probably fit in a person's mouth, though the idea of thrusting it down somebody's throat, dead *or* alive, was pretty repugnant.

"Was this what was stuck in her throat?" she asked.

Detective Jackson's expression remained impassive. He said nothing for a few moments, then queried, "Why do you ask that?"

"Because that's the only reason I can think of that you'd be making such a fuss over it. People all around the Court were whispering and gossiping, trying to figure out what was down her throat. It was in the morning newspaper, for heaven's sake, that something was found. Lots of curiosity. Everybody knows about it."

She looked at him, then shook her head in disbelief. "Am I supposed to be falling on the floor, now, making a dramatic confession? You're wasting my time and you're wasting your time, too. I don't really have anything pressing I need to attend to, so I guess my time doesn't matter much here. But you gentlemen are supposed to be finding out who killed Darcy, and that won't happen while you're browbeating me."

She was pleased at how firmly she made the statement. She just might get out of here yet.

Detective Ruiz stuck his head in the door just then. He gestured to Detective Jackson, who followed him outside. A few minutes later, Detective Ruiz returned alone.

He sat down and looked at her steadily. "What is your involvement in the Christmas party being held this afternoon at Dos Hermanas?"

"Involvement? In the *Christmas* party? What on earth are you talking about?" She had almost forgotten the silly party altogether. It seemed very far away, in a world she was feeling more and more detached from. "Well, I was planning to attend, and maybe to buy a few Christmas gifts. But as you know perfectly well, I've been here all afternoon. So it's a good thing that I didn't *have* any involvement in the party, isn't it? I'd have let down people who were counting on me if I had."

Detective Ruiz regarded her steadily, his hooded black eyes staring right into her own. He said nothing.

But Sheri had had enough. It was time to call it quits.

"I want to leave," she told the detective. "I believe I'm free to go?"

He hesitated just long enough to make her really nervous. "Yes, ma'am."

She started to stand, and stumbled slightly. Well, wouldn't you just know it? Her creaky senior joints had missed two days of tennis workouts in a row. Use it or lose it, her doctor always said, an easy enough statement for somebody who was pushing thirty-five. The doctors were all children these days, too.

"I can give you a ride back," Detective Ruiz told her. "We've just learned that there's some kind of problem at the Christmas party you're missing."

"You don't mean somebody else has died, surely."

"Not yet."

❧

**GEORGE** Wyman continued to be pleasantly surprised by the level of awareness that the young pup from Battle Creek had on what he had come to regard as a fairly esoteric topic: historical piracy. He wondered if young John Haedrich's wife shared his interest.

Probably not. Piracy was not a topic for the squeamish. Most women of George's acquaintance had no interest in men with poor personal hygiene whose career arcs often included bloody murders, endless plunder, serious injuries, and hanging, followed by long periods of gibbeting. The gibbet was a cautionary reminder to seamen. The body of an executed pirate was customarily coated with tar and then hung in a body-shaped metal cage that would support first the rotting corpse and eventually the skeletal remains. Gibbets were hung near ports where seamen passing in and out of harbors could be easily reminded that the penalties for piracy were generally swift and extreme.

He was concerned that the police had taken away Sheri McManus, who was nice enough and not nearly as silly as so many of the women in Little Sister Court. The residents here reflected the demographics of their age group. There were far more women than men, and when a married couple (or an unmarried one, this being Florida where even the elderly often lived together without benefit of clergy) was split by death, it was almost always the husband who expired.

Even after a year in residence, George continued to be besieged by the forward husband-hunters. He got more than his share of baked goods and extra whatevers—even an offer of a frozen Omaha steak, which he accepted while ignoring that its donor mostly wanted to grill his beef side by side with her own.

Come to think of it, that had proven to be a good tactic. She hadn't been back since.

## Chapter 22

**BY** the time Jenna and Dan got around to the crab claws, they had each put away a couple of beers. It was dark now, the night alive with sounds and breezes. The sky was filled with stars, a far richer display than LA or even Floritas. As they talked and laughed, Jenna had a vague sense of the natural world around them, and she was very glad she had slathered up with the mosquito repellent. Now and then there'd be a squawk or a squeal or a rustle from the nearby bushes, and she was working very hard at not jumping each time that happened.

Luigi the parrot continued to provide commentary, though his vocabulary seemed a bit limited beyond "crab claws" and some general pleasantries. If he wanted to make his way in the world socially, Jenna thought, he'd need to branch out a bit beyond "How you doin'?"

The stone crab claws filled a good-sized bowl, and Dan had some grocery store cole slaw and bread on the side. He'd covered the picnic table with a plastic cloth, and citronella torches burned all around the table. A pretty good spread for a young bachelor, assuming that he was a bachelor—marital status being a topic they had not discussed. In any event, this place showed no evidence of a wife or significant other.

"Where's the rest of the crab?" Jenna asked, as she surveyed the bowl of thick, substantial claws. Dan had demonstrated how to use a heavy metal mallet to wallop the hell out of each claw. The shells were surprisingly thick and resistant, but the succulent meat was well worth the effort.

Dan laughed. "Back in the bay growing more claws."

"What?!"

"They regenerate," he explained. "The fishing regs let you harvest one claw off a stone crab, provided it's big enough, of course. Put the crab back and he'll go off and grow another claw."

This sounded a lot like traumatic amputation to Jenna, appalling even if the victim was a crustacean.

He saw her consternation and smiled. "It's no different from harvesting a fruit tree, really. What do you do when an orange is ripe, or a bunch of grapes?"

"Grapes," Luigi put in. "Bunch of grapes."

"You take off the fruit," Dan went on, "and before you know it, the tree or vine or whatever'll bring you another crop."

He had a point. And it wasn't as if she worried much about the Dungeness or King crabs that were killed altogether, not merely maimed. She was a hypocrite, actually, and they both knew it. She extricated more crab meat and dipped it in melted butter. "They're awfully good," she admitted. "I'm kind of sorry I asked."

"Do your best to forget how they got here," he counseled, "and just concentrate on enjoying them."

So she did.

✀

I don't have any dessert," Dan said later, after they had reduced the crab to a pile of hard shattered chips, every last morsel of meat sucked greedily from inside its protective shells.

"I'd be too stuffed if you did," she told him.

"Ready for another beer?"

She shook her head. "I'm fine." She looked at Luigi's cage. The bird had been quiet for a while. "Why birds?"

"Why not? I just always liked them, the combination of beauty and intelligence. They're fun to be around."

"So did you always have them? When you were growing up?"

He shook his head. "Naw. Had some budgies when I was a kid, but they all died. You ever had any?"

Jenna shook her head. She could feel the beer, sense how relaxed she had become. The mosquitoes were pretty much ignoring her and she'd just plowed through a small mountain of crab meat. Life was good. "Nope. We had cats."

"Birds in captivity can co-exist with cats."

Jenna laughed. "Not with the cats we always had. Our cats were all incredible hunters. Show them a bird in a cage and it might take a day or two, but they'd figure out a way to get that cage open and catch their own dinner. But you were talking about your budgies."

"Actually the budgies never lived very long. Turns out, I find out years later, it was cause we were feeding them birdseed. Seems like a pretty logical thing to feed birds, no?"

"Well, yeah."

"Birds love seed, but it's not a very balanced diet. In the wild they eat fruits and bugs and stuff. You can give a bird seed, but you need to supplement it with fresh produce. Who knew?"

This explained the veritable salad bar he'd been toting when Jenna and her mother had first come upon him servicing the birds at Dos Hermanas.

"Was that true what you said about Churchill's parrot still being alive?" she asked. The mention had been tugging at her curiosity ever since that first encounter by the bird cages at Dos Hermanas.

"Have I ever lied to you?"

She laughed. "I just met you."

"Well, I don't lie. Not about stuff that's important, anyway."

"And how do you define 'unimportant'?"

"Bad word choice. I'm an honest guy. Honest."

Jenna could hear an automobile engine far off in the night, getting louder. Dan got up as a silver Toyota pickup truck pulled into the driveway.

"It's Roberto," he said. "Roberto Lopez who works over at Dos Hermanas. Give me a minute?"

Dan went over to the truck as Roberto shut off the engine. The night seemed remarkably quiet once again, as the two men spoke briefly in voices too low for her to understand. After a few minutes of this quiet discussion, Roberto fired up the pickup again and drove away, waving in her direction.

Dan started inside. "Sure you don't want another beer?"

"Sure, one more."

When he came out, carrying two fresh bottles, he moved toward a couple of Adirondack chairs. "Come sit over here, Jenna. It's more comfortable."

She slipped out of the picnic bench and moved toward him, knowing he was watching, This was definitely her last beer. "So what about Churchill's parrot?"

"Well, she's over a hundred years old," he began, "a blue and gold Macaw named Charlie. Churchill apparently loved animals, had all kinds of them, including a leopard at one point."

"Talk about bad pet pairing. A macaw and a leopard?"

"That's the way the way the story goes. Anyway, he bought Charlie, who was actually female, and he started teaching her to swear as soon as he got her. Taught her 'Fuck the Nazis' and 'Fuck Hitler' and never got tired of hearing her say them. She's the oldest bird in Britain."

"How can anyone possibly know that?"

He smiled. "I guess you've got a point there. But people in the bird world all seem to agree that Charlie is the real deal. She even cusses with an English accent."

She considered that for a minute. "How many of those birds at Dos Hermanas actually talk?"

"A bunch. They're all various species of parrot, and some of them are more likely to speak. The African greys are very talkative, and the scarlet macaw. Melissa the cockatoo is very affectionate, but you know that already. A lot depends on the species. Every now and then you get a bird you'd expect to be a talker and it won't say diddly. Birds bred in captivity are more likely to talk because they're exposed to people from the moment they hatch. They're also more expensive, but much easier to handle and play with."

Jenna had never considered a bird as the kind of pet one

would play with. "If you say so. But some of them aren't raised in captivity?"

He laughed. "Used to be just about none of them were. You'd have to capture them in the wild. Which isn't all that hard if you go to the places where they originate. Latin America, Africa, Australia."

"Australia?"

"Oh yeah. People always think of koalas and kangaroos when you bring up Australia, but they've got incredible birds there. When I was in the Navy stationed in the Far East, a buddy and I took a trip to Australia and I was just amazed. They've got flocks of birds there that are endangered anywhere else, and really strict export laws."

"But if they've got so many, why *not* export them?"

Countless stars glittered in the blue-black sky, and behind her the house was dark. The silence of the tropical night was broken only by occasional rustles or cries of what Jenna assumed were animals—animals she hoped weren't announcing they were being eaten by alligators. The torches continued to burn, providing the only real light, reflecting off the smooth dark planes of Dan's face. He was a very appealing guy, and she realized suddenly that if she weren't traveling with her mother, around now she'd be giving some serious thought to spending the night.

He shrugged. "Why do governments do anything? They've got birds there that we only see in zoos here. The natives actually kill a lot of them because they're too destructive. A guy there told me about what they call a 'snowstorm.' A farmer or rancher will warn the neighbors to lock up their domestic animals. Then they soak bird seed in sheep-dip, which is poison, and spread it by the side of the road. The birds eat the seed, take off, then fall out of the sky, dead."

"That's horrible!" Jenna shuddered at the image. "Do they do it so they can collect the feathers?"

Dan laughed. "They gather the dead birds up with back-hoes and throw them in a ditch. Feathers aren't the big business they once were. People around here killed each other over feathers once upon a time. Used to be that ladies' hats had lots of long exotic plumes, and back when this area was essentially untamed, almost uninhabitable, hunters would come down and wipe out flocks of particu-larly popular birds. The roseate spoonbill is close to extinct because its feathers were so popular. Piece of useless in-formation: You know Flamingo, over in the Everglades?"

Jenna nodded.

"Well, it was named for the birds the early explorers found there. Now there *are* a few flamingos over there, and probably were back then. But most likely the birds they saw were roseate spoonbills. Which before much longer, like I said, were all but wiped out by the plume hunters."

"I've seen them in Audubon prints," Jenna said. Over the years, Booker T had sold a number of high-end Audubon books. "He did a lot of work down here, didn't he?"

Dan snorted. "Don't get me going on Audubon. Do you know how that guy worked?"

Well, hardly. "No."

"He'd go out and observe birds in their natural habi-tats—see how they flew and sat and moved. Then he'd shoot a whole lot of whatever species he was working on and wire the dead birds into the positions he'd seen in the wild. From that he'd paint. Except that—and I'm sure you can see this coming—dead birds don't last very long in this climate. So he'd have to keep killing more and wiring them up till he finished."

"My mom was talking about going to the Audubon House down in Key West."

"Tell her to save her money. He didn't live there. That place didn't exist when he was here. He didn't even do all his own artwork. Other artists mostly did the backgrounds and even some of the birds."

"But the Audubon Society," Jenna protested. "It's a conservation organization."

"Old man Audubon is probably whirling in his grave, thinking about all the birds that people don't get to shoot because of those do-gooders."

❧

**AS** she lay propped on pillows in her room at Dos Hermanas and watched old sitcom reruns on TV, Diane Haedrich felt enormously disappointed.

It was so incredibly unfair that she should get sick at what might otherwise have been a very nice event. Up until the very moment that her stomach clenched, the day had been just sailing along, much nicer than the previous one—though as she reflected on it now, yesterday had pretty much been doomed from the get-go. Any day that began with coming upon a dead body before breakfast was clearly off to a very poor start.

When Diane was younger, she had helped her mother and aunts make Christmas ornaments to be sold at the annual church bazaar. She had mastered the use of the glue gun by the age of seven, and she liked nothing better than to be presented with a pile of small objects needing to be affixed to larger ones. She had come to realize that she wasn't particularly good at craft innovation, but if you gave her the right materials and adequate instructions, she was unstoppable.

In that respect, at least, it almost didn't matter that the Craft Fair had ended so abruptly. She probably wouldn't have bought much, since at least part of her goal in attending had been to cruise for ideas. She'd found one, too, and had come away with a perfect, timely, and relatively inexpensive plan for many of the people on the Haedrichs' gift list.

She'd get a bunch of inexpensive picture frames and some little seashells and glue the shells to the frames. For their parents, she'd insert prints of some picture, yet to be taken, of the two of them in the Keys, though his mother would probably say, *wink, wink,* that it would be just the right frame for a picture of a baby. For some of John's extended-family members—cousins they saw only on major holidays, people whose taste veered sharply away from anything natural or outdoorsy—she would then spray paint the shell-covered frames gold. And for his Aunt Veronica, whose decorating inspiration seemed to come from Liberace, she'd sprinkle on a bit of glitter, too.

Diane hadn't been surprised when John left the Craft Fair after taking a polite stroll around the room and piling a plate with cookies and appetizers. John had been excited by his meeting with that older fellow he met yesterday, and was anxious to talk to him again. And while she had been "shopping" inside and getting sick, the two had apparently shared an interesting conversation.

John was a half-hearted shopper under the best of circumstances, almost always deferring to Diane's judgment and going to significant lengths to avoid being tagged for a trip to the mall. She had promised him she'd take care of

Christmas shopping for both of their families while on this trip—and then, before she could make a single purchase, she found herself barfing into the bushes.

At least she hadn't gotten anything on her beautiful new holiday sweater—soft white angora embroidered with jewel-toned sequin ornaments. She had watched that sweater all through the Christmas shopping season last year, nearly buying it at 25% off in mid-December, then exercising restraint and keeping her fingers crossed. Her wish had been granted. It was still there on the day after Christmas, at half price, and she snatched it up with glee. She had tried it on, tucked it away, and brought it out with a thrill of anticipation when she began packing for this trip.

The bazaar had been the sweater's maiden voyage, the waters a bit choppy. And the day had really been too warm for angora anyway. She had stripped off the sweater and laid it out on the back of a chair on the cottage porch to air right after the debacle on the Dos Hermanas lawn. Then she'd slipped into a T-shirt and gotten into bed.

"You feeling any better?" John asked from the chair by the window. He had been mercifully unaffected by whatever bothered Diane and the others.

"A lot," she told him, hitting the MUTE button. She'd seen this particular episode of *Friends* several times, could almost recite the dialogue. "I was thinking maybe we could go out later, if you want. Maybe go into Key West and see what Duval Street is like at night."

"Are you sure you're up to it?"

She nodded. "Actually, apart from being kind of embarrassed, I feel just fine. I can't believe I did that."

"You were sick, sweetie. It's not like you planned it. And you certainly weren't the only one feeling ill."

Diane shuddered. The idea of planned nausea was too awful to contemplate. She had never been able to understand bulimia. As for morning sickness, something you heard plenty about when most of your friends were in their twenties and early thirties, she'd deal with that when it happened.

John sat on the bed beside her and picked up her hand, looking at the simple gold band on her third finger. "We find what I'm looking for, I've got the diamond all picked out."

Diane shook her head. "Don't talk like that, honey. I don't care about having a diamond, honest. And it won't make any difference to me if you don't find what you're looking for."

John's expression was stubborn. "I'm not a quitter, Diane. You ought to know that."

Well-traveled territory. "Honey, it's not about quitting. It's about being realistic."

"My father had a good head on his shoulders."

"But he didn't believe in this. He only told you because he'd promised *his* father that he'd tell you."

"Whatever. Anyway, George told me to come on by and check out his library tomorrow. You're welcome to come along."

Diane thought a minute. There was no getting around this. Might as well march right through. "This may be a silly question, but how will a library about pirates help with anything?"

"I don't know, exactly," John admitted. "But I just have to try."

"Did you tell him about what you're doing?"

After all this time, you'd think she would have come up with a simple way to categorize this wild goose chase. But that was part of the problem. All the shorthand names she came up with were things like "impossible dream" and "cockamamie scheme" and "ridiculous waste of time." As long as the quest made him happy, she didn't particularly mind, but she was starting to realize that if he didn't achieve what he'd hoped for on this trip, he was going to be extremely disappointed and discontented.

She just wished she knew some way to take this whole mess and resolve it happily.

*Chapter 23*

**LYNNE** sat in the Parkers' living room with Peggy and Sheri McManus, wondering what on earth was happening on this tiny island, why so much had gone so inexplicably wrong in less than forty-eight hours. Rick, while reasonably well recovered from the afternoon's upset stomach, had said goodnight and gone off to bed half an hour ago.

Peggy and Rick's single-story home was tucked away in its own heavily vegetated waterfront corner of the Dos Hermanas property. While much smaller than the places where the Parkers had lived while their kids were growing up, it felt just the right size to Lynne now. The comfortable living room was done mostly in rattan with bold, forties-style, floral upholstery and glass-topped tables, and the entire place had an understated but distinctive tropical atmosphere.

Peggy had good taste and disliked clutter and had never been one to keep something when there was a logical reason to discard it. Lynne remembered Peggy's annual garage sales, eagerly awaited in their neighborhood during the Parkers' Floritas days. She herself had always joined in, a collaboration that had moved some pretty nice stuff down the block to the Montgomery house over the years.

The Parkers seemed to have downsized their living arrangements without difficulty. The space wasn't overcrowded, didn't have that awkwardly condensed feel of some retirement households, where eight rooms worth of furniture have been shoehorned into five. There weren't too many pictures covering the walls, too many books crammed into looming bookcases, too many sets of dishes and glasses in an overflowing hutch. The kitchen counters were scrubbed shiny and free of appliances, while the bathroom vanity held only a water glass and a soap dish, with a couple of guest towels in a basket.

This was Lynne's first real opportunity to spend any time with Sheri, other than when they spoke with her briefly out near the boat ramp yesterday morning, as the paramedics tended to Darcy's body and police moved through the crowd, interviewing the loitering onlookers. Sheri was what Lynne had come to think of, in the genealogy of a mobile society, as a neighbor, once removed, having lived three doors away from Peggy in Atlanta. Sheri and her late husband had moved to Little Sister Key first. She had later steered the Parkers toward Dos Hermanas, when the resort went on the market a short time after a Parker Christmas card announced Rick's impending retirement.

Sheri was probably ten or fifteen years older than Lynne and Peggy, but the age difference didn't feel significant to Lynne. Still, Sheri looked downright aged just now, her face makeup free, lined with experience and sorrows. She was comfortably dressed in sandals and a fresh, peach-colored silk caftan, and had earlier confessed to standing under the shower for half an hour after getting home from the police station.

"I just don't get it," Sheri said, her hands cupped around a glass of Chardonnay.

Lynne noticed that she didn't appear to be drinking any of the wine, just taking solace from its presence. Warming it, too, not the optimal treatment for a nice white wine. But it was Sheri's glass and Sheri's awful day that was under discussion. Most people, under those circumstances, would be chugging right from the wine bottle.

"They didn't have any reason," Sheri went on, "to think I'd done anything really wrong. I mean, *nothing*. All along, they kept saying that they thought that Darcy's little business of getting the drugs from Mexico was a perfectly reasonable thing to do."

"Where did Darcy get the drugs?" Peggy asked. "Do you have an idea?

Sheri shook her head. "You're starting to sound like the cops. I don't know. Never knew, never asked, never heard. I know they came from somewhere in Mexico. Some of the paperwork and packing material was in Spanish. But I don't read Spanish."

"I wonder if Roberto Lopez had something to do with this," Peggy said thoughtfully. "Did the police mention him?"

"No, and neither did I." Sheri looked confused. "I thought Roberto was just a handyman."

Peggy held up both hands in horror, palms toward Sheri. "Never say somebody is *just* a handyman. That's like saying somebody is *just* a housewife. Roberto is an amazing handyman. I swear, he talks to machines the way some people communicate telepathically with animals. And he strikes me as very shrewd. It wouldn't surprise me a bit to find out he was involved in this. It's a perfect setting for him. He's around Dos Hermanas and the Court all the time. He's got a Boston whaler he keeps over on Big Pine Key where he lives, and that could certainly get you to Mexico and back, assuming there's no hurricane blowing. And he'd know all about how to avoid the Coast Guard. I think that's the first thing they teach in Florida Keys marine navigation classes."

"You're starting to convince me," Lynne said, "and I've barely met the guy."

Sheri was nodding now. "It's got to be Roberto. I can't think of anybody else that Darcy could use. And you left out the most significant detail, Peggy. Roberto is Mexican, not Cuban."

"Then I guess the question," Lynne said, "is whether Darcy's death had to do with the drug smuggling."

"Could you please stop calling it 'drug smuggling'?" Sheri asked plaintively. "That's the way the cops kept referring to it and I felt like some kind of hideous gangster, instead of a middle-aged lady counting pills into bottles. What was that awful movie where Al Pacino played the cocaine dealer?"

"*Scarface*," Lynne answered without hesitation. It always surprised her when something inconsequential that she hadn't thought about for decades immediately popped up from her memory bank, while the important things she'd been doing a week ago had somehow dropped off into oblivion. It was like hit-and-run amnesia.

"How do Darcy's kids seem to you?" Sheri asked.

"I haven't seen her son up close yet," Peggy said, "or spoken with him. I gave the daughter two keys and put them in a two-bedroom cottage. Ellen told me her brother would get in around dinner time, and I saw her get picked up by a young man out front, when we were all tied up in the nausea mess. The last time I looked, the lights were still out in their cottage. I'm assuming that was her brother who picked her up, and that they went to Key West for dinner or something."

"I wish I'd had a chance to talk to them first," Sheri said.

"I'm not sure what that would accomplish," Peggy told her. "Her daughter seemed pretty tightly wound. And she was extremely distressed that the cops wouldn't let her into her mother's place yet."

"In her position, I would be, too," Sheri said. "But I don't think the police are going to let anybody near that coach again for a long time. They've put actual physical seals on the doors. And they've got the last key I know of that was floating around, the one Darcy kept in a fake rock on her patio. Though I can't say I'm sorry I don't have a way to get in there again. It gave me the creeps being in her place, knowing she was dead. I kept thinking about the things that just *stopped* when she died. Like her grocery shopping list. The newspapers outside. And that was before I found that drawer full of stuff I was telling you about."

Peggy frowned. "Do you think her children know about Darcy's—I don't know how to—about the way she took things from people?"

"I don't see how they could *not* know," Lynne said. "I don't think you all of a sudden start randomly stealing in your seventies. If this is something she was doing now, I bet she's been doing it for a long time. The children would know. Though whether they'd be willing to admit it is another story."

"They're probably hoping that it won't come out, don't you think?" Peggy said.

"Are a lot of people going to be in trouble if the police don't give back those confiscated medications?" Lynne asked, carefully avoiding the D word.

Sheri nodded. "My guess is yes. Financial trouble, for sure. And a lot of these drugs—you just can't stop taking them suddenly. Of course, who knows what's really necessary in the first place?"

"Good point," said Lynne, who wasn't taking anything on a regular basis, other than vitamins and baby aspirin. She started taking the baby aspirin a few months after her seemingly healthy husband dropped dead on Floritas Beach. Her doctor said she didn't really need to, but that the aspirin probably wouldn't hurt. "That's why seniors are always told to take a brown bag of all their medications in when they have a checkup. Things prescribed by different doctors or at different times might interact or cancel each other out."

"Tell me about it," Peggy said. "People wonder why drug prices are so high—seems pretty obvious to me. Now that the law lets them advertise prescription drugs on TV, the pharmaceutical companies are spending millions on commercials designed to make people think they need drugs they've never heard of, for problems they didn't know they even had."

"For problems they probably *don't* have," said Lynne. "TV drug ads have sure come a long way since those black-and-white commercials in the fifties."

Peggy laughed. "*For headache, neuritis, and neuralgia.* What was that for, Anacin?"

"Yep. I never did figure out what neuritis and neuralgia were," Lynne admitted, "though I certainly didn't want them inside *my* head, with those little boxes that had the pounding hammer and the frazzled nerve and whatever the other one was."

"Do you guys remember the one with the totally fried housewife saying, 'Mother, please, I'd rather do it myself'?" Peggy asked. "My mom really hated that. And the one that described a headachy mother who turned into a 'raging stranger' to her children. I guess she wasn't the only one who didn't like it, 'cause they changed it later to 'unreasonably irritated.'"

"Not quite the same," said Sheri, who was smiling for the first time in the evening. "Me, I loved Speedy Alka-Seltzer."

"That irritating little twit?" Peggy asked.

Sheri nodded. "One and the same. I've pretty much loved all the Alka-Seltzer commercials. Remember, 'I can't believe I ate the whole thing'? But I saw some of these old ads on some documentary and they all looked incredibly primitive."

"Commercials *were* primitive back then," Lynne said. "In a way, I kind of miss that. I hate those ads that show active adults—young seniors, or supposed-to-be-seniors—and they're running across a meadow, or—"

"Or getting ready to get in the sack," Peggy interrupted. "Are there really that many people in the country who aren't getting laid? That many men with erectile dysfunction?"

Lynne shrugged. "I wouldn't know. But to look at prime time television, you'd think every man in the country had trouble getting it up." She smiled. "Though there's a real subtlety to those ads. Like the one that has the football being thrown through the tire."

❧

**LATER**, in her own bed in her own cabin, Lynne listened to Jenna watching TV in the other room. Jenna had just gotten in a little while ago, and she seemed quite cheerful, which pleased Lynne.

The conversation about prescription drugs bothered her. It was easy enough to be amused by the horny couples in their fifties, even as the ads warned against too much of a good thing. Erections of over four hours, the announcers cautioned, might lead to death, though they never quite said why. Where was Catherine the Great when you really needed her?

But it wasn't just about sex.

There were all those other things that the giant drug companies would like you to believe you are suffering from. High cholesterol? Got a pill. Hypertension? Ditto. Depression? Fix you right up. Obesity? Lose weight without those annoying stomach staples. Osteoporosis, gout, rhinitis, gastric reflux, arthritis? Taken care of. Not to mention neuritis and neuralgia.

The goal here was clearly to change the power balance in the doctor-patient-pharmaceutical triumvirate. In TV ads, the doctor was almost an afterthought. There was a certain sameness to most of the ads, with the swiftly spoken disclaimers often the most interesting part. Any list of "possible side effects" invariably led off with minor ailments like stomach upset and drowsiness, while hoping to distract the listener with film of former sufferers now living *la vida grande*. Then long lists of horrific possibilities were presented in what often sounded like a speed-reading competition. Finally, when the viewer was bored, or channel surfing, or slipping into the powder room to take a pill, the announcers get down to the big stuff. Heart failure and death.

The oddest thing was that the people in these commercials seemed so happy.

All of them.

Lynne remembered the first colored Band-Aids that were introduced in the fifties, with a nice catchy jingle. They hadn't stocked "Stars and Strips" at the Exchange, which now that she thought about it was somewhat ironic. The Band-Aids were, however, available off base, in better drugstores. She had somehow managed to convince her mother that they needed a box, even though Lynne was not the kind of kid who suffered many cuts and scrapes. She'd manufactured or overstated a few at the time, though, just to be able to use some of those cool, color-coordinated Band-Aids.

Which, now that she thought about it, wasn't all that different from today's pharmaceutical ads aimed at people who didn't even know they were unwell. Society had moved from Band-Aids and Bactine to Viagra and Cialis.

As she drifted off to sleep, Lynne could hear the advertising jingle running through her mind.

> *Band-Aid Stars and Strips!*
> *Whistle-de-doo, they're keen!*
> *They're red, blue, yellow, too—*
> *Tootle-ee-toot and green!*

❧

**ELLEN** Gainsborough had barely slept in the past forty-eight hours, and she was beginning to despair of ever getting a decent night's sleep again. She was up and down through the night, brewing herbal tea, sitting out on the porch, wandering the Dos Hermanas and Little Sister Court grounds, attempting double-crostics from the book she'd bought after dinner last night in Key West.

Nothing worked.

She wouldn't have minded putting in an hour or two on a treadmill or elliptical trainer, but she had no idea where to find either, and Little Sister Key didn't offer a twenty-four-hour gym. As far as she knew, Little Sister Key didn't offer a twenty-four-hour anything.

This was a quiet place, and every time Ellen had been down to visit her mother, she had found herself bored silly after the first day. Usually she got around that by taking her mother into Key West for a fancy dinner, or a visit to some of the art galleries, or a sunset cruise. They'd taken a day trip to Dry Tortugas once, and Ellen remembered her mother on deck as they approached the island, smiling in sheer joy, leaning out into the wind by the rail. The anachronistic nineteenth-century brick fort had seemed to rise directly out of the ocean, left incomplete once it became clear that the entire island was sinking from the weight of the construction.

Ellen was furious with the police. Why couldn't she go in her mother's home? They'd been tight mouthed with her throughout the day. She knew more about her mother's death from the local fish-wrap newspaper than she did from the police. The cause of death was a blow to the back of the head. And the "foreign object" found in her mother's throat, that basset hound detective had told her, was a small vial used for packaging pills. And that was all he'd say.

Her insomnia made her even more annoyed at the uncomplicated snoring that came out of Ed's room. She needed his counsel, and his solace. She wouldn't even mind another argument about just how much to tell the police. It was one thing to protect Mother's privacy, Ed had said at dinner, and another to play into the hands of whoever had killed her by holding back.

"We don't know why she was killed," he had pointed out. "And without knowing that, we don't have any way to tell what is or isn't important."

"But her reputation," Ellen had argued.

Ed made a sharp gesture with his hand, brushing that argument aside. "She's a murder victim, Ellen, and that changes everything."

A murder victim.

Murder victim, murder victim.

Murdervictim, murdervictim, murdervictimmurdervictimmurdervictim.

With that uneasy mantra flowing through her brain, Ellen finally fell asleep.

## Chapter 24

**LYNNE** had nicked her finger somehow yesterday, and given the general level of catastrophe, she figured it was a wonder it hadn't gone septic on her. But despite the fact that the stupid Stars and Strips jingle kept ricocheting around her brain, she had managed to get to breakfast without dressing the minor cut.

The Orchid Lodge breakfast room was sparsely populated, and only a faint scent of antiseptic lingered as a reminder of the chaos yesterday afternoon. Lynne remembered seeing a first aid kit on the wall outside the bathrooms, and she went back to that hallway in search of a Band-Aid. The kit looked homemade, rather than pre-packaged, and it resembled a small bathroom cabinet, with enough small rust spots to suggest it had been there a while. Indeed, its metal cover didn't open easily, but once Lynne swung the door open, she found herself staring at its contents, her cut forgotten once again.

She thought about going out and looking for Peggy, then

realized that the fastest way to reach her friend was probably by cell phone. Peggy picked up on its second ring.

"I'm eating breakfast," Lynne said carefully, mindful of the others in the room. "Do you think you could come by here for a moment?"

"You sound . . . odd. Is everything okay?"

"Okay enough. But I think you're going to want to see this."

Peggy showed up a few minutes later, looking worried. Lynne set aside her doughnut and led her back to the hallway and the first aid kit.

"I just opened this," she said, "and look what's here."

Peggy frowned. "Looks like a pretty standard kit to me. It was here when we came and it seemed like a sensible thing to have, but I've never used it and I'm not sure that anybody else has, either."

The cabinet held all manner of bandages and gauze in different sizes, a packaged sling, alcohol pads, antibiotic ointment, cold and hot compresses that activated on opening, various types of tape, scissors, tweezers, and rubber gloves. It also contained Alka-Seltzer, Maalox, Tylenol, and a small bottle that Peggy lifted out and held, recognition dawning.

"Ipecac!"

"Exactly."

Neither one of them needed to be told what Ipecac was, or what it did. Though out of pediatric favor these days, according to Lynne's daughter-in-law, Lynne and Peggy and millions of other women had raised their children with this little bottle waiting in the medicine chest just in case. Ipecac was used to induce vomiting after ingestion of poison.

Peggy opened the bottle. "Empty," she said, frowning.

"But it could be that it just evaporated over the years. This first aid chest looks like it's been here forever."

"Do you think it's this simple?" Lynne asked, reaching in to get a Band-Aid. This time she wasn't going to forget. She smeared some of the antibiotic gel on her finger and bandaged it neatly. "That somebody just picked this up and dumped it in something people were eating or drinking—" She stopped, aware of the look on Peggy's face. "What?"

"I haven't had a chance to tell you this yet. It seems that the most likely source of the nausea was the crangria."

"Oh, no!" That would teach Lynne to help with other people's parties. Or to share her favorite recipes.

"Jim Tyler, my manager, talked to as many people as he could find who were at the party. He made up some kind of spreadsheet with all the info, and he told me this morning that the only thing that those who became ill had in common was drinking crangria. The people who were the sickest apparently drank the most. Now, there *were* three people who barfed but hadn't drunk crangria. He seemed to think, and I'm inclined to agree with him, that those people might have been part of the ripple effect that group nausea produces."

"Would this little bottle hold enough to do the job?" Lynne wondered.

"Who knows? But I called that Detective Ruiz this morning and told him about the crangria. He wasn't all that interested, actually. Nobody died, who cares? But I'm going to call him again and tell him they should test for Ipecac in the crangria."

"Do you still have some of it here?"

Peggy nodded grimly.

"Good. If he doesn't come up with something, let's find a private lab and get it tested ourselves."

"Do we do that before or after Rick and I brace for litigation?"

Lynne hugged Peggy. "Don't be silly. It was just a little incident. You might want to call your insurance agent to be on the safe side. But I bet that everybody will forget all about it."

She hoped she made her tone firm and compassionate, because she didn't believe a word that she was saying.

※

**WHEN** Jenna meandered out of their cottage midmorning, she found Dan finishing up his morning tasks with the birds. Jenna hadn't bothered to get up for breakfast, a meal she normally skipped anyway, and she'd stopped paying much attention to the time.

"Hey, sleepyhead," Dan told her softly. He had Melissa, the cockatoo, on his shoulder as he serviced her cage. "Didn't think I'd get to see you this morning."

"I'm on vacation," Jenna said. "And I'm also on West Coast time, though I think I've pretty much shaken that off."

"Hello," Melissa said. "I love you."

Jenna laughed. "What would happen if I asked to hold her?"

Dan frowned for a minute. "Well, she might poke your eyes out. She's very jealous, and she knows I spent most of yesterday with you." He put a hand up to his shoulder and Melissa obediently climbed on. He brought the bird over to Jenna's shoulder and set her down gently. "Or she might express affection."

"I love you," said Melissa.

Jenna chuckled as she turned her head to see the feathery creature just inches from her eyes. It was a good thing she wasn't wearing spaghetti straps. "Would this be a diversionary tactic while she takes aim at my eyes?"

He reached down into the box at his feet and came up with a small cluster of grapes. "You could feed her."

"Bunch of grapes," Melissa said, leaning toward Dan, her eye on the fruit. Jenna had always thought of birds as having beady eyes, but for some reason she found this gesture mildly appealing and the eye she could see rather pretty. This was getting out of hand.

Dan handed Jenna the grapes, which she offered to Melissa, who took the entire cluster of half a dozen, held it in one nasty-looking claw, and began to lunch.

"You up for a dive this afternoon?" Dan asked. "Chop's down around Looe Key, and I think we could probably get down to the *Adolphus Busch* with pretty good visibility."

"I'd love it. Would mid-afternoon work? I'm supposed to go into Key West with my mom today, but we ought to be back by three thirty or four."

Dan smiled, and Jenna realized that she was liking that smile a lot, hoping to see it often. "That'd be just fine. You want to call when you're back?"

"Sounds good. Anything I need to know beforehand?"

He furrowed his brow in mock concentration. "An appreciation for Budweiser is not required. But beer makes a pretty good dive chaser."

❧

**ELLEN** Gainsborough realized she was overdressed. Normally being in professional attire provided a sense of security, an anchor to her work and her world. Here in the Keys, it was kind of silly. Still, she wanted to be taken seriously, and women in well-tailored suits usually had an advantage in that regard.

Ed, however, had effortlessly managed to project just the right combination of professionalism and casual island attitude in Dockers and a pressed, long-sleeved shirt, open at the collar. He had left the navy blazer behind in their room when he realized how hot it was today. In the poorly ventilated interview room at the police station where the Gainsborough siblings sat with Detective Rafael Ruiz and Detective Jackson, it didn't matter much what the weather was. There were no windows.

"My mother has been murdered," she said, in her iciest tone, "and all you people seem to care about is this silly little drug distribution thing. Why aren't you looking for burglars, or drug abusers, not elderly pharmaceutical users? Have there been other murders like this one? And what about men she might have been seeing, somebody in a jealous rage or something?"

"We're doing the best we can, Ms. Gainsborough," Detective Ruiz said.

"That's exactly what I'm afraid of."

*Chapter 25*

**ON** her informal list of overrated writers, Jenna placed Ernest Hemingway in the top five. His writing seemed to her to be all boozy bravado and bull fighting and pointless exercises in alcoholism and machismo. His simplistic style left her cold and his personal life was deplorable.

She couldn't, however, be altogether negative about a man who had been so devoted to cats.

"It's a myth, really," Peggy had told her yesterday at breakfast, a meal that seemed to have occurred a week ago. "Those six-toed cats aren't really direct descendants from the original ones at his place. It's a nice legend. And sure, there were a few cats there when he lived here. There were cats all over the place. Key West is an island and a port. Ships and boats carried cats because they also carried rats."

"But everybody knows about it," Jenna had argued. "They're actually *called* Hemingway cats. I've seen pictures. Their feet look like fuzzy coasters."

"Oh, there've been polydactyl cats around Key West for a long time, no doubt about that. It has a fair amount to do with inbreeding, which is always a risk on an island." Peggy launched a discussion of the genetics of poly-dactylism—an overabundance of toes—that left Jenna's eyes glazed over and sent her mother back to the coffee pot.

"Hemingway actually had a lot more cats at his place in Havana," Peggy concluded, "with an undetermined toe count. That's not what they'll tell you when you visit the house, though. After the house here became a tourist at-traction, they started to make a big deal out of it. I under-stand that for a while they were even selling six-toed kittens to support the herd, but I don't think they do that anymore."

Jenna had spent some time looking at several framed black-and-white glossy photographs that Peggy had hang-ing on a wall of the Orchid Lodge. They showed Heming-way holding various cats, sometimes even in his lap while he appeared to be working. Jenna had lived too long in LA to be overly impressed with celebrity glossies, which hung everywhere but the offices of urologists, exterminators, and the IRS. Hemingway, however, had been dead a long time, and had lived in an era when taking publicity pho-tographs was unusual enough to be a big deal.

Remembering this morning that he'd cared enough about those felines to pose with them went a long way to-ward justifying the expense of the tour, which they discov-ered was significant when they arrived in Key West in late morning. Every time you blinked in the Keys, it seemed, somebody had a hand out to relieve you of another ten- or twenty-dollar bill.

When the official tour ended, Jenna told her mom she

wanted to stick around for a while, make friends with some of the cats. "That shouldn't be hard," her mother told her, "so long as you don't trip on them. I want to go down the block to the Audubon House, but I can wait if you want to come along."

Jenna considered sharing Dan's opinions of John J. Audubon, which she realized with a start she had appropriated as her own, without question. She contained herself and shook her head. "I was thinking I'd find a back corner here and call Larry. I promised him I'd call from the grounds here. He's a big Hemingway aficionado."

Larry owned first editions of all the master's works and had several books that were signed. In the modern era, when even works on plumbing repair and gallstones were occasion for book signings, it came as a shock to realize that the craze of author signings was a relatively new phenomenon. There weren't all that many signed books by authors who'd been dead nearly half a century.

After her mother left the grounds, Jenna headed to the gift shop, pausing to speak softly to a large cage full of adorable kittens, presumably polydactyl. In the gift shop she found what she'd been hoping for—copies of the same glossies hanging in the Dos Hermanas breakfast room. She purchased several as souvenirs for Larry, then wandered outside and found a tucked-away bench in a remote corner of the grounds. The bench was only half occupied by a sleeping gray cat, curled in a position that rendered toe-counting impossible.

She rapidly computed the time difference and figured he'd probably still be at home. He picked up on the second ring.

"Jenna! Twice in two days—we don't talk to each other

that often when you're home. So what's happening? How was dinner with the diver guy?"

"Quite nice," she said. "And right now I'm sitting under a palm tree on the grounds of Ernest Hemingway's Key West home."

"Tell me absolutely everything," Larry instructed, and Jenna could picture him pushing back in his big comfy armchair, lifting his feet onto the matching ottoman.

She told him about the swimming pool that third wife Pauline had chipped out of solid coral while Hemingway was in Spain during the Civil War, a $20,000 indulgence that took five days to fill and got funky fast with no chemicals in the water. She described the writer's second-story office, once reached by a hanging rope bridge from the second story, all very Tarzan. "It's hard to say how much it's been changed," she told him, "but I think it's probably a pretty safe bet that there weren't any *Reader's Digest Condensed Books* in the office when he was using it. His typewriter's there, and some very odd paintings that superimpose a Hemingway ghost on the room."

"Isn't it amazing how easily you can screw something like that up?" Larry asked. "How hard would it have been to get some real books?"

"Well, there are real books in the upstairs hall. Signed to 'Hem,' many of them. But his main library is still in Havana."

"Does Castro read English?" Larry huffed. "What a waste! They're probably rotting in some damp cellar."

"Now that you mention it," Jenna told him, "something like that happened here. Pauline or somebody boxed up a lot of his stuff and stored it in the back of Sloppy Joe's bar. When they finally opened the boxes, there were manuscripts and papers and letters and a lot of them were in pretty sorry shape."

"*Islands in the Stream,*" Larry said. "Published posthumously."

"Apparently so. And before I forget, there was something else that was moved here from Sloppy Joe's when the place was remodeled. They had the old urinals lying in the street outside during a remodel and Hemingway hauled one back here to put in the yard. He said he'd put so much money down it that it belonged to him."

"And it's still there? A *urinal?*"

"Uh huh. Gussied up with some tiles and a Mexican urn. You know, Larry, I bet Key West was pretty interesting back then. Hardly anybody was here, just artists and writers and reprobates."

"What else?" he demanded.

She told him about the wine cellar that Hemingway and some friends had emptied in a massive binge that went on for days as he moved out during his third divorce. Hemingway had, it seemed, selected a different wife for each of his major domiciles: Martha in Cuba, Hadley in Paris, Pauline in Key West, and Mary in Cuba and Idaho.

"And for some reason," she went on, "they framed fifteen cancelled checks and a delinquent tax receipt from 1931. Not special checks, either, just mundane housekeeping stuff."

"And the cats? I know you're just itching to tell me about the cats."

About a week before Jenna had left for Florida, Larry had happened upon her using the store computer to do some online research before her departure. He showed up as she was visiting the Hemingway House Web site, which featured photographs of a couple dozen cats. most identified by literary or artistic names: Zelda Fitzgerald, Pablo Picasso, Simone de Beauvoir, Archibald MacLeish, Charlie Chaplin.

They had all looked quite happy, those pictured cats, in many cases snoozing contentedly. Jenna hadn't been surprised to find the actual cats equally relaxed, ignoring the crush of tourists with the ease of long practice.

Jenna laughed. "I'm sitting here next to Emily Dickinson. They're everywhere, Larry. Mostly sleeping, of course. They *are* cats. But they're on chairs and beds that are behind ropes to keep the public away. They pretty much have the run of the joint. And the truly amazing part is that none of the furniture looks scratched and I haven't smelled cat pee once."

※

**JOHN** Haedrich wasn't the kind of guy who had premonitions, or intuitive hunches, or vague shadows of forewarning. He was a forthright and determined young man who had always functioned with a belief that the best way to get from X to Y was a straight line.

This made his reaction to George Wyman all the more puzzling. From that first chance meeting on the Dos Hermanas lawn, John had felt a strong sense of connection, an impression that he was coming into the home stretch of his quest. When he'd tried to communicate this feeling to Diane, she had encouraged him politely, making it pretty clear that she didn't share this excitement.

John had called Wyman this morning and made an appointment, figuring it was better to telephone than to just show up. Wyman had greeted John as an old friend and set their meeting for two o'clock. That would give John a

chance to go over to the rescheduled Craft Fair in Little
Sister Court with Diane first.

As they walked toward the Court now, he started second-
guessing himself. "Maybe this isn't such a great idea."

Diane squeezed his hand. "Who knows? You certainly
ought to ask. And anyway, sounds like you had a good
time talking to him."

"Oh, I did. I bet he could go on for hours. He's like a pirate encyclopedia. I used to think I knew a lot about piracy
and shipwrecks. He's like some kind of professor on the
subject. He said he's got a copy of *Buccaneers of America*
in its first publication, in Dutch."

"Really?" She didn't sound too interested.

Diane had agreed, before they heard about the reschedu-
ule, to come along for the meeting with Wyman, though
not with any kind of enthusiasm. But when John suggested
that maybe she could meet him at Wyman's mobile home
after she went to the Fair, she pounced on the idea.

"That sounds great, honey. How long do you think
you'll be?"

John shrugged. "No idea. I could be out of there in five
minutes or it could go on for hours."

"Well, I think he sounds like somebody you'd really
enjoy. If you hit it off with him, you can keep in touch by
email."

"Good point." He looked at Diane, who was wearing a
red-and-white-checked shorts outfit today. She had worn it
a lot last summer. "You sure you're feeling all right?"

"Just fine. Honest."

She did indeed seem to have fully recovered from yesterday's digestive upset. And so had most people, it
seemed. That had been the talk of breakfast today, folks
conversing back and forth from table to table, everybody

working pretty hard to forget that yesterday afternoon this place had been filled with suffering, heaving men and women.

As they walked between the rows of mobile homes now, holding hands, he regarded the dwellings with both curiosity and dismay. Diane's parents were talking about retiring, going someplace warm, and they had seemed almost more excited about this trip than their daughter. For a while, they had hinted about coming along, but nobody had ever come right out and suggested the idea, which he had allowed to quietly fade away.

The Florida retirement idea lingered, however. John wasn't sure how they would work it out. Jim and Leslie Corwin, Diane's parents, didn't have a lot of savings. Both of them had worked for decades at Kellogg's, Jim as a machinist and Leslie in production. Helping four kids through college had eaten up their meager savings. They could sell their house in Battle Creek, of course, but real estate in central Michigan was really cheap by Florida standards. The Corwins would be lucky to end up in a double-wide trailer in a place just like this. Which wouldn't be such a bad deal, actually. It would certainly be nice to have an excuse to come to Florida in the winter. And a place to stay.

He stuck his head briefly inside the Little Sister Court Community Room, kissed Diana goodbye, and headed out. Right on time. He had a feeling George Wyman would appreciate punctuality.

*Chapter 26*

JENNA had hoped to be able to dive the *Adolphus Busch,* and today the weather cooperated.

The winds had begun to slow yesterday in midmorning, and had died down altogether by the time they emerged from the water. Since then the air had remained still. Dan had predicted that there'd probably be fewer divers out later in the day, since most dive trips were only offered in the morning.

Even so, when they arrived at Looe Key mid-afternoon today, they found other divers, including a group dive.

Dan dropped anchor at a respectable distance from the others, sharing the mooring with another small boat. Jenna felt a wonderful anticipation as they put on their gear without saying a word. They reviewed hand signals, and Dan cautioned her to signal a stop anytime she was unsure. She'd be going deeper than she'd dived in years, and diving her first sunken vessel.

"Ready?" he asked then. She nodded, adjusted her

equipment, then dropped backward off the side of the boat into the water.

The world changed instantly. Part of the magic of diving for Jenna was the strange adjustment in vision that came from being underwater, regarding undersea life through a mask. This world moved with a slow and languid sense of suspension.

Today's descent was slower than yesterday's, stopping at intervals until they could see first the mast of the *Adolphus Busch* and then the rest of the ship. The mast was at fifty feet, the main deck at eighty. Jenna felt an exhilaration as they started below the water, her breath slow and easy. She had always secretly yearned to make this kind of dive. Or, even better, the type of dive where you needed a drysuit and a ton of specialized equipment. But for the moment, this was fine.

The *Adolphus Busch* sat on the ocean floor, a bit askew, settled into the sand. It wasn't difficult at all to make the mental leap from this retired freighter to a sunken Spanish galleon, a foundered pirate sloop, a storm-ruined Nantucket whaler. The boat stood upright, home to schools of brightly colored fish that moved through its open passageways, along its sunken staircases. Dan had told her to watch for a huge Jewfish— variously reported to weigh anywhere from three hundred fifty to four hundred fifty pounds—that hung around the *Adolphus Busch.* She hoped to see it before it came close enough to startle her. She didn't want to seem too much of a landlubber, after all.

Time disappeared.

**BACK** on the surface, Jenna felt a stronger bond toward Dan than she had the first time they'd dived. Whether this had to do with having spent more time together exploring and decompressing, or a heightened physical attraction or the shared danger of being far below the surface of the ocean she wasn't sure.

Stripped of her wetsuit, minus flippers, wearing only a bikini and a smile, Jenna felt utterly at home.

Dan took care of the equipment and directed her to an ice chest that turned out to hold an assortment of imported bottled beers. As Jenna pulled out two, Dan handed her his Swiss Army knife. She opened both and handed his over.

"I love watching sunset on the water," Jenna said.

"It's pretty amazing," Dan agreed. "My favorites are the ones when you're on the water and there's no land in sight anywhere. Those are the purest sunsets and sunrises—just you and God's ocean."

Jenna hesitated a moment, then decided not to be coy. "You feel like getting some Cuban food tonight?"

He smiled. "I'd love to, but I've got to go take care of some business for the next couple of days. I'll be heading out pretty soon after I get you back. You'll still be here day after tomorrow?"

"Yeah."

"Then how about a rain check?"

She agreed, surprised at how disappointed she felt.

❧

**JOHN** hesitated for a moment outside of George Wyman's mobile home.

It was well-tended, if a bit barren, which was unusual in this land where almost everything was smothered in green. Gravel instead of a lawn, one cactus in a clay pot as vegetation, no chairs set out as an invitation to stop and chat. By contrast, the place right next door was swallowed by a jungle of palms and vines, the vigorous vegetation hacked away at the windows to allow light into the building. That place had a little fountain bubbling outside its door, by a white plastic table and chairs.

The walk from the Community Center, where he'd left Diane on the far side of the complex, had made it clear that Little Sister Court had no particular rules or standards, at least not that were enforced. He'd seen everything from a forlorn, silver Airstream trailer, detached from any vehicle and looking utterly abandoned, all the way up to a fourplex with topiary landscaping, shrubbery cut to look like poodle tails.

He'd have to find out more about that place. *You don't want to be the nicest house in your neighborhood,* his Uncle Geoff had always said. Uncle Geoff was a Realtor, and presumably knew what he was talking about. In any case, being the nicest house on the block hadn't been an issue for John and Diane or either set of their parents.

Wyman opened the door just as John balled his fist to knock. "Come in, come in." He stepped back to let John inside, then closed the door carefully behind him.

There was no foyer, no entry hall. The door opened directly into what seemed to be a combination living room/family room, nearly as Spartan as the exterior. His furniture was angular and tightly upholstered in various shades of brown. A nice leather armchair was aimed at a plasma television hanging on the wall.

The real focal points were on the walls. Four black-and-white Jolly Roger flags were displayed flat on the wall facing the doorway. A broadsword and a cutlass were each mounted on a solid mahogany backing, and a half dozen daggers were displayed on additional wooden bases. The flags and weapons were complemented by framed prints and paintings of piracy. The smell of cigarettes hung in the air, and beneath the décor the walls seemed a bit dingy. A chunky glass ashtray stood beside the chair on a sturdy, solid stand. It was empty, wiped clean, and shiny.

"It was nice of you to take time for me," John said, moving instinctively toward the bladed weapons. Then he looked to his right and found a room that made him blink in wonder.

"Aha! You noticed my playpen," Wyman said, with a smile. "Feel free to take a look."

John had already started toward the room. A five-foot-diameter central table was covered with a detailed and authentic-looking diorama. A small town nestled around a protected harbor in a tropical bay. The lush tropical greenery disappeared off the edges of the table, making it uncertain whether this represented a Caribbean coastline or an island. The focus was on a pair of pirate ships, one facing out of the harbor, the other lying on its side onshore as small figures swarmed around it.

"This is incredible!" John exclaimed, moving in to examine the scene more closely. "Did you do this?"

"Yes." The note of pride was unmistakable.

"It must have taken you a really long time. This is amazing." Each of the dozens of small figures was intricately painted. Here was one with a peg leg, another carrying a parrot on his shoulder. All the figures showed intense and meticulous attention to detail. "And I really like the way you've got the ship careened."

"Not a particularly exciting aspect of pirate life," Wyman said. "But that's why I wanted to feature it. Teredo worms would eat their way right through those wooden hulls. Sometimes they'd have to career a ship three times a year to keep ahead of the little suckers. Of course, they were dangerously exposed while this was going on."

John moved in closer, saw the businesses and houses in the small town. "Does this represent a particular place?"

"Not really. Though some of these other models do." Wyman pointed to some deep shelves along two of the walls. "All of them are accurate in as much detail as possible."

For the first time John noticed that there were other, smaller dioramas, dozens of them, shelved along the wall like so many fancy decorated cakes waiting for pickup in an upscale bakery. "How long have you been working on these?"

He moved close enough to see that while the individual scenes were smaller than the one on the table, the scale was the same and they were equally detailed. He also noticed, for the first time, a work table against one of the walls without shelving. A plundered and burned Spanish galleon was midway through its first coat of paint. "And where do you get the info so the details are accurate?"

Wyman lit a cigarette with a silver lighter. "The information and details come from various artwork and maps of the time. In addition, I have a comprehensive library, which I often consult. Would you like to see it?"

"Absolutely," John said. That was, after all, the ostensible reason for his visit.

John followed Wyman through the open area and down a short hall to the building's end, the relatively large room that would be identified on standard sales brochures as the unit's master bedroom.

It was set up with three sets of double-sided wooden shelving running perpendicular to the end of the unit, nearly from floor to ceiling. A dehumidifier hummed just inside the door. George Wyman flicked on some fluorescent lights, casting everything into unnatural brightness. Most of the shelves, John could see now, were full. And the books—could this really be?—appeared to be organized by the Dewey decimal system. Each aisle of shelves had a pair of numbers at its end.

The size of this collection floored John. There were shelves and shelves of history books, all neatly aligned at the edge of the shelves. It was overwhelming.

"You've got a lot of chemistry books," John noted.

"That's how I made my living. My vocation." Wyman gestured toward the shelves of pirate books. "And these are my avocation."

This section, the largest of all by far, dealt with piracy, shipwrecks, and buried treasure. As John tilted his head to the side and began reading the titles on spines of books, Wyman moved to a large shelving unit with closed glass doors, next to a small oak reading desk. He donned white gloves, then one by one removed cherished old volumes and set them carefully on the desk.

"These are my pride and joy," Wyman said, and John came to look, holding his hands together behind his back so as not to touch anything he wasn't supposed to. Wyman's white gloves spooked him a bit.

Wyman showed off his prizes with a fervor that took John aback. An early English translation of *Buccaneers of America* by Esquemeling. Chatterton's *Romance of Piracy.* Captain Charles Johnson's *A General History of the Robberies and Murders of the Most Notorious Pyrates.* He had several editions of this, including one from the eighteenth century that was kept along with the Dutch version of *Buc-*

*caneers of America* in an even more protected environment, a special climate-controlled bookcase.

"Where did you get all these?" John asked.

"I've been collecting for a long time, son. Never married, don't have any children. That's what eats up your paycheck. I put my money into history instead."

"I don't know what to say," John said, wandering down one of the aisles, passing a large section of true crime books, then moving into fiction, which consisted mostly of mysteries and thrillers.

"Don't have to say anything. It's nice to be able to show this all to somebody who understands what it's about."

John had a sudden flash of sadness. George Wyman wasn't old, really, but he wasn't young, either. If he didn't have any family to appreciate his collection, what would happen to it? It would be awful to just set these beautiful old books out in a yard sale.

"Esquemeling has a particularly complete biography of Sir Henry Morgan, one of several pirates who managed to achieve knighthood and avoid execution." He carefully replaced the book in its sealed case. "Why don't we go back out to the main room?"

The main room. Not the family room, because this man evidently had no family to consider. He was so clearly solitary, so obviously alone.

"Would you like a pop or something?" Wyman asked as they returned to the main room.

"No thanks, I'm fine."

Wyman sat in his leather chair and John perched awkwardly on the edge of a brown sofa covered in a coarse, nubby weave.

John took a deep breath. "I guess this is going to sound crazy," he began.

❧

**ELLEN** had braced herself for her mother's presence when the police finally let her and Ed into the coach. She had feared that the interior would seem somehow forlorn, but what she hadn't anticipated was the swath of disruption that crime scene technicians had created through the place. Dark fingerprint powder was scattered everywhere except the black lacquered dining room furniture, which was dusted in white.

Ellen gasped in dismay as she looked around the place and pictured her mother's disapproval. Mother had always been a fanatic housekeeper. This disarray was enormously unsettling.

"Is there some reason why the air conditioning isn't turned on in here?" Ellen asked Detective Jackson. "Or at least the windows opened? This place is musty, and I know that Mother wouldn't have kept it that way, not to mention all this mess."

"We've tried to leave things alone as much as possible," Detective Jackson told her. "But I don't see any problem with opening a window." He crossed to the kitchen and opened a window over the sink. The view through that window was solid green with an occasional splash of color. Beyond the foliage, Ellen knew, was the next coach over. Darcy had created her own tropical tableau with a mixture of exotic and ordinary plants.

"There wasn't anything about people breaking in here, was there?" Ed asked. "Are you satisfied that Mother wasn't killed in here?"

Ellen stifled a gasp. Ed was being much more plainspoken here than he had been at the station. He had his hands in his pockets, she noticed. He'd suggested that she do the same, but she didn't have pockets in the more comfortable slacks and blouse she had changed into after the session at the police station. At least not pockets sufficiently large for her hands.

"Not at all, sir," the detective said. "We just left things exactly as they were. We removed a few things from the dining room, but there wasn't anything to suggest violence in here, and the crime scene analysis didn't come up with any surprises. We're hoping that the two of you might look around and notice details that we wouldn't recognize as significant."

Ed agreed for both of them. Ellen was finding it difficult to speak. She trailed her brother throughout the place, down the hall, into the bedrooms, back to the kitchen and living room and dining room.

At the end of this brief trip, Ed turned to the detective. "I didn't see anything that would help. Ellen, did you?"

She shook her head, still struck mute and fighting tears.

❧

**LYNNE** watched as John Haedrich deposited his wife Diane and fled the relocated Craft Fair. The young man looked as if he were dodging a bullet when he darted out the doorway, and perhaps that was exactly what was happening. This wasn't the kind of function that most men found appealing, or even tolerable.

Diane appeared to have fully recovered from her bout with nausea the previous afternoon, as had several of the women who were working at the relocated Craft Fair. Diane was dressed more comfortably than she had been yesterday, and more casually as well. She had a way of holding herself that made Lynne imagine that Diane would look cute and friendly in brown grocery sacks, taped together.

Today's presentation was stripped down a bit from yesterday's setup in the Orchid Lodge. Bing Crosby sang "Christmas in Killarney" from a boom box near the door and the mood was deliberately festive. People were once again dressed in their holiday finery and some women, Lynne noticed, wore different holiday outfits altogether. It made her wish that she had brought some of her holiday clothing along.

She went first to the Charity Christmas Tree, which she had intended to visit yesterday, before being pre-empted by the group barf-a-thon. The tree, she thought, was a great idea—a four-foot artificial pine standing on a table, laden with a wild array of ornaments. Many folks from the Court and a few from Dos Hermanas had donated ornaments—some new, some hand-crafted, others very old. Yesterday, Lynne had just missed out on the chance to buy a trio of beautiful blown-glass ornaments from nineteenth-century Germany. She'd overheard a woman telling the lucky buyer that the translucent globes had belonged to her husband's family, but none of their kids wanted them.

The mechanics of the charity tree were quite simple. Each ornament on the tree was for sale, and all were priced just a touch below retail. All proceeds from the purchase of these ornaments would go to an environmental group based in Islamorada, up in the Middle Keys. Lynne, who hadn't noticed much to indicate an interest in environmentalism down here, found this a welcome change.

Lynne went to the tree now and carefully removed an intricately carved and meticulously inlaid wooden, three-dimensional snowflake—an alien concept here in the land of eternal summer. As she removed it from its space between a glass angel blowing a golden trumpet and a rather creepy Santa head that seemed to be made out of a desiccated apple, she was conscious of someone beside her.

"That sure is pretty," a young female voice said.

Lynne turned and found Diane Haedrich.

🌿

**JENNA** was annoyed with herself nearly as much as she was annoyed with Dan. She had no reason to expect him to stick around, after all. She'd paid him for two dives and accepted a crab dinner. That didn't constitute any kind of commitment.

But she didn't like the casual way he had brushed off her invitation for dinner tonight. Would he have mentioned his unavailability if she hadn't made it an issue? Or would he just have been gone, leaving her to notice that somebody else was tending the birds tomorrow morning?

And what made her think that some Florida boat bum had any particular interest in her?

*Chapter 27*

**GEORGE** Wyman was thoroughly enjoying the afternoon.

John Haedrich's interest in piracy seemed both genuine and well-researched. Better than George would have expected, to be sure. So many people seemed to have gotten their perceptions of piracy from *Peter Pan* or *Treasure Island* or even that recent film atrocity, *Pirates of the Caribbean*. The use of computer-generated ghouls went far beyond the limits of responsible portrayal.

John reminded him of another young man he had once known, a fellow who'd also been intensely interested in Caribbean buccaneers. So he wasn't entirely surprised when John sat down awkwardly after visiting the library and said, "I guess this is going to sound crazy."

"Maybe, maybe not. No way to tell until you spit it out now, is there?"

John's smile was awkward and tentative. He was slight and a bit gangly, the sort of guy George had seen a lot in his corporate days—supervisors, accountants, behind-the-scenes management types. The comparison wasn't surprising, actually, since Kellogg's was a corporate entity similar to Kimberly-Clark.

"You were asking me before how I got so interested in piracy. Part of what I told you is true, but there's more to it. I remember always being drawn to stories about pirates as a little kid, and as far back as I can remember, my grandfather was really interested as well. He was always talking about buried treasure and pirate booty, and I guess my grandmother just wasn't very interested."

John leaned back a bit on the couch. "Nobody was, to tell the truth, except me. So I read books about pirates and watched old Errol Flynn movies with Granddad on TV. I made myself a buccaneer's sword, and some daggers. You know how they say, 'armed to the teeth'?" He stopped and grinned. "Well, of course you know! Usually I have to explain what—Anyway, my dad cut the sword and cutlass and knives out of plywood and I figured out how to file and sand them so that when I painted them they looked like actual blades."

"Sounds fascinating," George said, and he thought it did. What would it have been like to grow up in this kind of environment? He had been an adult when he came to the world of shipwrecks and buried treasure and adventure on the high seas. His own childhood had been dominated by a strange mix of getting in trouble and sports, sports and getting in trouble. Participating in street softball as a kid, all the while following and watching local teams. He'd always had an encyclopedic recall for baseball statistics.

He remembered now, with a certain detachment, how television had arrived in the middle of his life, and changed everything. Now he could watch games endlessly on TV. No more radio announcers, no more waiting for the next day's papers to find out who won.

His TV habit had grown like a hydra over the years. Here, at Little Sister Court, his satellite dish system allowed him to get pretty much any sporting event in the world. When he first got cable back in Appleton, he had binged on sports. After a while, though, he focused his interests.

Any televised hockey. The Green Bay Packers, of course, and the Braves, for sentimental reasons, decades after they deserted Milwaukee for Atlanta. The Cubs and the White Sox. No basketball since Michael Jordan retired. No tennis, no golf.

The satellite dish fed one part of his personality. The other part lived and breathed history. And the two coexisted pretty well in one body and one brain.

"I just found all this out recently," John went on, "when my father died. He had cancer and he was sick for a long time. Toward the end, he called me into his bedroom and gave me a letter that his father had given him when he died. Dad said that he wouldn't have given it to me at all, except that he'd promised his own father he'd either act on the information or pass it on to me. He chose Plan B, and here I am."

"What do you mean?"

"Well, it sounded so screwy that I can see why my father didn't do anything. Dad was a very serious man and I think my grandfather embarrassed him sometimes. He was very . . . exuberant. Heck, he even embarrassed *me* sometimes. Anyway, the letter said that my grandfather knew where there was buried treasure on an island in the Florida Keys, under a banyan tree at a fish camp at Mile Marker

Twenty-Six. Which is here, of course. Little Sister Key. And Dos Hermanas was originally a fish camp."

"Very interesting," George said. It was way beyond interesting. It was downright astonishing. "And how is your search going?"

"Well, that's the thing. I've got a pretty good metal detector and I've been systematically covering land here and around the key. I do it mostly at night so I don't have to answer a lot of questions about what I'm doing. Diane—my wife—says I'm crazy to be doing this."

"She may have a point," George told him. "And there's been a lot of development here over the years. When did your grandfather tell your dad about this?

John stopped to think. "Granddad died when I was about twelve. And Dad passed away a year and a half ago, on Memorial Day weekend."

"What happened to your grandfather?"

"He fell off the roof. He was cleaning leaves out of the gutters and somehow he slipped. It broke his back and he was in the hospital a long time. We thought he was getting better, but then he took a turn for the worse and passed away. But before he died, he made my dad take a solemn vow that he would tell me when I turned twenty-one. He didn't, though. Waited till he knew he was dying and even then he was reluctant."

"Sounds like a pretty cold trail. As far as you know, did either of them—your father and grandfather—come to look for whatever it was?"

"Not that I know about. Doesn't mean it didn't happen, of course."

"Did your grandfather say anything about whatever it was that was buried here?"

"Not that my father told me. I always figured it was pirate treasure. And I thought that maybe you'd know something. You know, a local legend about some pirates leaving a treasure here. Or something about a fortune that somebody already found."

George shook his head. "Don't know about any local legends, son, about fortunes lost or found. And it would be tough to bury anything on this key. Coral's mighty hard, and you'd really have to really work at chipping out a place deep enough."

"Oh, well," John said, disappointment turning the two syllables into a lament.

"Hate to burst your bubble, but Little Sister Key is coral for the most part. I suppose it's possible. But the other problem with this buried treasure idea is that it wasn't easy for any ships to reach shore past all the reefs in the Keys, even in a sloop or schooner that didn't need much depth. Those reefs were just as treacherous for pirates as for anybody else. That's why the wreckers did so well."

"I hadn't thought about that," John said slowly. "But I guess it makes sense."

"A couple of centuries ago," George went on, "when the Caribbean had a lot of pirate activity, it was mostly to the east of here. It made more sense to stay around the Dominican Republic and Haiti, Tortuga, Jamaica, the Bahamas, et cetera. Cuba, too, south of here. Those places all had plenty of pirate activity, both on land and at sea. Up around Fort Myers there was Jose Gaspar, and there are rumors about where he hid his fortune. Quite a few islands up there, actually, but none of them are near the Keys. He did say the Keys?"

"Yes, sir."

"And Mile Marker Twenty-Six?"

"Yes." John sighed. "I guess I've known all along this

was a wild goose chase. I should have listened to Diane." He looked at his watch, startled. "I probably ought to go find out where she is, what she's spending all our money on. Thanks for"—he waved an arm—"all this. It's really very interesting."

"Come back any time. Bring the little woman along if you'd like. The pleasure was all mine," George Wyman said, and he meant it.

※

**LYNNE** was pleased to have connected with Diane Haedrich by the Charity Christmas Tree, with its wide range of donated ornaments.

"These are pretty amazing ornaments, aren't they?" Lynne said. "I think that a lot of them probably tell a story."

Diane laughed as she removed a six-inch parrot that seemed to be covered in actual feathers, vivid bits of emerald and turquoise and scarlet. "The story this one is telling is, 'Buy me!'"

"It's a beauty," Lynne agreed. "Do you think somebody made it from molted feathers from the birds over at Dos Hermanas?"

Diane examined the parrot carefully. "Actually, I think it's probably from feathers that were clipped to keep the birds from flying away. See, this is shorter than you'd expect from how wide the feather is. A feather this wide would be six inches long." She pointed to some feathers on the bird's belly. "These, on the other hand, look like something the birds molted or picked out. One of the parrots is a feather picker. It's a hard habit to break, unfortunately."

"You know a lot about the birds," Lynne said.

Diane shrugged. "I guess. I've always loved them, and these birds here are just astonishing."

"I've been watching for some of the wild parrots that they say live around here, but I haven't seen any yet. Somebody told me that after Hurricane Andrew, all the birds in the Miami zoo flew away."

It seemed to Lynne that if a storm was sufficiently strong to destroy buildings and cages at the zoo, it would be equally hard on small feathered creatures. But it made a nice story and there probably were some emancipated parrots living in the area, as freed of their former responsibilities as any of the people who had landed down here in the Keys, on the edge of nowhere, as far south as you could go without leaving the country.

Lynne and Diane chatted some more, moving from one table to the next. Lynne liked the girl's openness, her enthusiasm, her—more to the point—willingness to attend the Craft Fair at all.

Jenna had been singularly disinterested, not unlike John Haedrich. Jenna had returned from diving this afternoon in a poor mood, apparently miffed that Dan the parrot wrangler wasn't going to be around for the next couple of days. Lynne thought Jenna's irritation moved beyond simple annoyance at being unable to dive, and she wondered a bit what had and hadn't happened last night.

This trip was a reminder that most of the time she had absolutely no idea what her daughter was doing, or where she was doing it, or with whom.

Jenna now lay basted with coconut oil out by the Dos Hermanas pool, wearing the world's tiniest bikini and listening to music on her headphones. To Lynne, this tableau felt like a flashback to her daughter's sullen-teenager phase, which had presented pretty much the same view and had mercifully lasted less than a year. Jenna looked good when she was tan, and she knew it. Since achieving adulthood, she generally kept enough of a tan base so that she could build on it without too much trouble. Already her skin was darker than when they'd arrived, taking on that deep golden tone that went so well with her blonde hair and blue eyes.

※

**LYNNE** shook herself back to now, to the Craft Fair. She and Diane continued to circle the room together, admiring various items, chuckling at others, building a camaraderie that Lynne found appealing.

Diane was a crafter, it turned out, and Lynne felt her own nascent crafting tendencies rising. "I was a scout leader for years," she confessed, "and even now when it gets to the beginning of December, I find myself wandering the aisles of craft stores, stopping now and again to consider whether a certain project could be done by ten girls in one hour."

Diane laughed. "My mom is the same way. She's a weaver, kind of."

"Kind of?"

"Okay, she's a weaver. What I meant was that it wasn't her job, it was more of a hobby."

They had pretty much exhausted the Craft Fair offerings when Diane looked at her watch with a guilty expression. "I ought to go. I promised John I'd come see the pirate man with him."

"The pirate man?"

"Oh, he's some old guy who lives here. John met him a couple of days ago and they've been talking about pirates.

John has a *major* interest in pirates." She looked at Lynne with a what's-a-girl-gonna-do expression.

"You must mean George Wyman," Lynne said.

"I guess."

"I met him the other day, when he was delivering some kind of trivia game questions to Peggy, the owner of Dos Hermanas. He seemed very knowledgeable. And very full of himself."

Diane cocked her head and looked at Lynne straight on, the brow between her bright dark eyes furrowing. "Really?"

Lynne shrugged. "That was my impression, anyway. I probably caught him at a bad time. It was shortly after we came upon the—" She hesitated, then went on. No need for euphemisms here. Diane had been there by the dock herself, after all, had even offered to do CPR. "The body."

"That sure was creepy," Diane said. "I never saw a dead body before."

Lynne had seen too many. "The best thing you can possibly do is try to forget about it, put it out of your mind. It'd be a shame to spoil your vacation." She realized she was slipping into tour guide mode, and consciously backed away. This was her *own* vacation, dammit. She wasn't under any obligation to help anyone have a good time. Truth be told, she'd been feeling tempted to walk up to somebody at random and be rude, just because she could.

But Diane was already agreeing. "I hear you."

"Would you mind some company?" Lynne asked. "With George Wyman?"

Diane's face reflected hesitation. "I'm not sure—"

"Never mind, that's okay. Didn't mean to put you on the spot. I'll walk back with you, though." She lifted the white box that had come with her wooden filigree snowflake. "And I got my dream ornament."

Diane lifted a brown lunch sack that had been stamped with Christmas trees and pulled out the parrot. She mimicked a bird voice, then. "Pretty bird, pretty bird."

They were both laughing as they left the Fair. Outside the air was warm and balmy, the palm trees swayed in gentle breezes, and exotic floral aromas wafted through the Court. It was a glorious day, in a place where glorious days were taken pretty much for granted.

"I can't believe it's December," Diane confessed. "I keep thinking I'll wake up and be back in Michigan, with my car spinning out on ice."

"Believe," Lynne told her. "And enjoy."

They continued making small talk as they meandered through the Court. They passed the yellow crime scene tape that criss-crossed the entryway at the unit whose mailbox announced: GAINSBOROUGH. NO SOLICITORS.

Diane shuddered. "What do you think happened to her, anyway? I know you said to not think about it, but it's not that easy to forget something like that. I mean, she was just lying there, her legs kind of floating, her arms raised up like she was reaching out to somebody."

"The official cause of death is blunt trauma to her head," Lynne said. "Lots of ways that could happen." As she said it, she realized that while this was technically true, Darcy Gainsborough probably hadn't been kicked by a horse, or thrown into a tree after an auto crash, or dropped from a balcony—though actually, that last wasn't entirely implausible. Second-floor balconies were plentiful around Dos Hermanas, though surely that kind of fall would make noise—a very nasty noise, at that—that somebody would hear.

As they rounded the corner past the Gainsborough trailer, Lynne saw John Haedrich just emerging from a trailer that might have belonged to a desert rat in Plaster City, California, a hamlet near the Mexican border. His back was turned, and he was saying something to the man she recognized as George Wyman. Then Wyman pointed at them and John turned, his face breaking into a broad beam as he saw Diane.

Lynne waved in greeting and stayed with Diane as she crossed the gravel road.

"He's got some great dioramas, Diane," John told his wife. "Incredible pirate scenes. Pirates in the Caribbean."

"If you'd like to see—" Wyman offered.

"We'd love to," Lynne said, making a snap decision. Pirates were interesting, something she hadn't given enough thought to.

She followed Diane and John into the trailer.

❧

**GLORIA** Parker could remember periods of her life when she had been continually exhausted.

When the boys were young, for instance, it had been all she could do to keep up with their car pools and sports teams and laundry and lunches. Not a day went by that she wasn't sorting socks and making PB & Js, usually a dozen at a time, spread out on the kitchen table.

Jamie had been an accident, actually, the last two boys coming so close together that they were almost Irish twins—an expression Gloria would never have known were it not for the shanty Irish maid she had employed full time during those years. Irish twins, Colleen had told her, with a bawdy wink suggesting that her employers were mating like minks, were two babies born within the same twelve-month period. Tom hadn't heard the expression either, but he loved it and to this day referred to Tom Junior and Jamie that way.

A nice stroll down memory lane, she told herself irritably now.

Now, once again she was sleepless and distraught. Tom wasn't around to help her, and that quack in Key West had been so self-righteous when he questioned her need for so much Xanax that she had foolishly stormed out of his office. She had gone straight to Darcy Gainsborough, who promised to add Gloria's pharmaceutical needs to the next order at a price significantly lower than what Gloria had been paying. Tom's health insurance and its COBRA extension had now expired completely, leaving Gloria essentially uninsured. She had been pleasantly surprised by how reasonable Darcy's rates were for what she assured Gloria were U.S.-manufactured medications. Darcy, bless her soul, had even come up with a few pills to hold Gloria over until the next shipment arrived.

Without her prescription, she paced the room. Then, looking out a window, she saw something odd below. She had thought the first time that this caught her attention that it might be somebody walking off sleeplessness akin to her own. The second time the figure had turned and seen her watching, even though she had withdrawn completely.

This time she had her lights off and she could see much more clearly. Yes, it was that young man who had the pretty young brunette wife, the one who teetered on the edge of sluttiness. She was probably a nice enough person, Gloria supposed, if you liked that type.

What was he doing? Moving along with some kind of rod that he swung from side to side the way blind people did as they walked, tapping those long white sticks on the pavement. Some kind of light on his head.

He had no business out there, she knew that for sure. Tomorrow morning, first thing, she was going to inform the authorities.

**JOHN** Haedrich was startled by the knock on their door at seven forty-five in the morning. Surely it was too early for maid service. He and Diane were just getting ready to leave for breakfast, actually. He was trying to contain the disappointment he felt after yesterday's conversation with George Wyman. He'd hoped for some kind of help, some hint that the older man might offer to make sense out of this murky mess. About the only positive note he could take from their conversation was that Wyman hadn't heard of anybody else finding a treasure. Then again, Wyman had only lived here a short period of time.

It was a remarkable mini-museum, however, that otherwise nondescript trailer.

All those books, thousands of them. Those weird miniature island and pirate ship dioramas, the Jolly Roger pirate flags hanging on the walls, the cutlass and broadsword and daggers, all mounted as if there might be an emergency needing fancy blade work.

And buoyed by Wyman's unspoken support, John had gone out again last night and re-examined all the areas that had not responded to his previous tests with the metal detector.

Now, as he pulled open the door in answer to the knock, he saw in the cold, unrevealing eyes of Detective Jackson that his day was about to take a turn for the very worse.

"John Haedrich," the detective said. "We'd like you to come with us down to headquarters so that we can talk."

"About what?"

"We'll have that conversation there."

Diane stepped forward. "What if he doesn't want to go with you?"

Where did she get her nerves? John couldn't imagine standing up to a cop that way. But when he saw the look of condescension that Detective Jackson gave her, he felt the warm rush of rising anger.

The detective addressed John directly. "Will you come with me, sir?"

The "sir" was laying it on a bit strong. But John hadn't done anything wrong. All he was guilty of, really, was following a dream.

"Where are we going?" John asked. "Write this down, Diane. If I'm not back in a couple of hours, come find me."

As if it would do any good.

❧

**LYNNE** was at breakfast, lingering over a second cup of coffee beside the shell-bedecked Christmas tree when Diane Haedrich came into the Orchid Lodge and headed right for her table.

"Morning, Diane," Lynne said. "Where's John?"

She was not expecting Diane to burst into tears, but as the girl choked out the story, it was easy enough to see why she was so upset.

"They just left?" Lynne asked. She was having a hard time imagining anything that might make a pale number-cruncher from a cornflake company of interest to the police. "And they didn't say *why* they wanted to talk to him?"

"No, but I know why. At least I think I do. John has this letter that his father gave him a couple of years ago when he was dying, that came from *his* father, if you can follow this."

"So far so good," Lynne said. "One letter, handed down from grandfather to father to son. Is John an only child?"

"No, but he's the only boy in his family."

"Okay. And this was about—"

"Treasure. I know, I know. It sounds crazy. But that's why we came here, so he could look around and try to find whatever it was. The pirate treasure. The information he had said it was buried under a banyan tree at Mile Marker Twenty-Six. That's Little Sister Key. I thought it was silly, but I figured it was a Florida vacation in the winter, so why not? But ever since we've been here, John's just been fanatical about looking. He's been going at night so people wouldn't ask him what he's doing. He even has one of those hats like miners wear, with a light attached in front."

"And this—the police—has something to do with pirates?" Curiouser and curiouser.

"I don't think so," Diane said, sounding bewildered. "I mean, it's all kind of mixed up in my mind, but the business of what his grandfather did or didn't do couldn't possibly be related to pirates. That all ended centuries ago. Except John says there are still pirates in the South China

Sea, but *that* certainly wouldn't have anything to do with this."

"If John's been out at night, could he have seen something that would incriminate somebody? Did he see anything or anybody the night that Darcy was killed?"

"Not that I know of, and I'm sure he'd have told me. John isn't as rigid about authority figures and right versus wrong as his father was, but he certainly wouldn't keep anything like that to himself. The woman was murdered. And anyway, I *know* John. One time he was driving and a cat ran out in front of the car and he killed it. It was *totally* not his fault. I was in the car with him and there's no way he could have known it was going to happen or been able to stop. But he was depressed for weeks. So even if he did know something about that Mrs. Gainsborough and he was trying to keep it to himself, I'd be able to tell something was wrong. I could tell he was depressed last night, disappointed that Mr. Wyman couldn't help."

Lynne considered. She and Diane had just stepped inside Wyman's mobile home briefly, leaving almost immediately because John had seemed eager to go. She wouldn't have minded sticking around a bit, actually. Anybody who had four different black pirate flags hanging in his living room would probably be pretty interesting. But John had hustled them away. Why? And what could she do to help this confused young woman now?

"Have you eaten anything?" Lynne asked now, her mom genes swinging into action.

Diane shook her head. "I couldn't eat."

"Is your stomach still upset from the other day?"

"Oh, no. I just don't think I could eat."

"Well, let's give it a try. Do you want tea or coffee?

Bagel or muffin? You just stay put and I'll take care of you."

As Lynne bustled about getting Diane a bran muffin and a cup of Earl Grey tea, she wondered what the police could want with John Haedrich. Once Diane had calmed down a bit, she declined Lynne's offer to accompany her to police headquarters. But she did program Lynne's number into her cell phone, and promised to call.

"If he needs a lawyer, what should I do? We can't afford one."

"Then tell them you want an attorney from Legal Aid. Will John be smart enough to ask for a lawyer?"

"Not if he thinks he's innocent. Will they let me talk to him?"

"I have no idea. Probably not. But if you're planted out there in the lobby, it will at least show that somebody's paying attention. Sheri McManus was there for a long time the other day, by herself, and when she finally got back here, she said she wished she'd asked for a lawyer."

"So maybe I ought to get one? Is that what you're saying?"

Lynne took a deep breath. "What I'm saying is that I don't know. But you're sure John doesn't know anything about Darcy Gainsborough's murder?"

"Of course not!"

Lynne was pleased to hear the indignation in Diane's voice, a spunky restoration of what she had observed to be the girl's personality. "Then I'd suggest you go on down there and make yourself at home. Fuss a bit. And if you need anything, call me."

※

**JENNA** couldn't quite believe what she was doing. She was fantasizing about Dan Trenton, missing him, wondering where he was today and why he wasn't available.

It was silly, of course. Beyond silly.

She had no claims on Dan or his time, no reason whatsoever to expect this near-stranger to be at her beck and call. He was an employee, somebody she had paid for diving sessions. He'd been nice to her at Dos Hermanas because she showed an interest in the birds, and because he was a resort employee who was expected to be congenial with guests. He'd offered her dinner because somebody had given him a bunch of stone crab claws.

None of this amounted to anything.

But there was something about being away from home, in the tropics. Even when you knew there was nothing to it, it seemed not only right but almost obligatory to have some kind of romantic dalliance if you could.

She had spent the morning lying in the sun, her headphones playing Sheryl Crow and Sarah McLachlan. She was starting to build up a pretty nice tan, which always gave her pleasure. Sun-streaked blonde hair, bronze skin, blue eyes, bright white smile. It was a combination that had served her well over the years—though not much lately, she had to admit. The dating scene had been pretty grim the past six months or so.

A few months earlier, Jenna had broken off with a guy she was barely interested in, recognizing that she had liked the idea of having a boyfriend much more than she had liked the reality of having this particular boyfriend. The moment she stopped trying to justify an interest in him, a flood of his flaws had washed over the memories of their time together.

Now, woozy from the moist heat but significantly browner,

she stumbled into the Hyacinth unit at Dos Hermanas and showered. What next?

Although her mother seemed quite content to stick around Dos Hermanas, leaving only for the occasional horticultural side trip, Jenna found the place a bit too quiet for her taste, even if it *had* apparently been the scene of a murder. Her mother felt a loyalty to Rick and Peggy Parker, an obligation to help out as their guest. But surely it wasn't reasonable to expect any such assistance from Jenna, and in any case, there was nothing she could do.

She got dressed and left a note announcing her intention of going for a drive. The afternoon sky had clouded up a bit, so she grabbed a light jacket, then headed toward Key West with the top down.

In town, she parked and set out on foot, not headed in any particular direction, not seeking any particular goal. As she meandered around downtown, she began to feel a stronger sense of why this place had been so appealing to so many people, particularly young people. When you got away from Mallory Square and the endless throngs of cruise ship tourists, she began to realize, there was a nice atmosphere.

The explanation seemed to be tolerance, a sense that you could do whatever you wanted so long as you let everybody else do whatever *they* wanted.

The streets were lined with small hotels and B & Bs, and for the most part they appeared quite charming. Nobody was in a hurry, nobody was rude, nobody assumed she was a tourist. The last was particularly nice, because she hated to think she had that bull's eye on her chest announcing she was on vacation. She'd much rather remain anonymous.

In her wanderings, she worked up a bit of a thirst, so it

seemed perfectly reasonable to stop for a beer at a small, mostly open-air bar called Sunset Saloon, despite its lack of any sort of view for experiencing sunset. The bartender poured her a draft beer and brought her a basket of peanuts.

This was different from going alone to a bar in West LA, she quickly realized—less pretentious and less pressured. Poseurs abounded in LA bars, whether you paid attention to them or not. Here nobody seemed to be putting much on. A couple of guys approached her and she deflected them politely. They stayed deflected, which she appreciated. This was the sort of place she could imagine Dan Trenton hanging out, actually, though he wasn't here and finding him hadn't been her intention when she came to town. She tried to remember if he had mentioned the Sunset Saloon, and didn't think so.

Then she decided that maybe she didn't care after all.

After a couple of beers she decided to head on back to Little Sister Key, and it took a moment of concentration to remember just where she'd parked. It was easy enough to get around, but Key West had all kinds of alleyways and mini-streets and dead ends. Not to mention the one-way streets when you were actually driving.

She had almost reached the block where she thought she had left the car when she ran into Diane and John Haedrich, that couple who were staying at Dos Hermanas. They appeared equally startled.

"What are you guys up to?" Jenna asked. She hadn't interacted with them much, other than to acknowledge they were the same general age and in residence at the same resort.

"We're celebrating freedom," Diane said. "John just spent hours talking to the police."

Jenna frowned. "What happened?" She was thinking auto accident, witness to auto accident, car burgled—the kind of things that might involve cops while you were on vacation. Drunk and disorderly would be another, but the Haedrichs didn't seem like that type.

"They thought I might have killed Darcy Gainsborough," John said.

"No!" Jenna's astonishment was genuine. "Why?"

John Haedrich took a deep breath. "Because I've been exploring the grounds with a metal detector at night, trying to find a treasure that my grandfather claimed was buried here."

"What?" Maybe she'd had more to drink than she realized.

He repeated the information and provided more details. "Your mom was really nice to Diane this morning after they took me away for questioning. She was a big help."

Jenna was still trying to process this. There wasn't one single aspect that sounded like normal behavior, except for her mother being in the thick of the fray. Whatever this particular fray had been.

"I'm sure Mom is relieved that you've been released. Are you guys staying here in Key West for a while?"

John laughed. "I plan to just walk up and down the streets breathing fresh air as a free citizen."

"Then have a great time, free citizen."

## Chapter 29

**BY** mid-afternoon, Lynne had almost succeeded in forgetting about all the problems of the last few days.

It was easy to feel cut off and restored, sitting out on the Parkers' patio with Peggy, the warm afternoon sunlight tempered by soft balmy breezes. She had briefly debated going back to her room to put on a swimsuit and work on her tan, as Jenna was doing with such striking results. She had decided she didn't want to bother. She was comfortable in her T-shirt and shorts. That was good enough.

She heard a knock inside, followed shortly thereafter by Rick Parker's greeting.

"Sheri, hey there! C'mon inside, or outside, actually. Peggy and Lynne are out on the patio."

Moments later Sheri came onto the patio, looking a bit the worse for wear, her hair a little disheveled, her makeup limited to lipstick, her sundress wrinkled. As Lynne and Peggy greeted her, Rick stuck his head out. "What can I get you to drink, Sheri?"

"Well, what I'd *like* is a triple margarita, but I think what I'll ask for is—is there any more of that great fruit punch from the first Craft Fair? Now that we know it was the crangria that was making people sick?" A lab had confirmed Lynne's suspicion that the remaining crangria had been liberally laced with Ipecac.

Rick made a face. "You had to remind me. Yes, we actually do have some of the fruit punch, about ten gallons of it. Peg? Lynne? More iced tea?"

Both shook their heads as Sheri pulled a chair over and sat at the round glass table, moving her hands nervously. "It's times like this," she said, "that I really miss smoking. I would purely love to have a cigarette now. Ten cigarettes. I'm kind of frazzled."

"I could put a little vodka in that fruit juice," Rick suggested.

Sheri smiled. "Well, maybe a little wouldn't hurt. I just don't want to talk to anybody anymore. Except you guys," she added hastily. "But you would not believe how many people have made it a point to 'drop by' today. Some of them have a valid concern: they paid Darcy up-front for pills that are now in the custody of the Monroe County Sheriff."

"That would be tough," Peggy said. "Makes me glad we never climbed on that boat."

"We didn't need to," Rick said, handing Sheri a tall frosted glass with a swizzle stick topped by a glass palm tree. He sat down and sipped from a glass of ice water. "But that's just a fluke, that I got really good medical insurance as part of my golden parachute. It would be tough enough to pay for those prescriptions once, and these people are going to have to do it twice. Right before Christmas."

Sheri nodded. "This is all so confusing, and overwhelming. I feel like some wispy little leaf swirling around in a hurricane of rumors. Just on the way over here, I must have run into half a dozen people who wanted to know what was going on. As if *I* had any idea! I'm just the one they hauled in for interrogation. And I don't think I know anything more since that happened. Maybe less. It can be tough to know what's true and what's not and what's unsure."

"We could try to hash it out," Lynne suggested. "Start with what we know for sure. One thing we know for sure is that Darcy Gainsborough is dead."

"And that she was murdered," Peggy said. "What else?"

"We know she was some kind of sneak thief or kleptomaniac," Sheri said. "That one I know for sure. I couldn't believe it when I found that drawer. And my silly little dish in there with all the condoms and matches and odd little things."

"Were there any odd little things that seemed out of place?" Lynne asked. "I'd love to have seen the inside of her home."

"I'd happily have given up the experience for you," Sheri said. "But the thing is, everything in the drawer was kind of odd. There were parrot feathers and fish hooks and a crab mallet."

"About those condoms," Rick said. "There were different brands?"

Sheri looked a little uncomfortable. "With initials on some of them. But I'd rather not talk about that."

"Maybe Darcy took something that really mattered from somebody," Lynne suggested. "Something that she wouldn't have realized was special at that time."

"Hmm," Peggy said. "Perhaps. Or maybe she did realize it after the fact and she tried to do something about it."

"Like blackmail, you mean?" Sheri asked. "That would fit with the kind of woman she was. She liked to gossip."

"So do I," Lynne said, "but I've never blackmailed anybody."

"She claimed she wasn't making a profit from the drugs," Sheri said. "But she was. She was even collecting extra from me, and I was doing all that work, counting and packaging stuff, helping her out month after month."

"But it wasn't unreasonable, was it?" Lynne asked. "The extra charges."

"Depends on your point of view, I guess," Peggy said. "If she was gouging her assistant, then she was probably adding even more to other people's bills. There's probably a lot of wiggle room between the lowest price you can get importing prescription drugs from Canada and the best deal you can get in Mexico. And it sounds like Darcy wiggled quite a bit."

"Sheri, do you think the cops are going to give the drugs back to the people who ordered them?" Rick asked.

Sheri shook her head. "They told me no. But they seem to think that she was killed because of the drugs somehow. They kind of made it sound as if she was just the latest in a long line of gangland drug murders."

"She did have that pill vial jammed down her throat," Rick reminded. "A gangland kind of signature. Except that there's no gang involved. Do the police know who was actually bringing the drugs into the country?"

"I don't think so," Sheri said, "but my money's still on Roberto Lopez. They questioned him, I know."

Rick nodded. "That makes sense. He's Mexican, isn't he? Not Cuban?"

"Yeah," said Peggy. "And, he goes away for a few days now and then. But so what if he's smuggling prescription drugs from Mexico? Nobody around here is going to care about that. Smuggling is a way of life down here in the Keys. And it always has been."

"There's no way to know what else Roberto's involved with," Rick said. "There are a lot of drugs coming into this country that aren't in the *PDR*. For all we know, he had some kind of falling out with Darcy about money himself. But I want to go back to those condoms. Only one of each kind, with initials on them—those have to be trophies."

"Well, surely the police are looking into those initials, don't you think?" Lynne asked. In the sky above the bay, birds coasted on thermal breezes. As she watched, one of them made a dramatic dive into the water, emerging with something silver in its beak. "I'd assume they're mostly from men who live in the Court."

"Except for some of the people who've stayed here," Peggy said. "Like those fishermen from Louisville. I saw her talking to Nate Washburn at one point. I don't think he's very appealing myself, but who knows? And I have to say there aren't very many men I've seen at Little Sister Court that I'd want to sleep with, either."

"Thanks, I guess," Rick said.

Peggy blew him a kiss. "I already have the man of my dreams."

"They're mostly married over in the Court, aren't they?" Lynne asked. "The men, I mean."

"Pretty much, yeah," Sheri said. "There's a few bachelors and widowers. Tim Talbot, George Wyman, Eddie Westcott. And now that I think about it, it wasn't just the married guys ordering Viagra."

"Well, I haven't noticed anybody from the Court stepping forward to say they were screwing Darcy," Rick said. "But keep in mind, she was a tease, with a lot of people."

Peggy looked at him. "You, my love?"

"Absolutely," Rick said. "But in a way that didn't seem serious."

Peggy shook her head. "You men are such dullards. If you had seemed serious, as you put it, I bet Darcy would have tried to follow through. She was very determined."

"But still, nobody's come forward," Rick said. "Not that there'd be anything but hassles if somebody did. Still, it's possible that these guys, whoever they are, have enough intelligence or integrity not to want to sully a dead lady's reputation."

"Or fear," Sheri suggested. "At least the married ones."

"Good point," Lynne said. "I'll tell you what, though. I'd like to know why they hauled in young John Haedrich this morning. He's not an old geezer, and there's no way that *he* was going to get involved with a woman twice his age, not while he has that gorgeous young wife. Who is, by the way, terrified."

"You've seen him?" Sheri asked.

"Not since yesterday," Lynne said. "But you were here when Diane called and said they were releasing him. She told me they were going to Key West, and that maybe after that they'd check out and go home."

"Another customer down the drain," Rick said glumly.

"Maybe not," Lynne said. "I had the impression that John really doesn't want to leave here when he hasn't covered every inch of the key. Every exposed inch, anyway. I don't think that metal detector is going to do much good going through buildings and driveways and stuff."

"I still don't understand why the police took him in," Peggy said.

"Diane had no idea," Lynne said. "He came here on some kind of goofy treasure hunt, she says, related to something terrible that his grandfather did. He's looking for something buried under a banyan tree at a fish camp at Mile Marker Twenty-Six."

They all turned to look at the banyan on the side of the property, surrounded by piles of lumber, fenced off from the resort.

"Has he been around here?" Rick asked.

"Diane says that's the first place he looked," Lynne said. "But you know, the growth pattern of a banyan with aerial roots coming down—that might get something all tangled up in its roots."

"But he didn't find anything?" Rick asked.

Lynne shook her head. "Anyway, all that Diane says is that John was out in the middle of the night with it, so he wouldn't have to explain himself to anybody," Lynne said. "I was with her yesterday and we stopped at George Wyman's to meet him. A very weird place, actually. George has got a room full of pirate dioramas and Jolly Rogers hanging on the wall with swords and cutlasses. John says he knows everything you could possibly know about pirates."

"Who don't seem to be hanging around here, just now," Rick said. "But I can't help but wonder if this treasure stuff is related to the problems we've been having here."

Oh yes, Lynne thought. The aquarium of bleached salt-water fish. The crangria mixed with Ipecac, found in millions of medicine cabinets across the nation, years ago. The slashed tires and power failures and unlocked bird cages.

"Are people still checking out early?" Sheri asked.

"None today, so maybe there won't be any more. We're

not holding anybody to the usual penalty procedures for leaving early, or breaking a reservation," Peggy said, "even though it's costing us."

"Money, maybe, it's costing us. The goodwill is priceless," Rick said in a tone that suggested this discussion had been underway for quite some time.

"What about the false rumors going around?" Lynne asked. "Things we're pretty sure aren't true, like that Darcy was planning to move away on the earnings from her drug operation."

"She wouldn't make it past Marathon if that were all she had to operate on," Sheri said. "But it does seem to be a pattern. One of the rumors that I do believe is that Darcy was still collecting Social Security on her husband's account as well as her own, even though he's been dead for a long, long time."

"How can that be?" Peggy asked.

Rick smiled. "Not difficult if you've got things set up so the check goes into a direct deposit account. You just 'forget' to notify Social Security of the death, and unless it's your hometown bank and the bank employees are all at the funeral, nobody's going to know what's going on. Social Security has this little bitty one-time death benefit, and I'm sure it's to learn who died so they can cut off benefits."

It was an interesting conundrum. With Darcy's death, all sorts of people stood to lose. But who had anything to gain? Lynne decided it was time to switch to margaritas.

❧

**BY** the time Jenna reached the car, the sun had vanished again behind a bank of clouds. Feeling suddenly chilly, she grabbed her jacket from the trunk. Something heavy banged against her hip as she slipped on the jacket. When she stuck her hand into the pocket, she came out with Dan Trenton's bright red Swiss Army knife.

Instantly she remembered being out on the boat, opening bottles of imported beer. She must have come away with the knife then. She transferred it to her straw purse now, then carefully eased out of a parking spot that seemed much smaller than it had been on her arrival.

She had become sufficiently familiar with Key West to not need any map to get around, though she made a point of driving very carefully. In her travels around the Keys she had noticed a ratio of approximately one police cruiser for every two bars, a connection that seemed crystal clear to Jenna.

The sun came back out and as she headed back out on the Overseas Highway, the sun at her back, the air bright and fresh, the road uncrowded. This might be a good day to check out the Key Deer on Big Pine Key, she decided. Everyone kept talking about how cute they were, that they looked like Disney mini-deer, which probably wasn't the world's best endorsement. Still, Jenna was curious. She'd been told her they came out around sundown, which wouldn't be for a couple more hours. Still, there were supposed to be hundreds of the little fellows, enough so that the authorities had put chain-link fence along Highway 1 on Big Pine Key to keep them off the road.

But how many deer did she really need to see, even if they were the cutest deer in the world? One would probably be enough.

Now as she drove around Big Pine Key, however, there didn't seem to be even one around. Maybe they actually did come out only at sundown. Perhaps they didn't exist. Why had she left the Sunset Saloon? Now that she was in the general neighborhood of Dos Hermanas, she was in no hurry to get back.

Almost without realizing what she was doing, Jenna found herself back on the highway, then taking the semi-familiar exit leading to the road where Dan Trenton lived. This was ridiculous, she told herself, but she seemed powerless to turn the car around without actually seeing his place. In high school she and her friends had sometimes detoured to drive by a guy's house. Dude-watching, they'd called it. But this wasn't high school.

She told herself, later, that she truly hadn't intended to go there, much less to stop.

But she did.

And when she came down the road—the road that narrowed approaching Dan's place and ended, he had said when she was out here, not far beyond his place—she had a surprise. She wasn't expecting to see him.

But she did.

At first it wasn't clear what she was looking at.

Dan's truck was there, backed up toward the house. Roberto Lopez's truck was also there, by the side of the road. Both trucks had camper shells on them. The two men were outside and looked up at the sound of her arrival, with expressions of surprise and consternation.

Oh, hell.

She kept on going a couple hundred yards more and the road really did end, just as Dan had told her it did. She turned around and started back. She already felt stupid. The best she could hope for was to joke a bit and then slip away, pride damaged but not destroyed.

Dan was out at the road when she came back. So she stopped.

He leaned in the passenger side. "Hey."

Up to her. "Hey. Just riding around, seeing what the Keys look like when you're not a tourist." She pulled the knife out of her bag. "I found this in my jacket pocket. I guess I took it by mistake when we were diving the *Adolphus Busch*."

"I was wondering what happened to it." Then silence as he took the knife and stuck it in his jeans pocket.

Now what?

Beyond Dan, she could see Roberto snapping some kind of large sheet open, and using it to cover . . .

To cover bird cages. Parrot cages. Parrot cages containing parrots.

She looked at Dan, saw anxiety in his eyes.

"What's going on?" she asked.

He didn't say anything at first. Then, "Some stock for friends up north."

"They stock parrots?"

Again he was slow to respond. And she suddenly felt like the world's stupidest woman.

"You're *smuggling*. Oh, hell. Smuggling parrots." She tried to regain her composure. "Listen, I'm sorry I bothered you. I'll go now."

Nothing. Then he offered a faint smile. "No need to go, Jenna. You're here, you see what's going on. Might as well get out, don'tcha think?"

One beer more or less and she'd have squealed away at that point. But Jenna felt just about right. She pulled off the pavement, such as it was, and got out of the car.

As she moved toward the stacked cages, filled with a bewildering array of brightly colored birds, she felt an overwhelming sense of confusion.

❧

JUST for the heck of it, Diane Haedrich turned on the cell phone after they got settled and had placed their order at the Margaritaville Café. There was a message waiting, and she called in for it.

"This message is for John Haedrich," a strong male voice said. "This is George Wyman, speaking, John. I understand that you have been with the police today and I apologize for any discomfort that I might have caused you."

Diane was baffled. Apologize? Discomfort *he* might have caused? John seemed quite taken by Wyman, but this sounded pretty loopy.

"Please come by my home this afternoon anytime after three thirty. I do regret the inconveniences my actions may cause you, but I see no other way. Thank you very much."

"I don't get it, John," Diane said, punching buttons to replay the message and handing him the phone. It became clear from his expression that he didn't get it either.

"It sounds so—"

"So final?" she suggested. "I'm going to call Lynne. Maybe she knows what's going on."

But she didn't.

※

JENNA had switched to soda and was drinking a Diet Coke that Dan had found inside somewhere and poured over ice for her. Probably drinks he kept for girls. He was drinking Classic Coke himself, and most guys didn't drink diet soda if there was any other choice at all. Seeing Dan and Roberto with all those parrots had sobered her artificially, so that even though she was probably legally drunk, she didn't exactly feel high. She was also, she realized, probably in violation of more laws than those connected to driving while intoxicated. Suddenly she was an accessory to smuggling, theft, endangering wildlife. The list went on, but why bother?

"They come from Mexico," Dan said obliquely.

"And that's where you've been? Picking up parrots in Mexico?"

"I'll take the fifth on that one, I think. But here they are. They'll go to some people in Miami who do the actual placement. We're more like brokers. These birds will have good homes and provide much pleasure to people who will be happy to get them."

"To pay for them, don't you mean?"

"Well, of course."

"You told me that smuggling was really bad for birds."

"I guess I did, didn't I?"

He sat down at the picnic table and gestured for her to sit opposite him. "A lot depends on the type of smuggling and who's doing it. There are folks who bring birds into the U.S. inside hubcaps of the trucks they're driving. That's bad smuggling, and most of those birds die. There was a guy in Australia who tried to smuggle a bunch of macaw eggs into this country. He had them in his nice warm jockey shorts and they started to hatch right around the time he hit U.S. Customs."

Jenna laughed. She couldn't help herself.

"These birds," he said, pointing in the direction of the covered cages, "are what I think of as good smuggling. They were captured in the jungle and kept in cages until it was time to ship them here. They come in by boat, inside lengths of wide-diameter PVC pipe. Air holes in the pipe, and the birds are put in gently. I've seen it done. I've helped with it on occasion."

Behind him, Roberto was working with the birds. She could see him actually holding a length of pipe inside a cage, gently shaking it as a bright green parrot emerged with an angry squawk.

"How many birds die in transit?" Jenna asked. This seemed to be the central truth here, she thought.

"Very few. Sometimes none. They're not in the pipes a minute longer than necessary, on either end."

Jenna considered. It did make sense, and she had watched Dan handle birds with gentle respect and appreciation. "And when do they go to their next stop? Which I assume is some gated community on a fancy island."

He shrugged. "Often, that's probably the case. We're middlemen here, Jenna. We're not getting rich off this, just keeping our heads above water. It costs a lot to live down here, and you can't make a living tending the birds at a resort and making the occasional dive with paying tourists."

Now she *was* sober, she realized. She stood up.

"I don't know quite what I think of all this," she said. "I'm not going to turn you in to anybody, if that's what you're concerned about. But I don't know if I want to see any more of you, either."

"There's a lot of the reef you haven't seen yet."

He was trying to tantalize her, she realized, and it wouldn't be hard.

"I'm going back to Dos Hermanas," she said. "Maybe I'll see you around there."

When they walked back out to her car, she got in without making any attempt to physically say goodbye. He leaned over the closed driver's door and kissed her on the tip of the nose.

"I hope so," he said.

She could see him standing there by the road in her rearview mirror until the road turned and trees blocked her vision.

## Chapter 30

**AFTER** Diane's call, Lynne decided to go over to George Wyman's. Simple curiosity, she told herself, and Rick invited himself along. They left Sheri at her own coach and continued to Wyman's place.

Lynne caught her breath when they walked into the private side area.

On the door, visible only when you walked up to the entrance, a black Jolly Roger flag had been carefully thumbtacked in place. Lynne recognized the flag as one that she'd seen on the inside wall yesterday. She also recognized the gleaming silver dagger that had been hanging near the Jolly Roger. It had been thrust through an envelope addressed "John Haedrich" with sufficient strength to hold it steadily on the door.

They knocked. No response. Knocked a second time. Still no answer.

"What do you think?" Rick said. "Do we try the door?"

He did. It was locked.

"Do we call the cops?" Lynne asked.

"And tell them what? That there's a flag on somebody's door with a letter?"

"I see your point. But when Diane called, she sounded spooked by his message."

"Then why don't you go back over and wait for her. I'll stay here until you get back."

Feeling a growing sense of dread, Lynne went back to Dos Hermanas and found a chaise situated so that she'd see the Haedriches when they returned.

It seemed like a long time, but by her watch it was only ten more minutes before she saw their car pull in. She walked to greet them, and hugged Diane first. She'd been driving and Lynne was relieved that the girl seemed only a bit shaken by the strange events of the day. John didn't seem to want to be hugged, but he submitted, his body rigid.

"I waited for you to get here before doing anything," Lynne said, "but I think there may be something wrong at George Wyman's."

Diane's color drained and she clutched at John's arm. "Like what?"

"Rick Parker is over there waiting for you," Lynne said, addressing her comments to John. "After your call about that message, we decided to pay him a visit. There wasn't any answer when we knocked, and there's an envelope addressed to you on the outside door."

"Why don't you wait here?" John said to Diane.

"I don't think so," Diane answered. "Let's go."

**RICK** was standing by the door as the three of them walked around the corner. "I knocked again a couple times, but nobody answered."

John pulled the dagger out with one hand and took the envelope with the other. Lynne caught her breath when he slipped the blade into the sealed envelope and sliced it neatly open. It was such a casual gesture, one he clearly hadn't even thought about. Diane took the envelope from him after he pulled a sheet of paper out of the envelope.

A key dropped to the ground and Rick Parker picked it up.

"Dear John," John read aloud. "Please do not call the police until you have read the letter I left you inside. Do not allow your wife to accompany you inside. Sincerely, George Wyman."

Diane had seemed anxious before, but now Lynne watched her become indignant. She might not have wanted to go inside, but tell her she couldn't and there was no way to keep her out.

John tried the key in the lock and the door swung slowly open.

"George?" John called. "George, are you here?"

Rick took a deep breath and his eyes clouded. "Maybe you should stay outside," he told John.

"Nonsense."

The main room was empty. On a small table in its center sat a cassette player. On it was propped an envelope reading: "For John Haedrich. Listen to tape before contacting authorities."

John paid no attention to the table and its contents as he marched in, glanced to his right into the diorama room, then turned to look down the hall. He stopped abruptly.

Lynne moved up beside him. At the end of the hall, in

the library she had been shown briefly the other day, George Wyman was dangling by a noose on a jerry-rigged scaffold, a heavy piece of lumber resting on the tops of two large bookcases. He was facing down the hall toward them, his head at an odd angle, his face an ugly bluish purple. His hands appeared to be tied together and he held a wilted bouquet of tropical flowers in his grip.

Rick pushed past them and strode down the hall, put his fingers up to the man's throat looking for a pulse. He turned to face them. "He's dead."

Lynne was watching John.

"It's an execution," he said softly. "They'd tie the hands of a condemned pirate together and put a nosegay in them. He's executed himself."

He walked slowly down the hall. When he was about six feet from the body, he stopped and looked up at the purpled face for a moment, then turned around and came back to the main room.

"Shouldn't we cut him down or something?" Diane asked.

Lynne remembered the practical and concerned Diane on the morning they'd found Darcy's body, worrying about performing CPR. "I think the police would rather have you leave everything exactly as it is, Diane. Except for that envelope on the door, that's what we've done. It's up to John whether we listen to the tape before we call. My guess is that he's probably been dead since right after he left you that phone message."

John picked up the envelope left with the cassette, then sat on the ottoman in front of the large leather chair that Wyman had angled toward his television. He opened it and pulled out a smaller sealed envelope and a sheaf of papers. "It's all addressed to me," he said, dumbfounded.

Diane walked over to the cassette player. "Shall I?" she asked. John nodded. Diane pushed the play button, then returned and sat beside him, pushing him a bit to one side on the ottoman. There was plenty of room for them both. She took John's hand as the deep gravelly voice of George Wyman filled the room.

*This message is directed to John Haedrich of Battle Creek, Michigan, a guest at Dos Hermanas Resort. John, I've left you a letter with a holographic will. Please see that a copy gets to Webster Groves, an attorney in Key West. I have previously met with Mr. Groves and I am mailing a copy of this will to him, but I don't want to create any more problems for you than I already have. The will was witnessed by Peter and Eleanor Simpson, who live next door.*

*My name is not George Wyman.*

*I assumed that name fifty-one years ago when I decided to make a clean start at life. I had been in trouble previously and had spent time in a hospital after an automobile accident that killed my best friend and my girlfriend. I was not the driver, but I felt responsible for their deaths. I was being sought by law enforcement officials for another reason at that time, but they didn't know where to look.*

*I was born Thomas Carlson in 1930 and raised outside Saginaw, Michigan. My family had a dairy farm and it was expected that my brothers and I would take it over. I wasn't sure what I wanted to do, but I was quite certain that I didn't want to spend my life milking cows at 5 A.M. I enlisted in the Navy and served four years in the Mediterranean during the Korean War era. It was there that I learned about the corsairs and the Barbary pirates, and began what turned into a lifelong passion for piracy.*

*When I was discharged from the Navy in Virginia, I decided to stay and go to school on the G.I. Bill. While I was a student at UVA, I met a couple of fellows who changed the course of my life. I won't try to pass off the blame for my actions on anyone but myself, but if the three of us hadn't come together as we did, I wouldn't be writing this letter to you today.*

*My buddies were Mike Tracy and Joey Haedrich.*

*Joey was your grandfather, John. I knew it the moment you told me your name, that very first day we talked at Dos Hermanas. I could see his features in your face and I had no idea what to say or do. By then it was too late anyway.*

*Mike Tracy and Joey Haedrich and I shared an apartment in Charlottesville. Mike was from out West, but Joey was a Michigander like me, from Pontiac, outside Detroit. His folks wanted him to move back and get on the line at the auto plant, but Joey had other plans. I never felt comfortable in the South, and I guess Joey didn't either. After a year in Charlottesville, we headed back to Michigan.*

*Joey and I both went to work at the Pontiac factory, and it didn't take long for me to realize that in its own way, this was even worse than dairy farming. Joey started scheming on ways to make money fast. I think it would have been idle talk and nothing more, but then Mike Tracy blew into town. He'd been out West and was hitchhiking around the country. He had a plan where we would get some fast cash and then split* up for good. One time and a clean break. After a few months on the line at Pontiac, I was ready for anything.

Mike's plan was to hold up a bank one morning near another auto assembly plant on pay day, when they still had a lot of cash on hand. We had a lot of choices, but we settled on Flint. Mike picked up an old Chevy, cheap. He was free to travel so he did all the reconnaissance. Joey and I were going to stay on our jobs for a few weeks afterward and then quit. Mike would hold the money while we did that. There was no reason not to trust Mike, Joey and I decided.

Joey went on a different shift as part of the preparation, so that our absence on the same day wouldn't be so obvious. Mike planned a route in and out of Flint. He was going to steal a car that we would use for the robbery and leave his own car in a parking lot a few towns over. Then we'd abandon the stolen car and leave in Mike's own car. He'd drop us off back in Pontiac to go to work again.

We thought we had everything worked out for the holdup. Mike would wait outside with the engine running while Joey and I went in to get the money. That was how I always thought of it: "get the money." Not steal, or rob. Nobody was supposed to get hurt. Joey had a gun he was going to wave around, but he swore he wouldn't use it, that he wouldn't even load it.

The robbery went pretty much as we planned it, until Joey started to improvise. He made all the people who were inside the bank take off their watches and jewelry and put them in the bag I was holding where we'd put all the money we'd collected.

That slowed us down just long enough for an officer on the Flint Police Department to come into the bank as we were leaving. He wasn't looking for us, he just happened to walk in. It was just bad dumb luck. And it got worse fast. The officer started to pull his gun, but Joey already had his out. He shot the policeman four times and killed him. The gun was loaded after all.

I'm sorry to have to tell you that, John. But you need to know it to understand the rest of what happened.

We had the money and we decided to stick with our original plan. We'd all get together in a month in Detroit. Mike would hold the money while Joey and I went back to work at Pontiac. After two more weeks, I quit my job on the line and went home to the farm. Joey stayed another week after that before he quit. Joey was never really the same again after he shot that cop. Something twisted inside him. Even after he became religious, though, when I worried a bit that he'd turn us in, he kept his word.

When I quit and went back home, I took up with an old girlfriend, Lois Ledbetter. My best friend from high school, Walt Beeman, was still around. Lois and I spent a lot of time with Walt and his girlfriend Blanche.

We were all out one night in February, riding around, a bit drunk, not a care in the world. I remember we were passing a flask around in the car. We had just dropped off Blanche and Walt was driving. I never saw what happened. I was kissing Lois in the backseat when I heard Walt shout, "Oh my God." I could feel the car spinning out on ice, really fast, and that was the last thing I remembered.

I woke up a month later and learned that Lois and Walt were both dead. Blanche was alive, but she didn't want to talk to me. I took a while to heal, but I decided that I had been spared for some reason that night. Otherwise I should have been killed as well.

The time had come. But Mike had disappeared, just like Joey worried he would. I had no way to find the money, no way to even ask. The money was gone. We'd counted it that last afternoon we were together. It was over $55,000. In cash. Plus the jewelry.

I kept a watch that had belonged to an older gentlemen in the bank. It was a pocket watch, with a picture of him and his wife, engraved with his name. Wayne Fosberg. I kept it hidden and I brought it out only when I needed to remind myself of what I'd done and what I had to lose. If we had come to trial in Michigan for killing a police officer, we would have been executed by the state. That statement is probably as true today as it was then.

With no way to get the money, I figured it was up to me to make something of myself. I couldn't forget the expression on that dead policeman's face. So I told my family I was going to California to make my fortune. It didn't work. I never told them that I didn't like it out there, and that I missed the Midwest. I just didn't contact them again. I came back and started over in Appleton, Wisconsin. The only person who knew where to find me was Joey Haedrich.

I changed my name to George Wyman and went to work as an assistant in the chemistry division of Kimberly-Clark, the paper company. The lady in the personnel department even filled out my paperwork to get me a Social Security card.

I liked chemistry. I liked winter. I went back to school and started taking college classes, and a few years later I wound up with a degree in chemistry. I spent my entire working life at Kimberly-Clark. I made contributions to good causes. I lived a life that was as exemplary as possible. I had a second chance and I wanted to take full advantage of it.

Six months after the robbery, Mike Tracy turned up again. He went to see Joey because I wasn't around. Mike said he'd gotten mixed up with some guys in Florida and he was afraid they'd take Joey's and my money. He'd taken his third and buried the rest in a metal ammunition can under a banyan tree at a fish camp at Mile Marker Twenty-Six in the Florida Keys. Mike was heading back to Wyoming when he died in a single car crash in South Dakota. I found that out much later when I tried to write him a letter and a note came back from his mother.

Joey and I met in Chicago to figure out what to do. It was the last time I ever saw him. We agreed that whoever went and got that money would bring it to the other person. At that point, I didn't even want it and I don't think that Joey did either. But he never brought it to me and I never stopped being curious.

Joey had a provision in his will to notify me that

he had passed away. His lawyer did so. I did nothing with this information. It all seemed too long ago to matter anymore, though I continued to be haunted by the face of that dead policeman in Flint.

I retired from Kimberly Clark five years ago, but I didn't have any desire to leave Appleton. I liked it there. It was my home. And then I was diagnosed with lung cancer. No surprise, really. I always smoked and always liked it. But it got me thinking about that money down in Florida. It would be nice to make amends somehow, to the family of that policeman.

The only problem was that I couldn't find the money. But I'm getting ahead of myself.

I visited the Keys and realized that the fish camp Mike had mentioned had to be Dos Hermanas, in its earlier, more basic era. Little Sister Key simply isn't that large. And as luck would have it, there was a mobile home park right next door. I sold my house in Wisconsin and moved down here.

When I saw your appreciation for my library, John, I decided that you should have it. Provision is made for this in my new will. Please don't feel that the books have been tainted by my death. They were all purchased with money I earned honestly and they should go to someone who will appreciate them.

I've had no luck in finding any banyan tree other than the one beside the house where the Parkers live, and before they moved here, I spent quite a lot of surreptitious time poking long metal sticks into the ground. Like you, John, I tried a metal detector and found nothing. I started to realize that my time was limited and that Dos Hermanas was rapidly filling up for the winter. The Parkers were too enthusiastic about running the place, and too successful. I hoped to discourage business by performing a series of relatively harmless pranks. These I regret sincerely, and restitution is provided for in the aforementioned will.

I probably should have gone back to Wisconsin, but I didn't know how long my health would hold out and by then I rather liked it here. This was the type of place where all the pirates I had read about lived and died. Somehow it seemed like I was meant to come here.

This next part is very difficult.

Darcy Gainsborough was an attractive woman who approached me almost before I was unpacked to ask if I had any interest in purchasing low-cost pharmaceuticals. I told her no. I had more than enough money to meet my own medical needs. I didn't tell her that before much longer I wouldn't have any medical needs anyway.

I cannot pretend I was innocent when Darcy seduced me. Mine had been a rather monkish life. The details of the relationship I had with her are irrelevant, other than to say that it was consensual and enjoyable. There was no form of coercion on either side.

You may remember the watch I had kept from the bank robbery. I had it in a velvet box in a drawer of my dresser. I had a ritual on the first of every month of taking it out and contemplating my life.

When I opened the box this December, the watch was missing.

*I had no doubt where it had gone. I am a loner by nature, almost a hermit. The only person who had been inside my home in the previous month was Darcy. I didn't know what to do.*

*Then she was over here one night and she asked me who Wayne Fosberg was. She was coquettish and coy about it, and I felt quite comfortable in berating her for having violated my privacy. That just made her more curious. She was rather adept at using the Internet, a subject we had discussed at some length. She laughed and said she'd just go online and find out. I told her I'd tell her all about it the next time we were together.*

*The next time we were together, she taunted me. She said obviously I had something to hide and that she loved playing hide-and-seek. We were in the kitchenette here and she was drinking a martini. She said something to me. There is no point in telling you what she said, only that it angered me enough to strike her. As she fell, the back of her head hit the side of my kitchen counter. I had every intention of calling for help, but then she made a horrible noise and died.*

*From here on out, I took the coward's path. I waited until it was late at night and I brought her over to the boat ramp at Dos Hermanas. It was actually quite close to my trailer and she was light enough that I was able to pretend we were walking with my arm around her. Once I got to the boat ramp, I put her down and hurried on home.*

*You know what's happened since then. I realized when I learned that you had been taken for questioning by the police that I didn't want anyone else* to suffer for my crimes. There was only one honorable thing I could do. If I had done that back when we robbed the bank, none of this would have happened, but I don't believe in retrospective history. What happens, happens. That's true whether it is William Kidd striking and accidentally killing a ship's gunner or George Wyman, formerly Thomas Carlson, striking and accidentally killing a female neighbor and paramour.

I take full responsibility for the death of Darcy Gainsborough.

I am sorry not to have made restitution to the family of that policeman, but I have made provision for them in my new will. Beyond that bequest, John, I have left you all of my assets, including the library and all of my pirate memorabilia. As I told you one day when we were speaking of the library, a single man has few major expenses. I hope that you will use some of this money to buy your wife the bird you mentioned she wanted.

Beyond that, I apologize for complicating your life. I thank you for the courtesy and interest you showed an ailing old man.

I remain,
Thomas Carlson, alias George Wyman

**LYNNE** could hardly believe that it was just a week since she and Jenna had arrived at Dos Hermanas. Tomorrow they'd be going back home to California, with not much time to get ready for Christmas. She was looking forward to both Christmas and to being home.

The last few days in the aftermath of George Wyman's suicide had been incredibly busy.

The police had been angry that they had not been called immediately, though their behavior made it clear that John had been wise to listen to George Wyman's tape before calling anyone. John might never get to hear it again. There were all the normal complications and responsibilities caused by any death, coupled with notoriety that had occasioned a brief media frenzy. And there probably would be more to come, as the search for the banyan tree continued.

There was promising news on that front. When word of the missing treasure beneath a banyan tree became public, an elderly couple who were longtime residents of the southern end of Little Sister Key came forward, with their memories of a second banyan at Dos Hermanas. This tree had been larger and older than the one that remained, they recalled, but it had succumbed to a root rot thirty years ago.

Nobody was precisely sure where that banyan had stood, but the couple believed it was in the area currently covered by the tennis courts. Rick and Peggy agreed to let John use part of his inheritance to remove the courts, attempt to locate the missing money, and then repave the area. Any money discovered would go to the descendants of the dead Flint policeman, in addition to what George had left them in his will.

※

**ONCE** again they were on the Parkers' patio for grilled snapper at sunset, but this group was a little different. Gloria Parker had declined to attend, a plus all by itself. They were joined by Sheri McManus and John and Diane Haedrich. Jenna was with them but kept to herself. She had been moody for the last few days, but unwilling to discuss whatever was bothering her. Lynne had noticed, however, that she no longer was spending any time with Dan Trenton. Jenna said she didn't want to talk about it, and so they didn't.

"What do you plan to do now that you're wealthy?" Rick asked John.

"I'm not sure," John said. "It's a lot more money than I imagined. Provide for that policeman's family, of course if we can find the buried money. We want to buy a house back home and I think we can get a pretty nice one. And I'd like to get a macaw for Diane, if she still wants one."

Diane grinned. "She does."

Lynne looked around the group and lifted her glass. "I'd like to make a toast. To good friends, old and new. And to tropical adventures, wherever they may lead."